30 Nights

Christine d'Abo

KENSINGTON BOOKS
www.kensingtonbooks.com

KENSINGTON BOOKS are published by

Kensington Publishing Corp.
119 West 40th Street
New York, NY 10018

All Kensington titles, imprints, and distributed lines are available at special quantity discounts for bulk purchases for sales promotion, premiums, fund-raising, educational, or institutional use.

Special book excerpts or customized printings can also be created to fit specific needs. For details, write or phone the office of the Kensington Sales Manager: Kensington Publishing Corp., 119 West 40th Street, New York, NY 10018. Attn. Sales Department. Phone: 1-800-221-2647.

Kensington and the K logo Reg. U.S. Pat. & TM Off.

eISBN-13: 978-1-61773-957-6
eISBN-10: 1-61773-957-X
First Kensington Electronic Edition: June 2016

ISBN-13: 978-1-61773-956-9
ISBN-10: 1-61773-956-1
First Kensington Trade Paperback Printing: June 2016

10 9 8 7 6 5 4 3 2 1
Printed in the United States of America

Always for you

Part 1

An Interesting Discovery

1

"You are the biggest coward in the world."

Yup, that's me—Glenna Marie O'Donald—stellar research assistant and consummate romantic coward.

Jasmine, my best friend since my first year of college, fell into the chair opposite me at our table in the lunchroom. I wasn't bothered by her comments; she was right, after all. My history with guys was shaky at best. I liked them and they seemed to like me for a time. Then inevitably things devolved when my job took priority over hanging out.

Your boss is taking advantage of you.

You work way too much.

Why can't you spend as much time with me as you do at the school?

This sucks. I'm out of here.

Honestly, when you get burned more than a few times for the same thing, you tend to back away. I didn't *need* a man in my life. Jasmine never believed me when I told her that I was quite happy on my own. She'd snort, roll her eyes, and wave away my comment without a second glance.

It did get annoying.

I *didn't* need a man.

Even if I sometimes wanted someone special in my life. Occasionally. Every so often.

"I'm telling you, the staff barbecue is the perfect place for you to talk to him." She opened her lunch and the smell of kimchi rice filled the room.

The *him* she was referring to was Professor Eric Morris. The tall, dark-haired, super-fit sociology professor had a voice that could melt hearts and drop panties with a simple *hello.* Professor Eric Morris, who had more female students in his class than anyone else on campus. A man who rarely smiled, but when he looked at you there was no doubt he not only saw you, but every thought and feeling that flitted through your head. He starred in far too many of my nightly fantasies for me to admit without sounding like a crazy, obsessed stalker.

The man, who in the year and a bit that he'd been teaching at the college, I'd barely managed to say two words to, because I was, as Jasmine put it, a coward.

"I love you like a sister, Jaz. But there is no way I'm going to say anything to him. Ever."

It was the Friday before the Labor Day weekend, the last workday before the start of the school year. Most of the professors from the college were gone, taking their last bit of vacation to play golf, read, or do whatever their passions happened to be. I loved working this time of year. The school was quiet. It always felt as though someone had taken a deep breath and were waiting to exhale. A collective pause before the chaos to come.

This year was going to be especially awesome. Professor Mickelson, my boss, had already been away for three months on his semester-long sabbatical. I still had four more months of only communicating with him via e-mail. Heaven!

"Are you insane?" Jasmine threw her napkin at me. "This is the perfect time for you to do it. He'll be there. You'll be there.

Your crazy boss *won't* be there. You might even be able to relax and have fun for once."

She was my best friend in the whole wide world, but there were times when Jasmine scared the shit out of me. I looked down at my hands and picked at the dry skin around my nail. "I just can't."

"What's the worst that can happen? He'll say no. At the very least you'll have an answer and you can move on to someone else."

A grad student chose that moment to come into the kitchen. He didn't even look at us as he made his way to the coffee machine. I leaned forward to close the distance between me and Jasmine. "I'm quite happy with my fantasies, thank you."

"I bet you are. I bet you dream about climbing up his body and licking every inch of his skin."

The grad student looked at us wide-eyed before he spun away quickly. I got the impression he was still listening, no doubt wanting to get some dirt that could be passed around the student lounge. Great, like I needed *that* kind of attention.

I nodded my head in the direction of our friend. "Can you keep your voice down a bit?"

"Not if you're not going to listen to my advice." She leaned back and crossed her arms, her eyes locked onto mine. "You need to make a move before someone else snatches him up."

Now the grad student wasn't even pretending that he wasn't paying attention. Jasmine must have picked up on it too, because in the next instant she turned around and glared at him. "Don't you have someplace to be, Stuart? Like running your tutorial?"

"Ah, yeah. Yes." For a moment I thought his eyes were going to bug out of his head.

"Then move your ass." Jasmine pointed at the door and narrowed her gaze.

I'd never seen a person move that quickly before in my life.

When she turned her glare back on me, I knew I wasn't going to be spared anything. "Glenna, I know you don't believe me, but this is the truth. You are not meant to be alone. You and Eric would be cute together. He's serious, you're serious. Just think about what sex would be like with him. Jesus, if I weren't gay even I'd be tempted to take him for a ride myself."

And there was a mental picture I so didn't want—my best friend and my crush fucking.

"I hate you." I pulled my tuna sandwich out of my container and took a giant bite. "He doesn't even know I'm alive. Saying hello to him at the barbecue isn't going to do anything to help get him into my bed."

"Well, you can't expect him to fuck you if you can't at least have a simple conversation." She took a big bite of her kimchi and waved her fork around. "Maybe you can get drunk and then grope his ass. Then you'd have to go apologize. There might be groveling. 'Oh, please Eric, how can I ever make it up to you?'" She batted her eyelashes at me before laughing. "You should see your face."

"You're an asshole. Why are we even friends?"

"Because I showed you how to shotgun a beer our first week of college."

"Only after I saved your ass with that essay."

But as she knew, my brain does this thing that as soon as someone puts a thought out there I can't help but picture how things will work out, all the way to their natural conclusion. In my head I saw myself at the party. Eric would walk by on his way to the food table or something. I'd "accidentally" bump into him as he passed me and look into his eyes all surprised. Maybe I'd even spill a drink on myself. He'd think he'd done it and would help me clean myself.

I'm sorry, Glenna. How can I make up for this?

Oh nothing. It was an accident.

I can't stand by while I've done you wrong. At least let me give you a clean shirt.

I'd blush, of course, because who wouldn't. *Thank you.*

Why don't you take mine? His voice would be that low rumble that always seemed to turn me on. His eyes would be locked onto me as he'd slowly unbutton his shirt.

Wow, Eric. Your chest is so firm.

Would you like to see the rest of me?

And bam, crazy-monkey sex!

If only.

I cleared my throat and quickly took another bite of my sandwich. "I don't think Eric likes anyone. Or has sex. Or anything. He's always on his own."

"Baby, I've seen that man. He's having sex. As much as he wants with whomever he wants to do it with. I keep telling you all you need to do is go after him."

"He doesn't know I'm alive," I said again. And I was essentially a coworker. That went against so many things on my mental "don't touch" list I couldn't fathom it.

"Whose fault is that? Not his. If you want someone then you need to do something about it. Life doesn't reward the cautious."

"Sometimes it does."

"You don't believe that."

I hated when she was right. "Maybe."

"You're a research assistant who lives in the world of studies and observations. Talk to him—hell, I was serious about the groping. I'm sure you could chalk this up to some exceptionally hands-on research project."

"God, you're a child sometimes. I don't need a man to fulfill me when I have a perfectly good vibrator at home to help—"

"Baby, all you do is masturbate."

"—live out my fantasies. I'd be scared that the reality would never live up to the imaginary Eric that I've created in my head."

It was in that moment that my skin began to tingle. We were still alone in the kitchen, but I could have sworn someone was there. It was probably Stuart standing outside in the hall trying to get some more dirt. Well, he was out of luck because I was done being browbeaten by Jasmine.

"I need to get back soon. Professor Mickelson left me a pile of books to pull and outline for him. He'll be chasing me through e-mails if I'm not done soon."

Thankfully, she sighed, signaling the end of her teasing. "When does the old goat get back?"

"He's off all term, but he's threatened to come back around the end of October for a check-in. Then I'm sure he'll have me buried in another bunch of new projects before the next term starts."

"I'd better head out too. I have a one-thirty meeting. Apparently the CS profs want to do a study on online learning again. I have to pull some old case studies so they don't rehash an old thesis."

"Blah."

The echo of our chairs scraping as we stood filled the room. One second I was picking up my garbage and taking it to the garbage can, and in the next I was face-to-face with the object of my lust.

Professor Eric Morris stood in the doorway, coffee mug in hand. Well, *stood* isn't quite the right description. It's more like he *loomed*. He's probably only a smidgen over six feet tall, but being only five foot four myself, it makes for a huge difference from my perspective. Mind you, being eye level with his chest was no hardship. His dress shirts fit him perfectly, but they couldn't hide the muscles beneath. As usual, I was paying more

attention to his pecs—Were they really as firm as they looked?—
rather than his face. That was why I didn't immediately notice
him staring at me. Which he totally was.

And there was my blush. "Umm, hi, Professor Morris."

Woot, go me! I finally spoke to him.

"Glenna."

God, his voice! It was a lot lower than any other man's voice
that I knew and had a way of seeping into my body when he
spoke. Could the sound of a voice be an aphrodisiac? If so, then
I could listen to him read the phone book and probably have an
orgasm.

Jasmine cleared her throat and I realized that we'd been
standing staring at each other for longer than was normal. I
looked at the garbage in my hand and then at the garbage can
directly behind him. "Umm, sorry. I just need to . . ."

I'd half-expected him to move to the side so I could reach it.
Instead he stayed put, forcing me to step awkwardly around
him. I clamped my mouth closed as I moved so he wouldn't be
subjected to the stench of my tuna breath. As I brushed past
him, I got a nose full of his aftershave. It wasn't a brand that I
knew, but he smelled awesome and it always made me a bit
giddy when he was nearby. I could always tell when he'd been
in a room, my nose keenly aware of his lingering scent.

It was only after I finally dropped my garbage into the bin
that Eric moved over to the coffee machines. I wasn't a close
colleague to him and hadn't worked on any of his projects since
he'd come to the school, so I didn't have much I could say to
him. Not that he was particularly easy to speak to with his back
to us. I scampered over to the table and grabbed my things. "I
need to stop and get some paper for my printer."

"Cool." Jasmine was clearly trying to fight off a laughing fit.
"Want to grab a coffee before we go? You look like you could
use one."

I'm going to kill her. "No, I'm good for now."

Just before we left the kitchen, Jasmine piped up. "Have a great day, Professor Morris."

"You as well, Ms. Houng, Glenna."

Yes, she was going to die in the most painful way possible.

Somehow I managed to keep my mouth shut until we were out of earshot. "I hate you."

"Are you kidding me? For a second I thought he was going to throw you over the table and fuck you in front of me."

"You're high. He doesn't know me."

"Don't be so dramatic. He knew your name, which means he knows who you are. And you couldn't see his face the way I did. Not only does that boy know you're alive, but he's interested."

"Whatever." She was just trying to get me going. He couldn't be interested.

As we were about to turn the corner, I looked back down the hall toward the kitchen. Eric was standing there, coffee cup in his hand, staring back at me.

He wasn't interested, was he?

Until today I didn't even think he remembered my name.

We were almost back to the office when I heard my cell phone ringing. I missed it, but when I finally got to my desk and checked, I saw that there were four missed calls from my mom. "Shit."

"What's wrong?" Jasmine turned her seat to face me.

"Not sure yet. Sec. Hey, Mom. Sorry, I was at lunch."

"Glenna, hon." It took no time to realize that she'd been crying.

"What's wrong? Is it Dad?"

"No, your father's fine. It's Great Glenna."

I closed my eyes and felt the blood drain from my face. "Oh no."

"She's in the hospital, but the doctors aren't sure she's going to make it through the night. Can you come?"

"Where are you?"

"They took her to St. Joseph's."

"I'm on my way."

Jasmine was on her feet standing in front of me when I hung up. "Hon, what's wrong?"

"It's my great-grandmother. She's dying."

2

I was named after my great-grandmother—Great Glenna. She was the type of person so full of life, of silliness, that you'd forget her age. I hoped to be so lucky as to live into my late nineties.

As a kid I'd hated that my dad named me after her. It's not easy to carry around a name like Glenna when you're a child. The teasing I endured . . . man, kids can be cruel. Still, the older I got the more I appreciated the connection I shared with her. Not to mention that I also loved the extra attention she always paid me as a result. Special treats, books, trips. *Sorry, you can't come if your name isn't Glenna.*

It was awesome. So was she.

I've never been a fan of hospitals. I hated the chemical smell that hung in the air. To me it always announced that it was working hard to keep germs and other *things* at bay. I always did what I could to avoid coming here. Tonight, though, it didn't matter. Great Glenna was in the other room. And she was dying.

I sat with my nanna while the doctors were in with her, doing what they could to make her comfortable in her last hours. My dad was off to call the rest of his brothers so everyone knew what was going on. Mom had announced that she was going in search of coffees. Knowing her she'd have a good cry as well. It was going to be a long night, most of all for Nanna.

She'd been holding my hand for the past five minutes, but hadn't said much. My mind naturally drifted to the mortality of everyone I loved. It's a terrifying thing to be reminded of.

"Mum knew this was coming." Nanna gave my hand a squeeze. "She'd been writing letters to people for months now. Saying good-bye properly, as she put it."

"Oh, Nanna." I leaned my head on her shoulder. "I'm sorry."

"It's fine, dear. Mum will be leaving this world with no regrets. That's the most any of us can ask for from this life."

I was twenty-eight years old and already there were things that I had shied away from doing, places that I hadn't gone to. Would I be able to say the same thing about my life when I was ninety-eight? No regrets?

"I've had them on me ever since she finished composing them." Nanna wiped a tear from her cheek.

"What? The letters?"

"Here in my purse. Let me give you yours."

I think I moved more from shock than anything else, giving Nanna room to fish through her bag. She pulled out a small bundle of envelopes, a name neatly printed on the front of each one. Within moments she set the one with my name neatly penned on the front on my lap.

Little Glenna.

My chest squeezed and I found it hard to breathe. I couldn't do that, not yet. She was still here, after all, just resting on a bed in the other room. I swallowed down the rising ball of hurt and smiled. "I'm going to read this later."

"Of course." Nanna suddenly looked horrified. "Maybe I shouldn't have given this to you yet. I should have waited . . . until . . ."

I set the letter on the seat beside me and hugged her hard. "It's fine. I love you."

"I love you, too."

Mom came back then, coffee in hand and her face streaked with dried tears. "There was a hell of a line at Tim Hortons. Sorry for the delay."

Dad came back shortly after that, his face tight and his gaze assessing how Nanna was doing. "Mom, Tony is picking up Brian and they're heading over to the house. Steven will come by here a bit later."

Nanna patted my hand. "Why don't you go for a walk, dear? Stretch your legs a bit."

"I got you a large double-double." Mom handed me a coffee as I got up. "I forgot how big these were. Dump it if you can't drink it all."

"Thanks."

Mom hugged me, holding me longer than she normally would. "I saw there was a nice little sitting area down the hall if you're looking for a quiet spot. We're not going anywhere, so come back in when you're ready."

"I will."

I left them and headed toward the direction Mom had indicated. My thoughts bounced around, remembering my times with Great Glenna. Her home had been a large old farmhouse in Antigonish, Nova Scotia. When I was a kid, we'd go to visit her sometimes, taking Nanna with us. I didn't remember much of the place, but even as a kid I knew that the house was more than a little run-down.

Some summers she'd board a plane and would make the trip herself to stay with Nanna for a month, usually July. I loved the lilt of her voice, the way her eyes would sparkle, telling you she was up to something. I loved her East Coast accent and the way she'd say certain words that made them sound oh-so-very Canadian.

"Dammit." It became hard to take a breath without my body shaking. I needed to sit down, to have some time to pull my shit together before I could even think of going back to my family.

The signs for the sitting area directed me down the hall. The coffee was starting to heat my hand through the cardboard cup. Mom never remembered to ask them to double-cup it. When I finally got to the room, there was a couple inside talking to someone who looked to be hospital staff. *Best if I stay out here then.* A quick look around and I discovered a chair against a wall a few feet away. That would be as good a place as any.

The hallway was quiet except for the hum of voices in the other room and the rattle of air coming through a vent. I sat on the over-padded fake leather chair and waited for the air to hiss from the cushion as my weight settled before I looked at the envelope.

Little Glenna.

It was dainty, small, so unlike the woman who penned it. I laid it on my lap, not ready to open it yet. Instead I drank my coffee, letting the caffeine, sugar, and cream do their best to boost my spirits and charge my body. It was artificial, but would hopefully help get me through the next few hours.

Great Glenna's letter waited.

I finished my coffee and set the cup on the floor.

I took a breath, then another before I finally picked it up to examine it once more. It was thin, probably only containing a single sheet of paper. Nanna had said this was a good-bye from the woman who was currently connected to life-support machines on the opposite end of the floor. She was still living, still holding on.

She was speaking to me even though she couldn't.

I closed my eyes and made up my mind that I would do this now. I slid my thumb beneath the lip and gently tugged the envelope open. I was right in that there was only a single sheet of paper, but wrong that it was the only thing inside. She'd folded it in thirds, as though it were hugging the other item—a picture. Before I opened the letter, I shook it to the side and the photograph slid out.

When I'd been very young, Great Glenna had taken me to the Eaton Center on one of her visits to Toronto. We'd gone into a photo booth and had our picture taken together—two generations bound by a single name. We'd divided them up, two for her and two for me. Over the years, I'd lost my copies. Having a replacement wasn't something I'd ever thought possible, having forgotten that she would have kept hers.

The tears that I'd kept at bay earlier now trickled down my cheeks. Why hadn't I spent more time with her? They'd moved her to a nursing home here years ago, available for me to see whenever I wanted. She was my Great Glenna, a woman whom I'd admired for years, and I'd always done my best to live up to owning her name. I was a horrible great-granddaughter.

Sniffing the tears away, I finally opened the paper so I could read her final words.

> *Dear Little Glenna,*
> *I know I'd told you this before, but I was always secretly pleased that you were the great-grandchild that bore my name. Not that I have any particular attachment to the moniker, but rather because the first moment I saw you as an infant, I knew we were kindred spirits.*
> *I'm so proud of you and what you've accomplished in your life. Working at a college? Well, that's certainly something that I could have never done. My biggest regret was that I never continued my education. Thank you for showing me what could have been.*

When I sat down to write these letters, there were so many people I wanted to offer some final passing thoughts to. Most of them it was simply a good-bye. For you my sweet girl, I wanted to give you something a bit more than that. I want to give you a tiny bit of advice.

I've watched you grow up into a beautiful, intelligent woman. You live your life with care and thought. I want you to stop that. Not completely, but just a bit. I want you to do something wild. I don't use that term lightly. I see you going down a path that is going to give you most of what you want from life. Eventually, I have no doubt that you'll marry and have children of your own. I want that for you.

But I want you to make sure it is with the right man.

I don't want you to get to be my age and be full of regrets.

Today, tomorrow, next week, I want you to go out and do something that will make you say, "Great Glenna would have loved this." I would hope this would involve a man, but only you can decide if that's right for you.

Regardless, I want you to know that I love you. Your mother often told me that you felt bad for not spending more time with me. I'm an old woman, but I'm not a petty one. The time we had together was precious. As you know, I'm a fan of quality over quantity. You always gave me that.

I love you.

Yours for eternity,

Great Glenna.

"Dammit." I wiped the tears away with the heel of my hand. "Dammit."

Every ounce of guilt and regret I'd had filled me. I crushed the letter to my chest and let out a sob that must have been audible to everyone close. She loved me, was proud of me.

She wanted me to take chances.

I leaned forward until my forehead touched my knees. Folded over, I was able to shut everything out, and for just a moment enjoy the darkness and let her words sink in. In so many ways, she was an observer the way I was. She had an uncanny ability to get to the heart of a problem by simply asking a few questions. While I put my skills to work in academia, she used hers to help people live better lives.

She was amazing.

It took me a while to pull myself together enough that I felt I could face my family.

When I returned, the doctor was out speaking with Mom and Dad. Nanna wasn't there. When Dad saw me coming, he met my gaze and gave his head a little shake.

No.

Oh no.

"Mom?"

She wiped her eyes and pulled me into a monster hug. "She's gone, baby."

"Nanna?"

"She's in there with her right now."

I held her a bit tighter. "I love you so much."

"I know. I love you, too." She pulled back and wiped away a fresh batch of my tears. "You got your letter?"

"I did."

"She really did love you best of all the children. And she knew that you loved her, too. Never worry that she didn't."

"Thanks, Mom."

The next few hours were the hardest of my life to date. I somehow held the rest of my tears back once Nanna came out. Dad stepped in and took over until Uncle Stephen arrived. It became easy to slip into the background then, to take a moment to catch my breath. I'd promised Jasmine that I'd give her a call to fill her in.

She picked up on the first ring. "Hon, are you okay?"

"Great Glenna passed."

"I'm so sorry. Do you need anything? I can pick up some things and bring them to your place."

"I'm going to Mom and Dad's tonight to be with them. I just wanted to let you know that I'll be out until after the funeral on Wednesday."

"Don't worry about a thing. I'll even e-mail Mickelson to let him know what's going on."

"Thank you."

"Go be with your family. Call me when you can."

It hurt losing Great Glenna, but what made it easier to handle was having people in my life whom I could count on, whom I loved and who loved me in return. Yes, the pain was there, but I knew it would fade eventually.

The best way I could honor her and her memory was to become the person Great Glenna knew I could. Somehow I needed to find a way to seek out and seize adventure the way she had. To live a life without regret, to do things that Great Glenna would look at and say, *That's my girl!*

Now I just needed to figure out how the hell I could do that.

3

The funeral was as lovely as one could be. It had been years since I'd last been to a service. My parents weren't particularly religious, so we didn't go to church unless Nanna asked us to attend. But Great Glenna had been a believer, and she'd been the one who, several months earlier, had picked out this particular church where she'd wanted her service to take place.

The hymns were ones I recognized as songs she'd often hummed to herself when she'd be knitting something or other. Aunt Sabin had me crying within a few bars of her rendition of the "Ave Maria." Uncle Tony gave the eulogy and Nanna even said a few words. The interment was at a graveyard a short drive away. I placed a flower on her casket along with the other grandchildren and great-grandchildren.

Before I knew it the service was over and we had nothing left to do but to carry on with our lives.

The days between her passing and the funeral gave me an opportunity to look at her letter again and take stock of my life. I couldn't help but think of Jasmine and her teasing. How I was a coward, never willing to put myself out there and take a chance. I thought of Eric and the upcoming barbecue. Jasmine was right in that it was the perfect opportunity to get to know him. There wasn't anything terrible that could happen from saying hello and asking about his classes this semester.

Great Glenna would certainly approve. Eric was kind of her type, except about sixty years too young.

I was thinking of Eric as we fell into groups and began heading back to the cars. The wind had picked up and my hair kept blowing into my face. I stopped to fix it, which was the only reason I saw the bag fly from the top of a gravestone and onto the ground. My cousins continued walking, chatting quietly with one another, and hadn't noticed that I'd fallen behind. I couldn't stand the thought of someone's memorial gift to a loved one lying on the ground. It would only take a second to put it back where it belonged.

"Hold up!" I didn't wait to see if they heard, knowing they wouldn't get too far ahead of me even if they hadn't. I jogged as carefully as I could in high heels on the grass over to the grave. It should have taken me all of two seconds to retrieve the bag and put it back on the grave marker. It would have too, if it weren't for the big black print that caught my attention.

No.

No, someone didn't . . .

I smoothed the wrinkles from the clear bag so I wasn't mistaken about what I was reading.

Day One
Masturbate

"What the hell . . ." My curiosity got the better of me. I pulled open the bag and quickly looked at the contents.

Sexting.

Lap dances.

Car sex.

Oh my God, these were sex cards!

At a graveyard!

"Holy shit."

"Glenna, you coming?"

I jumped and shoved the cards into my pocket without thinking. "Yup."

Sex cards at a graveyard? These couldn't have been intended to be here. Maybe someone was having some sort of kinky sex and these were accidentally left behind. The poor family whose loved one was resting here might get an awful shock if they came for a visit and discovered these.

Best to take them with me so that some other grieving person didn't stumble upon them. I was doing a public service.

Totally.

I caught up to my cousin Kristina. She gave me a quick smile and tilted her head toward the grave marker. "What was that?"

I loved Kristina, but she was a bit more conservative in her views on the world than I was. So not the type of person to appreciate sex cards, especially ones found here. "Oh nothing. Just some garbage. I didn't want to leave it."

"That's nice of you to pick it up." Kristina gave me another smile. "Think they'll have some food back at Nanna's place? I'm starving."

"I think Mom and Dad brought a bunch of stuff over earlier. I assume that most people brought things for her to have. Should be plenty."

The cards were practically burning a hole in my pocket. They were exactly the sort of thing to pique my curiosity: How did they get there? Who wrote them? Who would use them?

God, I didn't want to wait until I got home to take a closer look at them, but I had no choice. I couldn't help but think that Great-Grandma Glenna would have loved the idea of the cards and especially me finding them after her funeral. If I believed in ghosts or fate, I could probably be convinced to believe that she had a hand in me finding them.

But I didn't.

Even if she did.

It really wouldn't have surprised me.

I'd only caught a glance at some of what was written on them, but it was more than enough to know that whoever penned them had an active imagination.

The problem with having a packet of sex cards was, with the notable exception of card one, the necessity of a second person. That was certainly something I was currently lacking.

If I had a choice in the matter, I knew exactly whom I'd want to share them with: Eric. He'd be perfect, but it would require him knowing that I existed as a sexual creature and not simply Professor Mickelson's research assistant. Or however he thought of me.

Maybe these sex cards could help with that?

Yeah, no. I certainly didn't have the proverbial balls for that.

The family had gathered at Nanna's house. Laughter occasionally permeated the mutter of chatter, and the tension that had been present earlier in the day started to subside. I loved my great-grandmother to bits, but I was finding it difficult to keep my attention focused. My mind kept drifting to the clear plastic bag and the contents that I'd transferred to my purse from my pocket the first chance I'd been able.

Talking to my aunt Stephanie? I couldn't help but wonder who needed to be told to masturbate. Giving my cousin Kristina a hug and second coffee? Wondering about lap dances in graveyards.

Either the intended recipient of these cards was new to sex, or there was a lot more to that particular story than I first realized.

"Glenna?"

I jumped at the sound of my mom's voice. She'd been hovering by my dad for most of the day, who in turn had been hovering around his mom, making sure that she was handling things. Accepting her hug, I gave her a quick kiss on the cheek. "How's Dad and Nanna?"

"As well as to be expected." Mom hadn't dyed her hair in a while and I couldn't help but notice the long streaks of gray in her natural brown. Another reminder that we were all getting older.

"Do you need me to get anything?"

"No, I think we've got it all covered. I just wanted to see if you were staying over tonight at the house and if I should head over to make up the spare bed."

A quick glance around the room at my dad and his brothers and I knew they were probably going to dip into the case of beer I saw in the garage and drink to Great-Grandmother's honor. That would leave Mom entertaining the aunts and Nanna, who would probably have a drink or two of their own.

"I think you'll have a full enough house tonight. I'll head back to my place. Besides, I have to go to work tomorrow anyway."

"Oh baby, are you sure you're up for that? It's only been a few days."

"Not really, but I can't take any more time off." I'd already used my allotted three days of bereavement time that the school granted. As much as I'd like to take another day or two to mourn, I knew myself well enough to know that going back to work would be more helpful than sitting in my apartment moping. "I'll be fine."

"Of course you will." Mom tucked a strand of my hair behind my ear. "Well, it looks like I'll be busy tonight, but if you need anything you just call. Okay?"

"Thanks." I gave her another kiss. "I think I might actually slip out. Unless you need me to stay and help out more?"

"Go. Though make sure you say bye to Nanna before you do."

"I will."

I made my rounds, handing out hugs and kisses to people

whom I hadn't seen in years and enduring the bevy of *oh, you look so mature now* and *my goodness you're so beautiful* from the various aunts and uncles. I must have been one hell of an ugly duckling given the amount of comments I received. I spent an extra few minutes with Nanna. She kissed me and squeezed me a bit harder.

"Of all the grandchildren and great-grandchildren, you're the one who's most deserving to be her namesake."

Oh.

Dammit.

I wiped the moisture from my eyes. "Thanks."

She squeezed my hand. "Go on and no more tears. She wouldn't want you dwelling."

So that's what I did.

The drive from Nanna's house felt weird. I'd tried to listen to music, but only got annoyed when my Spotify feed kept dropping off. The silence wasn't much better though. Too many thoughts about mortality—my own and my family's— that threatened to push hard against my grief. What I needed was a complete distraction.

I hit the phone button on my steering wheel. "Call Jasmine."

The electronic flutter of numbers being dialed echoed in my car. It rang four times before the familiar pop of her voice crackled through the speaker. "Hello?"

"Hey, Jaz, it's me."

"Hey, you." I heard her pull the phone away. "Just a second, Mummy . . . Sorry. How was the funeral?"

"The service was nice."

"Good. How are you holding up?"

"You know, okay I guess. Actually, since the service finished it doesn't seem so heavy, if that makes sense."

"I get that."

I hit a bump and my purse fell to the floor. The contents

slipped out and I caught sight of the bag from the corner of my eye. *Oh!* "You had plans tonight, didn't you?"

"Yeah. I'm at Mom's right now. She has me painting her bathroom. It's pink." She made a gagging noise.

"That's too bad. I found something . . . unique at the graveyard."

"I'm actually terrified to ask. And that's saying something."

I chuckled as I switched lanes. "Let's just say it's something Great Glenna would have appreciated."

"A dildo?"

"Oh my God."

"You did *not* find a dildo there?" She laughed hysterically. "That's fucked up."

"No, not a dildo. But it's something almost as weird. I found a plastic bag that had what looks like a bunch of sex cards in it."

"Whoa, what?"

"Index cards with sex things to try. Threesomes and shower sex and stuff."

"You're shitting me? That's awesome."

"Seriously, it was as though Great Glenna were there trying to tell me something."

"That you needed to get laid?"

I snorted. "Well, yes. But she was always after me to get out there and do something wild. She would have loved it." The sudden tightness of my throat forced me to clear it. The last thing I needed was to start bawling while driving. "Today was harder than I thought it would be."

"I wish I could be there for you tonight."

"I know. I'll be fine once I get home and have a shower."

"Bring the cards to work tomorrow. I'm dying to see these now." Her laughter filled the car and eased the ache in my chest. "We'll have to take an extra-long lunch and talk dirty in honor of Great Glenna."

"That sounds awesome. We'll have to be careful with them. From what I saw I wouldn't want to wave these under too many people's noses."

"It's frosh week. Everyone is busy with their own shit, getting ready for the term. No one will even remember we're alive until the middle of the month. We should be fine."

We chatted for a few more minutes before I pulled into heavier traffic. The last thing I wanted to do was get into an accident with a rental car while trying to navigate the 401 as I got closer to Toronto, so I let her go. If nothing else, I had something fun to look forward to tomorrow to take my mind off more depressing thoughts.

Sex cards at a graveyard?

Clearly, someone else's life was far more interesting than mine.

4

It's strange how something can go from hilarious to a wee bit sad in the blink of an eye. After I'd gotten home from returning the rental, I poured myself a glass of wine and pulled out the cards. I wanted to check them out in closer detail before I made good with my promise to bring them to school. If they were too racy, I would leave them home and Jasmine would have to come over to see them. While I was trying to take Great Glenna's advice and do things that were adventurous, I wasn't about to get myself in trouble at work. Professor Mickelson was an okay boss, but he had very specific views on how people should behave at work. Sex cards were probably not on the "approved behaviors" list. It was better to be safe than sorry.

Plus, I really wanted to see them now.

I started flipping through them as I tried to relax and enjoy the moment. Masturbate. *Snort.* Dry hump your partner. *Snicker.*

And then it happened. One second I was drinking wine and giggling at what was written there, and in the next I felt guilty for laughing at someone else's pain. Which card so drastically changed my mood?

Day Seventeen
Reenact a scene from a porn movie
(ask Nikki if you need help)

Nikki must be someone whom the recipient trusted quite a bit in order for them to ask for help regarding a porn movie. I mean, who asks random people for help about that? That got my imagination going full speed ahead—who was Nikki, was it a sister or friend, how would the recipient feel when it came to needing help . . . and that's when it hit me.

These cards were intended to help a very real person. This wasn't some movie where a character was looking to spice up their life. No, a flesh-and-blood person had used these cards, most likely to get over a loss.

It had started out hard to think of this mysterious recipient as an actual woman—and I was certain that these were for a *she* and not a *he*. The longer I spent looking at the hand-printed words, the more I could clearly see her in my head. She was probably older, maybe someone who wanted to be adventurous but didn't know where to start. The author would have cared a great deal for this person and wanted to give her these cards as a gift.

You need to take chances, Glenna. You can't live your life scared of your own shadow.

Ignoring Great Glenna's voice in my head, I spread the cards across my coffee table and spent the better part of twenty minutes looking at them. I positioned them in their proper order, looking at their progression. I picked up the Day One card to examine it. On the back there was a faint impression of part of a sentence.

. . . here, I started this little project. I call it Alyssa's 30 Days . . .

Who was this Alyssa? Clearly these had been written by someone with a heavy hand. It was someone who I could only imagine wasn't around any longer. Someone who wanted her to have a lot of sexy fun.

I turned the card around again. It didn't look used, the corners weren't bent and there were no creases or spills distorting the card stock. Alyssa either hadn't used them, or else she'd gotten what she'd needed and left them behind.

Oh.

She'd placed them on a grave marker. She was saying good-bye.

Guilt washed over me and I fumbled to put them back into a neat pile. I shouldn't be looking at these. They were a private thing, something between Alyssa and her deceased loved one. God, I was a horrible human being.

No matter how bold I'd wanted to be, or how badly I wanted to do something that would make Great Glenna proud, I couldn't take advantage of something like this. It was wrong.

I shoved the cards back into the bag and then into my purse. I knew that I couldn't show these to Jasmine. What I really needed to do was take them back to the graveyard tomorrow after work and return them. Yeah, that's what I would do. It shouldn't be too hard to figure out where I'd found them.

Right?

I'd make it up to Jasmine somehow. She'd understand.

Jasmine pressed both her hands on the edge of my desk and leaned over. Her long, straight black hair swung forward to frame her face and highlight her scowl. "What do mean you won't show them to me?"

Dear God, she scared the shit out of me. "They're private."

"Umm, no. You found them at a graveyard. That means they're out there for anyone or their dog to take. You took and I want to see."

"It's not that simple."

"Yes it is." Jasmine groaned and stood up. "These are just some silly sex cards, right? From a store?"

"They were homemade, actually."

"And they're kinky? Like porno kinky?"

"Are you going to keep bugging me about these?"

"If you're going to keep holding out on me? Yes." She leaned back and crossed her arms, her eyes locked onto mine. "I was promised sex cards and I want to see sex cards."

Why I thought I could talk Jasmine out of something once she had her mind set on it was beyond me. I fished them out of my purse, but I still didn't hand them over. "I feel bad about this. It's like we're looking at something that was meant to be private. A diary or something."

Her gaze was locked onto the bag and I knew she was dying to get her hands on them. She was almost as excited as she got at Christmas. "Glenna, *please*."

I held them up just out of her reach. "You have to promise me you're going to be respectful."

"You have a look on your face. That *oh, I just figured this puzzle out* look. Which means you've already spent a shit-ton of time examining these things. So please tell me the reason why I need to be *respectful* about *sex cards*."

And that was how I lost most of my battles with my best friend—she was annoyingly logical. "You're right, I looked them over last night. These were written for a woman named Alyssa. I think she's a widow and these are from her late husband, written obviously before he died."

"How could you possibly know that? Other than 'obviously' guessing."

Holding up my hand, I ticked off the reasons. "I found them at a graveyard. They're not really used. The first card tells her to masturbate. The author is directing her to get help from this Nikki, who I would assume is a sister or good friend." I let my hand drop. "Maybe this was him trying to get her back out there. After he'd gone."

"You mean died?" Jasmine hummed into her coffee cup and leaned farther back against her seat when I nodded. "That's actually some pretty brilliant deduction, Sherlock. Other than the fact you're assuming it's a *husband,* I could buy that."

"Based on the faint handwriting on the back, I assumed man. But sorry, I'll try to be more politically correct. Significant other."

"Thank you." Jasmine grinned.

"Whoever she is, I assume she's finished with the cards and that's why she left them there. There was nothing that said anything about sex in a graveyard—"

"Not that I would know because you haven't shown them to me yet—"

"But I think I'm going to take them back." I sucked in a breath and held it. When Jasmine didn't have a snarky remark I let it out slowly. "Well?"

Other than my parents, I'd say Jasmine is the one person who knows me the best in the world. I can't think of a time since we'd first met that I'd been able to pull one over on her. Jasmine sighed and shook her head. "Do you know what I think?"

"I have no doubt that you're about to tell me."

"I think that you want to keep the cards. I think that you might even want to use them." Jasmine cocked her head to the side and seemed to be considering something. "Your problem has always been that you need someone to give you permission to do anything. At least, that's not related to your job."

"I don't need permission." What a stupid idea. I was a

grown woman. "I just don't want to take something that was meant to be private and use them for my own perverted pleasure."

I could tell from the look on Jasmine's face that I'd totally used the wrong word choice. "How perverted?"

From the moment I'd told her about finding the cards, there was only one way this conversation was going to end. Rather than fight the inevitable any longer, I groaned and held out the cards for her to see. "I'm still taking them back."

Jasmine waved her hand dismissively before snatching the cards and scurrying back to her desk. "Okay, my pretties, let's see what you have for us."

I didn't need to see the cards to know what was written on each one. I'd spent more than enough time with them the night before to remember their words. The first few were tame, as though the author wanted to gently nudge Alyssa into some fun. Then they get a bit wild. Not outside of the realm of things that I'd consider doing, but not boring old missionary position either.

"Oh I like Day Twenty-seven." She licked her lips. "I'll volunteer to be the woman you kiss."

"That would be like kissing my sister."

"You're breaking my heart." She didn't look even a little upset. "These are awesome."

"And they're going back to the graveyard." I held my hand out, but Jasmine shook her head and turned her chair away from me.

"That's a horrible idea. I mean, you haven't even tried Day Twelve, oh and Day Twenty-six . . . my God that's hot."

"Jaz—"

"A vibrator in you while you go to a movie? You wouldn't last ten minutes."

"Will you keep your voice down? They'll be able to hear you down the hall."

"No. And you can't return these."

God, here we go. "Why not?"

"Because you don't know where to put them."

"I know the aisle where I found them. It shouldn't be that hard to remember which one it came from."

"Really?" She crossed her arms and stared at me.

It wouldn't be that hard to figure it out, right? There were only ten or so grave markers in that section. I was pretty sure I could tell which one it was, even though I didn't see it from the front. Though, I didn't actually know the last name of this Alyssa person, or if she shared the same name as her late partner, so I couldn't even be certain.

And what if they were put there accidentally?

And some poor unsuspecting person picked them up.

Or a kid.

"Shit." I dropped my forehead to my desk. "I can't take them back."

Jasmine chuckled. "I love that brain of yours. I could actually see your thought process churning. So now that you've come to that conclusion, we need to figure out what to do with them."

"You should take them." I peeked up at her through my hair. "You could find some hot girl and have a lot of fun."

"I don't need some sex cards to help me with that. I have a few prospects lined up if I can't get Nell to forgive me for missing our date last month." She winked. "I do have an idea though."

"What's that?"

Jasmine leaned in until her face wasn't far from mine. "You should show Eric."

That was all it took for my imagination to kick in again. I'd walk past his office on my way to the library. He'd be coming out at the same time and we'd run into each other. The book that I had the sex cards hidden in would fall, spilling them across the floor. Naturally, he would help me pick them up and catch sight of what was written on them.

What are these, Glenna?

Oh nothing.

They don't look like nothing.

Sex cards. I'd blush then, knowing he'd think I was a naughty girl for having them.

I'd be bent over so his gaze would travel to my cleavage. *And are you using them?*

I don't have anyone to use them with.

I'd be happy to help you out with them.

And bam, crazy-monkey sex! I swore that someday I would actually know what crazy-monkey sex really was.

"Maybe. But I'm pretty certain that propositioning a coworker with sex cards at our place of employment is frowned upon."

"No one would believe that nice, quiet Glenna O'Donald would do anything so crass as to proposition anyone. Besides, it's perfectly fine to date colleagues or else Nell and I would have been fired two years ago."

Jasmine was having an on-off relationship with Nell, who worked in the registrar's office. They were too much alike in many ways, which did cause some of their tension, but when they were *on* they were cute.

"How *is* Nell?"

"No, no, no. Stay on topic. You, Eric, and sex cards. We need to figure out a way for you to show him." Jasmine gets a particular look on her face when she's about to suggest something she knows will get me going. "I have the perfect thing.

You should take them to the welcome-back barbecue and show him there."

Not this again. "You're insane."

"Hear me out. That party is the first time you met him, which was this time last year. It's been a whole frigging year of you wanting to get into this guy's pants. Take the cards to the party and show Eric. See what he says."

"No." But there was something in my head that didn't let that thought settle.

Jasmine must have picked up on it too. She stood and handed the cards back. "Just consider it, okay?"

"No." I was already wondering if it was possible to make that happen. Would others notice? How would Eric react? "Dammit."

"Oh look at the time. I have a meeting for the rest of the day. I better go." Jasmine took her things and flounced away.

There she goes, my best friend and chief tormentor!

I reclaimed the cards and went to shove them back into my purse. Folded neatly along the side was Great Glenna's letter to me. I pulled it out, holding it in one hand and the sex cards in the other. Maybe this was fate pushing me to where it wanted me to go. I needed to do something radical to break out of the comfortable shell life had cocooned me in. Acting on my Eric fantasies with some sex cards would certainly do that.

It could also be a horrible mistake with unimaginable consequences.

This wasn't something I could think about now. I had e-mails to deal with that had piled up when I'd been gone. My sex life would survive another day without me worrying about it. I carefully folded Great Glenna's letter, slipped it into the bag with the sex cards, and returned them to my purse.

At the end of the day, my work completed and with nothing else to do, I sucked it up and brought them home. I briefly debated taking the bus to the graveyard to return the sex cards even after telling Jasmine that I wouldn't, but realized that mistakenly putting them on the wrong marker would be a world of awful worse than keeping them.

For good or bad, they belonged to me now.

When I got home, I went straight to my bedroom, shoved them into my nightstand drawer, and did my best to forget about them. Tomorrow I'd go back to work and would concentrate on getting back into my routine.

Life should now get back to normal.

5

From the outside looking in, I don't have the most exciting of jobs. There's not a lot of running around or crazy business meetings. There aren't any products that I get to try out and make my friends jealous with. I read. A lot. I get to talk to people when I need to conduct interviews, but that doesn't happen as often as I would like. Basically, I'm Professor Mickelson's minion and I do all that I can to make him look good.

I'm a digger. The rummager of articles. The master of the microfiche.

I love books.

I hate Wikipedia.

And often I'm alone.

As a result, it becomes fairly obvious when someone is watching me. Well, maybe not watching me exactly, but certainly paying more attention than normal.

Friday had come and gone quietly enough. The weekend had been filled with family calls and the process of getting my life back to normal. Not once had I thought about the sex cards and how I might incorporate them into my life.

The Monday after the funeral—and my having brought the cards home—started out typical enough. I went off to the library and spent time in the stacks. With the students now back on campus, there was an influx of people milling around the building. It was so easy to pick out the freshmen and the post-grad students. Two very distinct looks on polar-opposite sides of the scale. Normally I'd take my time and do a bit of people watching, but I didn't want to get pulled into playing tour guide accidentally.

Once I'd found the articles I'd been looking for, I signed them out and trudged back to our office. Jasmine and I shared a decent-sized room on the main floor of our building. The concrete blocks had been painted a moss green that seemed to glow strangely when the sun shone on them. Every time I came from the library I'd take the staircase that was on the opposite end of the building from our office. I liked walking down that hallway, as it saved me having to walk too long in the heat or cold, depending on the time of year. It also had the unintended side effect of taking me directly past Eric's office.

Which, you know, total bonus.

His door was almost always closed, either because he wasn't there or he was in a meeting. Sometimes, though, I'd be able to hear him talking on the phone or to a student and I'd walk a bit slower. Not that I was stalking him or anything. Okay, maybe a little bit. There was a long, skinny window that flanked either side of the door, so I could always sneak a peek of him and his potential companion. Those fleeting glances had served as fuel for my fantasies for the past year.

Good times right there.

I took my normal route up the stairs and enjoyed the shiver of anticipation as I approached his office. There wasn't any sound coming from ahead, so I assumed he wasn't there. Which sucked. I do enjoy my Eric fix on a Monday.

I nearly stumbled when I realized that his door was open

and he was inside. I didn't turn my head even as I awkwardly continued forward, but saw him working at his desk out of the corner of my eye.

I could have sworn that he looked up and watched me go. My heart pounded and I barely made it to my office. In all the time he'd been here, he'd never paid attention to me like that before. I was a distracted mess the rest of the day, my mind wandering back over that moment until I was damn near crazy.

The next day I had to go back to the library. I wanted to see if we had any first-person accounts in the archives that would support a quote I'd discovered the day before. It took me a bit longer than normal because the staff was busy helping new students and somehow things were already starting to get misshelved.

Once finished, I returned to the office, climbing up the far staircase and walking slower down the hall than I ever had in the past. I could see light spilling across the floor from where Eric's door was open. The murmur of voices grew louder as I approached. That in itself was so weird, given that in the past year he'd been at the school he would always have the door closed if he was in a meeting.

This time when I passed I turned my head slightly to see Eric leaning back in his chair speaking to two students who looked terrified to be there. *Freshmen.* I barely caught Eric's glance at me before I was past his door. There was no mistaking the full-on glance he gave me on my way by. My heart once again pounded in my chest, and this time it was accompanied by a full-body shiver. I wouldn't have believed it, but yes, I was in fact turned on by a single look from a hot guy. Thank God Jasmine wasn't there or else I wouldn't have heard the end of it. Getting my literature review report done so wasn't happening. Tomorrow, I'd have to be focused and not let my mind dwell on what it would be like to step into Eric's office and feel the full effect of his gaze on me.

Wednesday came far faster than I'd hoped. I had absolutely no reason to go to the library, so I resigned myself to attacking my desk work. It was phone interview day, where I got to play the part of manager and grill potential student research assistants for my team in the upcoming semester. Professor Mickelson had given me the list of candidate names and contact information via e-mail, but little else to go on.

That was fine, I could totally rock the phone thing.

Except, I'd forgotten how mind-numbing interviews could be. It's one thing when you get a great candidate who's engaging, makes jokes, laughs at my corny lines. It's quite another when dead air and awkward pauses punctuate rambling theories.

Jasmine proved once again why she was my best friend by bringing me coffee and jelly beans when I didn't think I could take any more. There was a fan in the window going constantly in the summer because our building's version of air-conditioning was laughable. Despite the calendar saying it was September, temperatures hadn't yet turned and the fan was going full out.

I leaned back in my seat, the back of my neck exposed to the fan and my floor-length skirt pulled up to my knees. I was listening to a candidate telling me about their master's thesis when I looked up and saw Eric walking down the hall toward our office.

There wasn't much at our end of the building. The kitchen was on the basement level, the office supply room on the floor above us. We were the last office right before the staircase, which hardly anyone used. And yet, there I sat, listening to an actually quite brilliant theory about social media as a tool for the disenfranchised, and watched as Professor Eric Morris sauntered toward me.

He stopped in the hall in front of the door and looked at me. It wasn't the subtle glances that I'd been firing his way for months now. No, this was a full-out stare that should have been creepy if it wasn't turning me on so goddamned much. My hearing must have gone on me because I couldn't make out the words coming from the chipper voice on the other end of the receiver. My entire awareness became nothing more than Eric's rich brown eyes looking at me as though I was a strange puzzle that needed to be solved.

"Does that make sense?" The question from my candidate jolted me out of my lust-induced haze.

"Yes, it does." I sat forward and pulled my skirt down. When I looked up again, Eric was gone.

And with him went the remainder of my ability to concentrate. I hired the next student I spoke to, though I couldn't for the life of me remember their name until I received an email from them later that day.

I didn't have an Eric sighting at all on Thursday, but that did nothing to help me get him out of my mind. That night when I got home, I was completely restless, frustrated by my unfulfilled fantasies. I'd spent the entire night tossing and turning, my mind replaying the previous day's events with Eric in the hall over and over. When I would fall asleep, my mind continued to play out the scenario, with very different results. Eric coming into my office, taking the receiver from my hand and placing it on the phone before dropping to his knees and kissing me. Pushing his hands beneath my skirt and cupping my pussy. Pulling his cock out so I could suck on it.

So yeah, I didn't sleep much.

I didn't sleep, but I did masturbate. Plenty.

I guess you could say I completed the task on the first card to a T.

By the time Friday finally came, I was exhausted. It had been a whole week since I'd found the cards. The end of the week, the college was normally a quiet place. Students would take early classes and then would head over to the Social Club. This week was no exception, and our building had emptied out pretty early. From what I could tell, it was only Jasmine and me left on our floor.

Her phone rang. "Hello?" From the look on her face I knew it had to be Nell on the other end. No one else could make Jasmine grin like that.

I didn't even wait for her to say anything when she hung up. "Get out of here."

"It's only two. That's early, even for us." She was already standing and grabbing her purse.

"You know no one is here. And if by some weird twist of fate a student or professor comes looking for you, I have your back. Now go. Be flirty with Nell. Drink wine."

"How did you—"

"Oh please. Go."

Jasmine grinned. "I love you." She kissed the top of my head on her way out the door.

There I was, all alone on a Friday at the beginning of the fall term, sitting in a stuffy office. The piles of books on my desk were musty, and the heat of the office only made them smell worse. I would need to hang around until at least three before I could reasonably duck out as well. Not that I had any major plans for the long weekend. No reason to take off. Nothing but an empty apartment and a pile of sex cards that I couldn't possibly use.

I picked up my pen and began to tap it on the edge of my desk. The noise echoed in the office. With a sigh, I set it back into my R2-D2 decorative mug and looked out into the hallway. It was devoid of any life, human or otherwise.

I sighed again.

What I needed was a drink.

I'd have to settle for a club soda.

Rummaging through my purse I liberated some change that had escaped to the bottom and made my way down to the kitchen and the vending machines. The basement hallway was far cooler than my floor, and the change in temperature as I walked brought goose bumps up across my skin.

The kitchen was as empty as the rest of the building, save for the hum of the vending machines and the clicking snap of the coffeemaker heating up. This time of year was strange and wonderful here at the school. Things would switch from hectic to dead in the blink of an eye. Meaningful conversations were few as everyone was still settling into their new schedules. Not that I'd have to worry about making any small talk today.

The vending machines lined the back wall like sirens, calling out to their prey with the soft glow of their lights and the mechanical song of a compressor whirring. The clink of my money hitting the coin collector and the thud of the can landing into the slot held my attention. The can was cold and sweating by the time I fished out the club soda. I didn't bother to wait to get back to the office and cracked the can open, taking that first sip of fizzy goodness.

I smiled and turned to head back upstairs, only to stop in my tracks.

Eric was standing in the doorway. His gaze was locked on the can in my hand, and slowly rose up my body to meet my gaze. I swallowed hard, again shocked at the intensity of his brown eyes. Wasn't that supposed to be an earthy color? Gentle and kind? It shouldn't be hard, piercing, like a probe that could see to the back of my skull.

"Hello again, Glenna." Holy shit, his voice was a rumble that filled the space, even though he barely raised it.

I held the can a bit tighter. "Professor Morris."

We stood there staring at each other, unmoving. Jasmine wasn't here to act as moderator this time, meaning I would have to get out of this situation on my own. The urge to flee was strong, but my curiosity was far more intense. He was standing there looking at me, aware of my existence, the one thing that I'd wanted more than anything in the year since he'd unpacked his first box of published studies in his office.

But the longer he looked at me, that his gaze flicked from my eyes to my cheeks and down to my shoulders, lower, the more I wasn't certain that I could survive the power of his focus. I cleared my throat, finally looking away. "I didn't think anyone else was here. Most people have left for the day."

He took another step into the kitchen, off to the side. The doorway was now open and I could easily leave without having to push past him. Was this a silent invitation to go? Was he making it easy for me to escape his presence?

Why the hell would I want to do that?

"I got caught up reading a study." The sound of his voice was less of a shock this time. He moved another step to the side, circling me. "I lost track of time."

"Jasmine had a date so she took off early. I was going to use the opportunity to get some research done."

He nodded. The muscle in his jaw jumped before he cocked his head. "What field?"

Okay, I could do this. Have a normal conversation with him. "Communication and cultural conventions. Jasmine calls me Sherlock because I have an uncanny ability to find bits of information that support Professor Mickelson's crazy theories. He loves when I make him look like a genius."

Eric looked back at the coffee machine. "So you're good and he's lazy."

It was a statement and not something that I felt I could comment on. *Yeah, I'm awesome and my boss is an asshole. Thanks!* Instead I took a sip of my club soda and tried not to burp. "And what are you reading? The study?"

He tapped his finger on the tabletop before turning toward the coffeemaker. For a moment I thought he was going to get his mug and go. Maybe he did as well because when he turned back and crossed the distance that separated us, he looked almost as surprised as I was.

"Glenna." His gaze was locked onto mine. "Tell me about the cards?"

You know when you're younger and your parents catch you out doing something that you shouldn't? That overwhelming, surprised sickness that hits you like a wallop to your stomach, chest, and psyche, followed by the overwhelming urge to pee? That's exactly what his words did to me. I couldn't even remember how to breathe as I tried to accept that yes, he was in fact talking about the sex cards that I had hidden away at home.

I looked away from him and toward the door. It would be easy enough for me to leave, to say nothing and disappear back into my office. Hell, I could shut the door and I wouldn't even have to see him go past. It's not like I was worried that he'd track me down and demand answers.

I wanted another drink of my soda, but the fizzy bubbles were adding to the pressure growing inside me.

"Glenna?"

"Cards?" Wow, I really was a chickenshit.

"Yes. The ones I heard you and your friend talking about the other day."

"You were eavesdropping?" That would totally burst some of my fantasies if he had.

"Not at all. I don't think the two of you realize how well your voices carry when the hall is empty."

Shit. "Umm. Sorry."

His hands twitched at his sides. "Would you tell me about the cards?"

"Oh yes. Those. Well, you know, they're just cards. Thirty of them. That have suggestions for couples. To do things. With each other. And occasionally fruit."

His cologne was fainter than normal, but being this close to him I was still able to make it out. He was wearing a dress shirt, but didn't have on a tie. At some point during the day he'd rolled up his sleeves, exposing his muscular forearms and their dusting of hair. The top two buttons of his shirt were also undone, giving me the perfect view of his throat. There weren't many situations where I loved being short, but standing next to Eric was certainly one of them.

When he swallowed, I watched, fascinated by the bob of his Adam's apple. "What were the suggestions regarding?"

It would be wrong for me to lean in and lick the hollow of his throat, yes? I was fairly certain that was a social no-no. "Well, just some things that you would do as a—"

"Glenna."

"—sex cards. They're sex cards."

My heart pounded as a rush of adrenaline surged through me. He didn't move closer, but I watched as his pecs flexed beneath his shirt. It was as though he was holding himself back from doing . . . something. Maybe he'd regretted the question and was trying to come up with a way to get the hell out of here without seeming rude.

"Look at me?" His voice was soft now, but just as commanding.

I pulled my gaze from his body to look back into his eyes. The intensity had eased, only to be replaced with something else. I wished I knew him better so I could guess what he was thinking.

"What are you doing with sex cards?" It was a simple question, but the answer proved to be a bit more complicated.

"I found them." I groaned then and rolled my eyes. The restraint that had held me back for over a year snapped and the words came rushing from me. "Okay, this is going to sound weird and I don't want you to think that I'm some sort of a freak or anything. I was at my great-grandmother's funeral—"

"I'm sorry for your loss."

"Thank you. And on the way back I noticed something that

had blown off a gravestone and it turned out to be a bag with a bunch of sex cards in it and rather than put them back I stuck them in my pocket and I can't even really tell you why I did because I don't have anyone in my life to use them with. But I found them and then I told Jasmine and she wouldn't stop bugging me until I showed her. So I did."

Eric reached out and put his hands on my shoulders. My head spun at the gentleness of his touch. That simple contact was overwhelming and grounding in the same instant. With his thumbs he rubbed soft circles. "Stop. Just stop."

"Sorry." I laughed. "I don't know why I'm nervous."

"I make you nervous?" He cocked an eyebrow.

"A little."

"Why?"

Oh, you know, because I totally want to have crazy-ass monkey sex with you. "I don't know. You're kind of intense I guess."

His hands fell away from me and I immediately missed their warmth. "I've been told that before."

He did walk away then and get his coffee cup. I stood there watching, because what the hell was I supposed to do after that? The can of club soda was dented from where I'd been clutching it, the sweat on the can now dripping onto the floor.

Should I leave? Probably. What else do you say to someone after confessing to stealing sex cards from a graveyard? I took a step toward the door as he put creamer into his mug. I took another step when he slid the mug under the dispenser and pressed the button.

Okay, so whatever it was that had happened between us was clearly over. I nodded, more to myself than anything, straightened my shoulders, and walked away.

I'd just stepped into the hallway when he called out. "Glenna?"

My heart did a weird flippy-turny thing as I poked my head back around the corner. "Yes?"

"If you want," he said with his back to me, "to bring those cards of yours back to work some Friday afternoon, I'd be interested in seeing them."

Oh.

Oh my.

"No." I spoke the word softly, probably too softly for him to hear.

He must have, though, because he turned his head slightly toward me and nodded. "Fair enough."

I'm not ashamed to say that I ran as quickly as I could back to my office and shut the door.

6

Now, I'm not normally a person who lives in the future. I honestly would rather live in the here and now, tackling daily tasks rather than worrying about things that may never come to fruition. I have my retirement plan and a few investments set up only due to the harassment of my father. If you asked me to make plans for something a few months in advance I would do it, but then it would be gone from my mind. The excitement would only come once the time was upon me.

Eric was interested in seeing the cards *some Friday afternoon*. There wasn't a definitive date or time, no commitment to getting together to review them. No reason for me to get excited.

Never mind the fact that I was absolutely *not* going to bring them in for him. No way. I didn't know him, not really, and he didn't know me. Despite having a major lust-crush on him, I couldn't be reckless enough to do something like that.

It was stupid.

Totally idiotic.

I purposely ignored the cards Friday night, not certain that

I'd be able to make it through the night if I'd looked at them. My plan failed spectacularly because I didn't sleep a wink.

Instead I masturbated. Twice.

Saturday morning I debated calling Jasmine and filling her in on my weird encounter with Eric. I knew she was most likely otherwise engaged and I didn't want to do anything to ruin her time with Nell. I knew what she'd say at any rate: *What the hell's the matter with you? Take the cards and go get laid!*

That would be the opposite of helpful.

Instead I called my mom.

"Hi, sweetheart. How are you doing?"

"I'm okay. Just wanted to see how Nanna was making out."

"As well as to be expected. She's been talking a lot about her own arrangements, funeral expenses, updating her will and the like. It's been hard on your dad."

The realities of mortality and how quickly our lives are over before we have a chance to do everything that we want hit me. "Do you want me to come visit?"

"Not unless you want to. We're fine, but probably not the best company right now. You're doing okay?"

"I'm fine." Truth be told I was feeling guilty that I wasn't more upset than I actually was. "It's been a strange week."

"You need to get out and have some fun. I worry about you spending too much time in that library. You work at a college. I would hope there would be some bands playing at the pub or a faculty party you could attend."

Eric flashed to mind. "It's nothing but craziness this month. Students getting drunk for the first time running around campus and stuff."

"Well, that shouldn't stop you. You're in your twenties, not your eighties. I hate to see you all alone."

"Mom—"

"I'll stop. Still, you should go out and enjoy the weekend."

"I will."

"Good."

We chatted for a bit longer, but once I'd hung up the phone I didn't feel any better. Mom's normal prodding to get me out into the dating pool normally never bothered me. Combined with my run-in with Eric and my overactive imagination, though, I knew I needed to get out and do something or else I'd start to go a bit crazy.

I spent the rest of the weekend visiting parks and outside venues in and around my apartment. One thing that I'd always loved about Toronto was the number of things you can pick up and do at a moment's notice. So I went and did, hoping to burn off the rising tide of energy inside me.

It didn't help.

On Monday I arrived at the office a full hour ahead of Jasmine. I made sure to fix my hair before I pushed open the door and walked down the hall. I had to swallow my disappointment when I realized that Eric's office door was closed and he was nowhere in sight. Which was good, because I didn't want to see him.

Nope.

Not even in his light gray shirt and charcoal dress pants.

When Jasmine flew in, talking before she was even fully inside the room, I had to press pause on my mental fantasies and focus my attention on her. "My God, this is the best day ever. The weather is perfect and the birds were singing my song as I walked across the parking lot."

"Clearly you had a good weekend." I laughed at her dramatic sigh as she fell into her chair. "You and Nell?"

"My plan was a success. We're back on, baby!"

"That's good. I'm so happy for you, Jaz."

"I think we might actually have worked a few things out this weekend. I mean, we didn't argue even once. And the sex. Holy fucking God, the sex."

"Sure, brag to the girl who hasn't gotten any in months." Six months, three weeks, and a handful of days. But who was counting?

"I keep telling you you'll never find the right guy sitting around pining for someone who you refuse to chase after. You either need to get off your ass and do something, or join an on-line dating site so you can meet people."

That was my opportunity to tell her about what had happened on Friday. A natural transition from *Hey, you had great sex* to *Actually, I was eye-fucking Eric's forearms in the kitchen.* But I delayed too long and she'd moved on to talking about the interviews she was going to have to set up this week, so it didn't feel right to bring it up.

I tried to focus on my work, but my thoughts bounced between my research and wondering where Eric was. When I felt myself start to get depressed my gaze would wander out into the hallway toward where Eric would normally come in. Through the school year his office hours were in the morning as he taught in the afternoon. Not that I was paying that much attention. Nope, not me. When he wasn't in by noon, I couldn't help but wonder where he'd gotten off to. When he wasn't here by one, I had to admit that I was worried just a little. By two o'clock, I couldn't stand it any longer. I picked up a stack of books and stood so quickly that Jasmine jumped.

"I need to renew these. Right now. I mean before I have to leave."

"Okay." She stared at me for a few seconds longer before shaking her head and turning back toward her computer.

"I'll be back."

"Yup."

Eric's door remained stubbornly closed and his office empty both on my trip to and from the library, where my books did in fact need to get renewed. We'd shared only a handful of conversations over the year that we'd worked together in the same building, so it wasn't as though I should have known his schedule or any deviations to it. Still, I was annoyed.

How could what happened on Friday have happened and then he not be here on Monday? It was as though fate or some ancient gods were playing a horrible prank on me.

Here Glenna, here is this man who you've been lusting after for so long now.

And *POOF* he's gone.

Sucker!

When three thirty came, I had to put my Eric Watch on hold. I'd talked to Mom last night on the phone and promised her that I'd stop by after work. I did walk past his office one more time just to reassure myself that I hadn't missed him. Nope, the door was shut. I straightened my shoulders and forced myself to ignore the what-might-have-beens and get my ass to the bus on time. I arrived moments before the bus did, and quickly took my window seat. It gave me the perfect view of Eric getting out of his car in the parking lot and heading to the building.

Typical.

Tuesday morning I couldn't bring myself to come in early. I'd slept horribly again the previous night, without even the benefit of sexy Eric fantasies. Thoughts of the cards and Great Glenna's words kept me from sleep until the wee hours. It had taken two full coffees to get me to the point where I could leave my apartment and recognize the right bus line to take. Which meant I was going to be useless all day.

I don't want to be dramatic about the situation, but the main thing that kept me going was the hope of an Eric sighting. And if Great Glenna was out there pulling some cosmic strings for me, preferably a sighting of him with his shirt sleeves rolled up. When I stepped out into the hallway and saw the light from his open office door spilling across the tile, I smiled. Okay then, this was much better. A quick glance as I walked past showed three other professors crowded into chairs in the space, all leaning in and debating something displayed on his computer. Eric didn't even look up as I passed.

Shit.

Frustration wasn't a new thing for me, so I continued on about my day.

I sat down and stared at my computer before glaring back down the hallway. This sucked. I'd spent the night debating Great Glenna's words and finally came to the tentative conclusion that yes, maybe, possibly I would bring the cards in on Friday and talk to Eric about them.

Maybe.

My e-mail *blooped* at me and I knew that the real world was once again at my doorstep.

> **To:** O'Donald, Glenna
> **From:** Social Committee
> **Subject:** Welcome Back Social
> **Message:** Staff. Don't forget that this Friday is our annual Welcome Back Social. We'll be gathering at the alumni building for a barbecue and drinks. Please make sure you RSVP to this e-mail stating any dietary restrictions you may have. Vegetarian and gluten-free options will be available. We hope to see you there!
> The Social Committee

The reminder got me excited and it wasn't just for the chance to have some of Monique's home brew. Jasmine was right that the barbecue was the perfect opportunity to approach him. I didn't have to worry about him not knowing who I was any longer, so there was no reason to avoid him. Plus, Jasmine had been right that the event was perfect timing.

I wasn't so dramatic to think that it had been fate that had put Eric in my path last year at the barbecue. It had actually been Professor Mickelson. He'd been showing Eric around and I'd been surprised when he'd stopped to introduce us. I still remembered the race of excitement when Eric had taken my hand and looked me in the eyes.

Nice to meet you, Glenna.

There'd been something about the way he said my name, the way he always spoke it with precision, that made me hyper aware of him. That was the only time we'd spoken for months. I saw him, but he'd still been getting situated with the college, his new course, his students. I didn't mind hanging on the sidelines looking.

Maybe this year I'd do something more than look.

And the barbecue *was* on a Friday.

Maybe . . .

The rest of the week passed in a similar fashion, with each subsequent day bringing me closer to needing to make a decision. I hadn't taken the cards out from their hiding spot, but every night when I got home from work I became acutely aware of their presence. It wasn't until Thursday night, after I'd had my shower and put my hair into a long braid that fell down the middle of my back, that I sat on my bed and stared at the nightstand drawer.

He was curious about the cards.

He wanted to see them.

Tomorrow was the perfect time to approach him.

I knew that meant I didn't have to bring them with me. I suspected if I didn't approach him then that he would never say anything. He was a professor at a school and had a reputation to maintain. He didn't strike me as the type of person who would actively proposition a coworker, or make advances unwanted or otherwise. The ball was squarely in my court. But damn, it was so far beyond what I thought I'd ever be able to do, it seemed alien.

I opened the drawer but made no further attempt to retrieve my prize.

Eric's interest could be purely academic. What kind of sex cards would a person find at a graveyard? Were they risqué or standard fare? I would tell him about Alyssa and my theory on who I thought she was. He might very well have a theory of his own that would either support or refute mine. We could discuss, perhaps even debate our points. Then once we were finished, I would tuck the cards into my purse and bring them back home.

That was a very valid series of events that could happen. Though if there was beer involved, things might turn out differently.

I reached in and immediately put my hands on them. I held them in place, running my fingertips across the card stock, feeling its smooth surface. I imagined I could read ink simply with my touch. Day One. Day Five. Day Ten.

I didn't want Eric's interest to be academic. I wanted it to be carnal.

I wanted to have sex.

That was never going to happen if I didn't take Great Glenna's advice and go after what I wanted. If I didn't, I'd end up living my greatest fear—growing old alone. That really shouldn't matter so much to me. I was fine on my own, enjoyed it for the most part. I didn't *need* a man to complete my life. I had my job and I loved what I did. I was really frigging good at it too.

But I'd be lying to myself if I didn't admit that I wanted the company.

Getting my courage up, I pulled the cards free and set them on my lap.

Day One
Masturbate

Well, I was more than familiar with Day One. There wasn't much else a single girl could do, especially since my recent adventures into the dating pool had been less than appealing. So yeah, I needed to switch things up if I wanted to take these cards to heart.

I had to masturbate with a purpose.

And didn't that sound weird.

I set the stack on top of the nightstand and lay back on my bed. I needed to make this special somehow, different. No dildo, nipple pinch, and boom! It needed to be more than a simple sexual release.

Closing my eyes was the easy part. I had a number of fantasies that I'd invented over the years that would get me to that place I wanted to be. Things that almost felt rote now. I didn't want this to be the same old routine. I was going to embark on a journey—I hoped—that would take me on a different path from the one I'd been on up to this point. Eric had been the object of my desire for so long, a fantasy out of reach and therefore safe. Tomorrow could be the beginning of something new. Or more likely, it could be the event that finally popped the bubble.

Tonight I owed it to myself to have one more fantasy. One more night of make-believe before my world changed.

With my eyes still closed I pressed my hand to the side of my throat, letting my fingers rest lightly on my skin. I pictured Eric in the kitchen at the university standing in front of me as he had last week. This time I kept standing there, hand at my sides, looking up at him. His gaze had the same intensity to it, but my fantasy Eric looked at me differently. There was no curiosity in his gaze, only desire.

My hand became his. I did my best to mimic what it must feel like to have his large fingers slide across my throat and down to stop just above my breasts. His gaze wouldn't leave mine, even as his hands explored. He'd be gauging me, my reactions to his touch. He'd notice the change in my breathing, the way I'd blush when I realized he was about to cup my breasts.

When my fingers reached my nipple, I slowly dragged my thumb across the hard peak. The fabric of my nightshirt was soft and increased the pleasure I felt. I repeated the action several times, trying to fight the urge to simply plunge my hand between my legs and get myself off.

Eric wouldn't do that. Oh no, he'd tease me, draw things out until I was begging him to let me come. I don't know how I knew that about him, but I did. He'd be purposeful with his caresses. Keeping that in mind, I slowly slid my hand across to my other breast, teasing that nipple as I had the first.

My fantasy Eric would lean in and nip on my earlobe. His hot breath would make me shiver, would cause my pussy to dampen with need. He wouldn't say anything right away, knowing what teasing would do to me. He'd press his lips to the sensitive spot just below my ear, licking my skin.

I want to taste you.

I squeezed my already-shut eyes tighter as I pushed my hand beneath my nightshirt. My skin was soft, but no matter how hard I tried to picture my touch being Eric's I couldn't quite manage it.

The sound of his voice in my head was what really saved the day. I didn't need his hand on me, only his presence in my mind directing me toward the pleasure that I so desperately wanted.

Show me how much you want me. Glenna, show me.

I didn't stop then, didn't hold back. With one hand on my breast pinching and rolling my sensitive nipple, I finally slid my other between my legs. I hadn't bothered sleeping with panties on since I was a teenager, so there was nothing else preventing me from slipping two fingers on either side of my clit and pressing down on my mound.

A moan popped from me, which only encouraged me. My thin pubic hair was wet from my arousal, and I brushed it out of the way as I pressed on the base of my clit.

That's right, Glenna. Show me what you like. How you want me to touch you.

Yes, I'd show him. With my thumb I pressed down on my clit and slowly stroked the hood. I continued to tease the folds of my labia with my fingers, circling my opening. I didn't care what the reality was; my fantasy Eric had a wonderfully big cock. I used two of my fingers to mimic what I hoped he'd be like and pressed them deep inside.

I wasn't a virgin. I wasn't even particularly naïve about sex. I'd had several boyfriends over the years and had enjoyed myself with each one. But not once had I experienced any sort of deep emotional connection with them. We had fun for a time, but inevitably went our separate ways.

With Eric it was different. He'd barely looked at me and that was all it had taken for me to become obsessed.

Awkwardly at first, I began to fuck myself with my fingers as I continued to rub my clit with my thumb. I turned my head so my nose was pressed to my pillow and bit down on the cotton cover. Eric would laugh at the futility of that, his brown eyes would sparkle. *That's not going to help you.*

I pinched my nipple harder, a punishment and a treat. My arousal was cresting, my orgasm racing forward like an ignited fuse toward its powder keg. *Glenna, you look so beautiful.*

"Eric."

The fantasy slipped away then, as it always did and all I could focus on was my body and the release I needed. I rolled onto my stomach and thrust my body upon my hand, increasing the pressure tenfold on my clit. My nipples rubbed hard against the cotton of my shirt, a frantic back and forth as I drove my body onward.

There. Nearly there.

I was aware of the muscles in my face tightening half a second before my orgasm hit me. I cried out into my pillow as pleasure overrode every bit of reason and logic that lived inside me. It was heaven and lasted for far too brief a time. Within a few moments it had faded away and my body relaxed. I should have moved, gotten up and washed my hands, but I didn't. I wanted to cling to this moment, this final fantasy. It was possible that things would go better than I hoped.

In this moment all things were possible.

After some time, I slid my hand from between my legs. My eyes opened of their own volition and my gaze landed on the cards.

Of course I would take them to work tomorrow.

I would show them to Eric.

And I would hope for the best.

7

For the first time all week, I slept like the dead. I didn't know if it had been from the orgasm, or if the exhaustion had finally caught up to me, but either way I slept well. I also slept past my alarm.

"Shit!"

Getting dressed turned out to be an entire production. I wasn't the type of person to typically freak out over my wardrobe. Get up, get dressed, go to work. Done. End of story.

Oh no, today had to be the day that my inner teenager decided to come out to play games with my confidence. I wanted to look good for the barbecue, but not unprofessional. Sexy, but not desperate. Three sundresses and a pair of capris later, I forced myself to put on my navy blue flower-print skirt and a white dress T-shirt, grab the cards, and leave my apartment to catch the bus.

Which I missed. Because of course I did.

To make matters worse the light cloud cover turned dark by the time I was dropped off at my stop. The rain started with a light patter for all of thirty seconds before the heavens opened up and dumped their entire contents on me. I should have run to cut the amount of time I had to endure the rain in half. But there wasn't any point. I'd chosen to wear my hair down, which was now plastered to my body. Thankfully I had a hair elastic in my desk so I could put it in a braid. I just needed to get there first.

I was late and looked like hell, so there was no way I wanted to walk past Eric's office. Given how this past week had gone, he'd be holed up there talking to his students or something, so he would be easy enough to avoid. I'd have time to hit the bathroom and clean up and dry off before I'd see him at the barbecue. For the first time in ages, I took the staircase closest to my office.

The air in the building was cooler than outside. I hadn't expected the rain and didn't think to bring a jacket, so my damp clothing clung to my skin. My nipples were two bullets making their presence known from beneath my shirt for anyone to see. I pushed the door open and stepped out into the hallway of my floor.

Eric had come out of the men's washroom at the exact moment.

We both froze and stared at each other.

"Fuck." I groaned.

He was wearing a plum dress shirt, the shirtsleeves once again rolled up, exposing his forearms. Only one button was undone at his throat, making it impossible to see any of his chest. Oh, he had on the charcoal gray dress pants, too. That was a nice combination on him. Very sexy.

"Glenna?"

My gaze snapped up to his. "Yes?"

"You look . . . uncomfortable."

"I can honestly say that's the understatement of the week." I looked down at my chest and shifted my purse to hide behind it. "It's been a, well, a morning. A very wet and frustrating morning."

He nodded. For a moment I thought he might crack a smile, but instead he started to walk away.

I wanted to die. An earthquake could have come along and shaken the building down around me and that would have made me happy. Or a giant sinkhole! Yes, that would have been much better. I sucked in a breath and took a few steps toward my office.

"Glenna?"

I shivered. Damn cold clothes. "Yes?"

"Will I see you later? At the Social Committee event?"

Water dripped from a wet tendril and landed on my purse. The cards were safe and sound from the wet deep inside. "I'm not sure."

"I hope so." A beat of silence. "You better dry off so you don't catch a cold."

"I will."

His words were chased with the clicking of his shoes as he walked down the hallway toward his office.

Despite everything, he still wanted to see me.

Another shiver got me moving again and into my office. Jasmine was at her desk, and Nell was sitting against it. I'd clearly interrupted something because they pulled apart and Nell's face turned red. Nell's short blond bob swished as she scooted farther away from Jasmine.

Okay, that was cute.

"What the hell happened to you?" Jasmine laughed and tossed me the roll of paper towels we kept for accidents. "And you're late. I didn't think you were coming in, slack-ass."

"Thanks, Jaz. Like my morning was going so well, I needed to be harassed by you."

"I keep telling her she's too mean to people, but she doesn't believe me," Nell said as she stood up. "Do you have something dry to wear?"

"I have a sweater. I'm sure it won't take long for me to become less wet rat. Thanks though." I really liked Nell and hoped Jasmine didn't screw things up with her this time.

"Well, I'll let you two get to work." Nell looked at me for a moment before leaning in and placing a quick kiss on Jasmine's cheek. "I'll see you after?"

"Lunch. And then supper and a movie."

It wasn't until Nell was gone and I'd managed to pull my hair into something that wasn't a complete mess that Jasmine started in on me again. "Okay, when you walked in here you looked as though someone kicked your dog and stole all your candy. What's going on?"

"You two aren't going to the barbecue? I heard they got ice cream for dessert this year."

"No, we're not. Talk."

Why? Why did I choose her as my best friend? "I can't, Jaz. You'll just give me a hard time about it and then you won't leave me alone until I tell you more."

Which was completely the wrong thing to say to her. Jasmine was on her feet and leaning on my desk within a second. "Dude, what the hell? Spill."

"No."

"Glenna."

"*No.*"

"I'm not going to stop until you tell me. You said it yourself. So it's better to fill me in now so I leave you alone."

I didn't have the strength to fight her. That said, I didn't have to tell her everything either. "I took your advice."

"That's good. I give lots of excellent advice. What specifically did you do?"

"I realized that I needed to take a chance so I reached out to a man. Sort of. Well, I'm going to reach out to him. I think."

Jasmine's grin could have lit the room. "Anyone I know?"

Of course she knew who, but there was no way I'd give her the satisfaction of saying. "I don't want to tell you. Nothing might actually come of this, and I don't think I could handle your teasing if it doesn't." I turned to her and took her hand. "I love you like a sister, you know that. But things have been a bit weird since Great Glenna died. I've been, I don't know, soul searching or something. I decided that you were right and I needed to get out there and try a few things. So that's what I'm doing."

Jasmine squeezed my hand in return. "I know I'm a jerk at times. I don't mean anything by it. I worry that you keep yourself too closed off sometimes. When you brought those sex cards in last week I saw something in you kind of spark. Or something. That sounds stupid. I'm just happy to see you getting out there again."

"Speaking of sparks, you and Nell. That was some serious eye-fucking going on when I came in."

There was normally an edge to Jasmine and everything she did. But when I mentioned Nell, that edge melted away and every muscle in her body seemed to soften. "Yeah, Nell. I'm pretty certain that I love her."

"I'm really excited for you." For as long as I'd known her, when Jasmine was with Nell it was the happiest I'd ever seen her.

"Okay, I'll leave you alone about your mystery man. For now. But the moment things start to get interesting between you I expect to be brought up to speed. With diagrams if necessary. Got it?"

"Deal."

"Let's get to work then. You need to reschedule one of your interviews, by the way. Something about your ten o'clock student getting stuck at a resort in Cuba."

I rolled my eyes. "Life's so rough."

Jasmine's third degree was enough of a deterrent that I'd

forgotten my embarrassment about Eric seeing me this morning. I'd chanced a look in the small locker mirror that I had tucked away in my drawer once I'd gotten Jasmine turned onto other topics.

Holy shit I was horrid. Like *horribad*, horrid. Why Eric had wanted me to keep my meeting with him was beyond me. If his interest was solely in the cards, then maybe.

But I couldn't help but hope that he wanted more than that. More from me.

The day became a weird mix of fast and incredibly slow leading up to the barbecue. Meetings and interviews would eat the clock only to be chased by prolonged periods of the second hand crawling at a snail's pace when I had nothing to do. Jasmine was oblivious to my struggles, chatting away about summer students, professors, and changing course codes.

God, this was insane. *I* was insane for wanting to go down this road in the first place. But the wheels had been set in motion and, like everything else in my life, once I started down a path I had to see it to the conclusion.

Unlike the previous week, Jasmine stayed until three. I wanted to rush her out the door, but couldn't. So I was forced to bide my time and wait. Finally, Jasmine's computer dinged and a smile bloomed across her lips. "I think the rest of this can wait until next week."

"Oh? Heading out?" I should have been excited, but instead a wave of nerves fluttered throughout my innards.

"Nell said that the registrar has gone for the day and she's the last one in the office. Everyone else has already headed over to the party. I hate to see my wonderful girl all alone on a Friday afternoon."

"That would be terrible."

My excitement grew as Jasmine got her things together and headed out the door. It was still early enough in the day that there was lots of time for me to talk to Eric. I hadn't seen him since my arrival this morning, but a quick glance down the hall told me that his door was closed. He must have left for the event as well.

Shit.

I'd half been hoping to catch him before he'd gone so we could have walked over together. Yeah, that was a bit preteen of me, but it would have been nice to gauge his mood, maybe get a feel for what he was thinking before we were thrust into a group.

Even after Jasmine was gone, I didn't get the cards and head out to the party. There was nothing stopping me now, nothing holding me back. Instead of doing what I'd been dreaming about for days now, I sat in my chair and stared.

The cards were in my purse, waiting for me to free them, to bring them into the light of day. Eric and I might have a laugh over them. We'd share our thoughts over a beer and hamburger. There was no reason for me to wait, to procrastinate. No reason at all.

And yet I didn't move.

Coward. I was a big, stupid coward.

Great Glenna's voice, mixed with Jasmine's, echoed in my head. I was being foolish. With a growl, I fished the cards out of the hiding spot. My palms were damp now, and I had to rub them on my skirt to dry them off so the moisture wouldn't absorb into the paper.

Okay, I can do this. My hair had dried from earlier and the braid was still looking mostly neat. I'd just have to put the cards in my pocket and then I could get Eric alone for a few minutes and show him . . .

Shit.

When I got dressed this morning I didn't think of the practicality of wearing this particular skirt. I didn't have any pockets to hide the cards. And while I could take my purse with me, it was heavy and awkward and not something anyone else would have. Well then.

I took them out of the bag and flipped the front card around. There, no one would be able to see what was written on them. I attached a paper clip to ensure they wouldn't get loose and fly away. That was it then, I was all set.

Ignoring my nerves, I grabbed the cards and left to chase my adventure.

The crowd at the alumni building was surprisingly dense. This was the first big get-together of the year and people were all fresh from their holidays and excited to see one another. The smell of grilled hamburgers and buns mixed with the scent of charcoal. Laughter and talking overpowered the buzz of music playing from what must have been someone's phone.

I should have brought my Bluetooth speaker, because that was going to get annoying.

"Glenna!"

I was super proud of myself that I didn't groan, wail, or cry as Sasha marched toward me, a flimsy paper plate in hand and a Cheshire cat grin on her lips. Current president of the Social Committee, Sasha had this way of getting you to do things that you really didn't want to do, and feel completely guilty about the whole thing in the process. She only talked to me when she wanted something.

I was so screwed.

"Hi, Sasha. The party looks great." *Please don't ask me to flip burgers. Please don't ask me to flip—*

"I know you just arrived, but can you take over from Rachelle? She needs to step out for a phone call for twenty minutes and you're the only other person who I know won't burn the hamburgers. All that practice you had as a student working fast food, I know you wouldn't let it go to waste." She actually batted her eyes at me.

No, I make more than minimum wage now! "Sure, no problem. Same spot as last year?"

"Yes. You're a doll." And then she strode away.

My stomach growled as I walked past the table that held an array of salads on my way to the grill. Poor Rachelle was coughing as a plume of smoke blew in her face. "Dammit."

"I heard you needed a backup." I held out my hand for the spatula. "I'm here to save the day."

I didn't know Rachelle well, but I was more than aware of her problems at home. The look of relief was genuine. "You're a saint. I have to call Matthew's school. He's gotten into a fight already."

"Family always comes first. Go. I've got this."

Any chance that I was going to be able to sneak away and talk to Eric was now officially gone. Not wanting to ruin my outfit, I grabbed a discarded apron and covered up before going down the line flipping the burgers. There weren't any pockets in the apron either, so I had to settle for putting the cards on the table beside me.

Who thought working fast food didn't give you the opportunity to garner important life skills? Two undergrad degrees and one master's and my most sought-after skill was hamburger slinging. As soon as the burgers were cooked, I pulled them off and put them in a chafer to keep them warm before starting on another batch. It was weird, but one moment I was completely focused on not burning the food, and in the next I knew Eric was watching me.

It should have been far creepier than it actually was, me having this awareness of him. If he knew, he'd probably be terrified. Well, maybe not. I straightened and looked over my shoulder toward where I felt his gaze. He was standing with a beer in hand talking to a few professors, one of whom must have been new. When his gaze met mine I had to fight the urge to look immediately away. There was no reason to be ashamed. Instead I shrugged and turned my attention back to the burgers.

My servitude lasted well past my promised twenty minutes. When poor Rachelle came back she was clearly in no shape to be tied to a grill. "Go get a beer and relax. I'll cover this."

I've never seen someone look so relieved before. "Glenna, you're far too sweet."

Thankfully, I was only flipping burgers for an additional thirty minutes before Sasha officially freed me. "I can't tell you how much we appreciate this. There's still lots of food left for you so help yourself."

"Thanks." My stomach growled its approval.

"Oh, what are these?"

The next moment happened in slow motion. The second Sasha picked up the sex cards, I grabbed for them. Of course, she held on to the paper clip, which caused me to stumble backward. The cards fell between us and I immediately went into a panic.

"Oh no!"

"Let me help." It wasn't Sasha, but Eric who dropped into a squat beside me. "Are these the research cards you pulled together for me?"

I couldn't be sure, but he moved so quickly gathering them I didn't think Sasha had a chance to see what was printed on them. I blinked back unexpected tears and laughed. "Yeah. Sorry, I meant to give them to you when I arrived."

"That's my fault, Professor Morris. I scooped her up the minute she got here."

Eric stood up, helping me in the process. "It's fine. Glenna was helping me out as a favor. Is it fine if I keep these, or did you need to do something else with them?"

I couldn't think of any reason to keep them, so I smiled and hoped I didn't look insane. "Oh no, they're all yours."

"Thank you, then." Without looking at them, he tucked them into his shirt pocket, so only the tops were visible.

Sasha looked between us. "Well then. Thanks again, Glenna. Be sure to eat something."

Without thinking I stepped to the food table and blindly filled my plate. I was throwing a pile of croutons on my salad when a bottle of beer was held out for me. Naturally, it was Eric.

"You look like you needed this." His smile was tiny, but it did wonderful things to his eyes to make them sparkle and ease the tension that normally hugged him. "If it helps, I don't think she saw anything."

"Thank you." I drank down half the bottle before I even realized it. "That was nearly the most mortifying thing that has ever happened to me in my life." I took another long drink and finished off most of the bottle. "Wow, I didn't realize I was that thirsty."

Or apparently horny. Standing this close to him, my body tingled with awareness. My skin, already hot from the sun and the grill, vibrated. Or else that was the result of my almost panic attack. He had this wonderful smell of sunscreen, cologne, and sunshine. It was also the first time in the past year that he actually looked relaxed. Maybe he was simply one of those people who took his job super seriously and tried to block distractions out.

Which made me a distraction that he was failing to ignore.

Oh. I really liked that.

"That's an interesting grin." He took a swig of his beer and guided me away from the food. "It makes me wonder what you're thinking."

So not going down that road. "Just happy to have been able to help Rachelle. She's awesome, but is having a hard time with her son. Teenagers are terrifying."

Eric made a humming noise deep in the back of his throat. He leaned in next to my ear as we continued toward the back of the crowd. "I thought you were thinking about these cards of yours." And he patted his pocket that held them.

I stopped dead in my tracks. "Pardon?"

No one was paying us any attention. The closest group to where we stood was currently engaged in a debate about something or other and laughing as they drank and ate. Sasha was over talking to one of the registrar assistants and surveying the fruits of her social committee's labors. There was no reason for me to be nervous about having this conversation with him.

Nope, none at all.

Still, I looked everyone over, just to make certain.

"I was being serious earlier. If you want these back, they're yours. The last thing I want is for you to feel pressured."

He was reaching for them, but I gave my head a small shake. "It's fine. But there's no way we can look at them here. Despite what you said, Sasha is curious and would probably want to know what they were if we started looking at them intently. I don't want her to see them and think they're a party game or something."

"You've grown quite attached to them, haven't you?" There was an odd note in his voice. Admiration? No, that couldn't be right.

"I guess I have in a way. I've spent a lot of time wondering about them. Coming up with a theory about who they were for, where they came from."

He nodded again. This time when he spoke, he lowered his head so his mouth was close to my ear. "I haven't been able to get them out of my head either. Not since I overheard you and Ms. Houng the other day talking about me. I kept wondering what kind of sex cards a woman like you would have."

Yup, that giant sinkhole could come any time now.

I'd be here waiting for it.

8

"Glenna?" Eric stepped around in front of me, frown fixed on his face. "Are you okay?"

Was I okay? Lord, he was as cute as he was naïve. "Oh you know, just crazy embarrassed. No big deal."

"I didn't mean to make you uncomfortable." He reached out and gave my forearm a gentle squeeze. "Sorry."

"I'm sorry. It was totally not cool of me to be discussing you that way with a coworker. If the tables were turned and it was you and another guy talking about me that way . . ." Actually, I would have been floored because I didn't think anyone thought of me as a sexual creature. "Well, I'm sorry."

"Apology not necessary, but certainly accepted."

The seconds ticked on as we stood there awkwardly looking at each other. What the hell could I say now? *Hey, since you have those cards, do you want to see them? Why don't you come back to my place, eh? Crazy-monkey sex!*

Eric cleared his throat. "My original comment stands. I haven't been able to stop thinking about the cards." His gaze locked onto mine and he lowered his voice. "I would never pressure anyone into doing something they weren't comfortable with. I simply wanted you to know. That I'm interested."

In me? "In seeing them?"

"Yes." His gaze flicked down my body before popping back to my eyes. "Yes."

I shivered. "From an academic standpoint?"

"Partially." He held my gaze as he took another sip of beer. "I know I've said this before, but I think it's worth repeating. If you're up for it, you could come visit me in my office before you leave for the day. I have to head back there now to finish up some work. I'll be around for at least an hour. If you change your mind, that's also fine. I'll set them on my desk and leave my door unlocked so you can collect them."

That was, well, the sweetest gesture anyone could have done for me.

He looked around and waited for a group to move away again before he continued. "While you don't know me well, I want to say that I would never do anything to put you or your job in jeopardy. No means no. Not showing up means no. That is perfectly fine. It's your choice and they're your cards." With a single nod and smile, he left.

I've never been stunned into immobility before, but with those few words, Eric had managed to do that to me. There was no misinterpreting his thoughts on the matter. He'd extended an offer, twice now. There would be no repercussions for saying no. Showing up didn't mean we'd be having sex or anything—God, I'd probably explode from joy—but we could at least talk about them.

I looked down at my watch. The minute hand ticked announcing that it was now ten after five. What the hell was I going to do?

Go for it. Take the chance for once in your life.

Great Glenna was right. This was the best opportunity I had to have an adventure. I straightened my shoulders, flicked my braid over my shoulder so my hair lay against my spine, and walked over to Sasha.

"Thank you for another great event. I need to pick up a few things and head out."

"I'm so glad you came. And thanks again for taking over at the grill. It's nice to know we can always count on you."

Yup, that was me. Dependable, predictable Glenna.

Who just happened to be on her way to discuss sex cards with Professor Eric Morris.

Nothing unusual at all.

I'd made it to the building and headed straight for his office before I could chicken out. Eric was sitting at his desk when I knocked on his door and went in. He was writing something on a piece of paper. I didn't bother to clear my throat to announce my presence. I had no doubt that he was as aware of me as I was of him. I was tempted to take a seat, but he still hadn't acknowledged me and while I might be many things, rude wasn't one of them.

He finished his sentence before clicking his pen and slipping it into his penholder on his desk. When he finally looked up at me, the look in his eyes caused my breath to catch in my throat.

"Professor Morris." I was happy that my voice was steady and didn't betray my nervousness. "Is this still a good time?"

"Of course." My God, he actually looked a bit nervous himself. "Please call me Eric. I think we're past the formalities by this point."

"Sure. Eric." And that didn't feel weird coming out of my mouth. No, not at all.

It was strange being in his space and having his undivided attention like this. We'd never had a reason to engage in such a manner before now. He was more of a teaching professor than research-focused. Even if he was, we weren't exactly in the same field and wouldn't have had much reason to work together before now. I adjusted myself in the chair, trying for a more comfortable position and failing.

He pulled the cards from his pocket and set them between us. "So these are sex cards."

"They are." I stared at them, wanting to snatch them away and light them on fire before he saw what was written on them.

"Could you tell me the story of how you found them again?"

There was something in his voice, a note that gave me hope that this was more than idle curiosity on his part. I recounted the story again, being careful not to embellish the little details. It was something I couldn't help but think he'd appreciate.

"Sex cards. At a graveyard." He shook his head, but the expression on his face looked more amused than confused.

"I have a theory. About the cards." I scooted closer to the edge of my seat. "I think the woman these were intended for, Alyssa, I think she's a widow. That her husband wrote these as a means to help her get past her grief and begin a new chapter of her life."

Eric nodded. I was surprised when he stood and moved around his desk toward me. Similar to how Nell sat when I'd walked in on her and Jasmine, he sat on the edge of his desk in front of me. "Do you mind if I look at them?"

Why he was asking my permission was a bit beyond me. It wasn't as though I had any special claim on them, no more so than anyone else who might have come across them. But since they'd come into my possession, despite not having used them myself, I felt a certain amount of ownership over the cards. I didn't want to do anything that would detract from their specialness.

Still, the entire point of coming to his office was to share the cards with him. I looked down at them, laughing briefly before I pushed them toward him to take. "I haven't looked too much at them. It's weird but it feels like I'm reading someone's diary."

Eric's fingers brushed against mine as he took them. That

brief contact sent a shiver through me, one that went all the way to my pussy. I couldn't look at him and pulled my hand back far faster than I should have.

As his silence stretched on, my curiosity got the better of me. I chanced a glance at him and was surprised at the look of lust I saw on his face. He'd look at a card for no longer than a few seconds before he'd file it to the back and refocus his attention on the next one. Over and over he repeated this until he reached the end. Then he tapped the cards on his thigh, straightening the pile.

"These are . . . interesting." There was something in his voice, a note that I hadn't heard before.

I didn't want to stare at him, but I let my gaze travel quickly up his body. I couldn't be certain, but I swore he had an erection that tented the front of his dress pants. I looked away and briefly bit down on my bottom lip before making eye contact with him once again. "They are. And I think you can probably see why I think she's a widow."

"I do. Most likely she was someone who didn't have a lot of sexual experience."

Excitement flared inside me. "You noticed that too? The way the cards seem to be building her up for something. At least the early ones. It's as though she'd only had sex with a few people and her partner didn't think she'd know what to do."

Eric ran his thumb along the edge of the cards. He wasn't looking at me then, but somehow I knew that he was watching my every reaction. "What are your plans for these?"

"I'm not sure." I picked at a small spot on my skirt. "Originally I was going to return them, but as I said that's not really an option. I could leave them somewhere for someone else to find. The student union building, maybe."

Looking up I was surprised to see Eric was holding the cards directly in front of him on his desk, but his gaze was now directly on me. "You're not planning on using them?"

God, those eyes. I wanted to squirm in my seat. I wanted to push my hands between my legs and press hard on my clit. "I don't really have anyone to use them with."

"No boyfriend? Girlfriend?"

"Boyfriend, and not for a while now."

"Why not?" There wasn't any judgment in his tone. More like curiosity. And maybe a bit of hope.

"I'm not the most exciting person in the world. My past boyfriends got a bit bored. Well, the ones who didn't get annoyed by my work schedule."

He nodded once before frowning. "These cards are far from boring."

"There are a few creative things listed there." My nerves were growing with each passing moment. I didn't know where this conversation was headed and the longer it went on, the more I needed to move.

I hadn't realized I'd looked away until he reached out and lifted my chin. "Glenna?"

"Yes?"

The muscle in his jaw shifted. "Tell me who you want to use these cards with."

Nope. No way would I go down that road. "No one, really. They're just a bit of fantasy material—"

"I want to hear you say it again."

My mouth snapped shut.

He ran his thumb across my chin. "I've had your words stuck in my head ever since I overheard you two talking. The way you sounded . . . I need you to tell me, what do you want to do with the cards?"

My heart was pounding so hard that I could hear it in my ears and feel the beat in my throat. "I . . . umm . . ."

He leaned in so I had no other option but to look him in the eyes. His mouth was tantalizingly close and his lips parted before he spoke. "Please."

"You." I sighed as soon as I spoke. There was no going back now. "I wanted to use the cards with you."

"Thank you." He leaned back and I instantly missed his closeness. "Could I keep these for the weekend? To look them over."

"I guess. Sure. I'll get them back though?"

"On Monday." He stood then and offered me his hand. "I need time to think."

He was going to think?

Shit, I was going to buy a new vibrator on my way home and masturbate until I was blind. "Okay then."

I took his hand and got to my feet. This was unlike every other time we'd touched. It was as though an invisible current ran between us, one that set my hair on end and my body on fire. I held on a bit longer than was strictly necessary, but despite everything that had happened in this conversation, I didn't know when I might get another opportunity to hold and be held by him.

"Thank you." He lifted my hand to his lips and kissed the back of it, never once breaking eye contact. "Have a good weekend."

And the next thing I knew I was standing out in the hall and his door was shut.

What. The. Hell?

I looked at him through his window, but he was already back behind his desk reading an essay. The cards were on his desk, but presently forgotten. Uncertain of what had actually just happened, I drifted to my office, gathered my things, and left for home.

Maybe things would make more sense on Monday.

Maybe.

9

Life could certainly be unfair at times. After spending the weekend in a haze of hope and want, when Monday morning finally rolled around I got out of bed and immediately puked. I was rarely sick, so for this bug to hit me as hard as it did was weird. I wanted to blame food poisoning, but that would have required eating something beyond peanut butter sandwiches. I crawled back in bed with my phone and e-mailed Jasmine to let her know that I wouldn't be in.

As much as I wanted to know Eric's thoughts after he spent the weekend with the cards, my curiosity would have to wait at least a day. I doubted he would think anything of my not being around. I closed my eyes and fell asleep.

A few hours later, my phone chirped at me letting me know that I had a new message. My stomach was feeling better, so I pulled myself into a sitting position back against my pillows and checked the e-mail.

It was from Eric.

> **To:** O'Donald, Glenna
> **From:** Morris, Eric
> **Subject:** Are you well?
> **Message:** ?

No *hi, how ya doing*. Nope, not from him. Nice and straight-forward. The simplicity of the message didn't undermine the fact that he'd been concerned enough about me to e-mail me in the first place. I didn't quite know how to feel about that. Now that I was finally getting the attention I'd always wanted from him, I didn't know what to do.

Well, first thing was first. I had to send a reply.

> **To:** Morris, Eric
> **From:** O'Donald, Glenna
> **Subject:** RE: Are you well?
> **Message:** Just a bit of a stomach bug.
> I'm sorry that I won't be in today. I
> was looking forward to hearing your
> thoughts on our mutual project.

There, that was good. Wasn't it? I read my reply a few more times, adding a few more comments before deleting them again. Shit, I was totally overthinking this. "Idiot." My voice echoed in my empty room.

I hit send and banged my head back into my pillows. That would be it. He checked in on me and he now knows I won't be there. I didn't have to worry about him thinking—

Chirp.

> **To:** O'Donald, Glenna
> **From:** Morris, Eric
> **Subject:** RE: RE: Are you well?
> **Message:** I'm sorry to hear you're not
> feeling well. I hoped to meet with

you after classes ended today. I have
several thoughts regarding our
project. Specifics to discuss. Perhaps
even an experiment? I'll let you decide
if we proceed with that part. That can
wait. I hope you feel better soon.

Holy fucking shit! Professor hot-ass Eric Morris wanted to
do *experiments* with me? My stomach protested when I flipped
around and pulled the blankets over my head. This might not
be the appropriate time for blanket-forting, but I didn't want
the outside world to do anything to ruin this moment. I stared
at my phone screen in the darkness beneath my sheets and debated how best to reply. This was on the university e-mail system and I didn't want to say anything that could potentially
land either of us in any trouble.

To: Morris, Eric
From: O'Donald, Glenna
Subject: RE: RE: RE: Are you well?
Message: I would be open to helping
you conduct some practical
experiments in regard to our project.
If my stomach agrees, I believe I have
time in my calendar tomorrow around
four o'clock. Does that work for you?

I hit send and immediately closed my eyes and started counting back from one hundred. I only got to ninety-four when my
phone chirped.

To: O'Donald, Glenna
From: Morris, Eric
Subject: RE: RE: RE: RE: Are you well?
Message: I have an opening. I believe that an off-site location might be best for our initial conversation. I'll set that up. Thank you for helping me with this. I appreciate it.

I read that message three times before I set my phone back on my nightstand. Oh how I wished my body were feeling up for a spin with my vibrator. Eric's voice echoed in my head, reciting the message over and over.

Thank you for helping me with this. I appreciate it.

Come hell or high water, I was totally going to work tomorrow. Nothing was going to stop me from meeting him.

Fate finally cut me some slack. Whatever stomach bug had haunted me the previous day was gone by the time I woke up the next morning. Not having any idea what Eric had in mind for us that day, I went once again with a skirt and T-shirt to wear. I even made sure to check the weather just in case there were any showers being called for. As much as I didn't think he minded seeing me impersonate a drowned rat, I didn't want to give a repeat performance.

The workday was as normal as ever. I went up the far stairs so I could catch a glimpse of Eric. He was working and didn't acknowledge me as I passed. Jasmine teased me, but I could tell she was happy that I was feeling better and back in the office. Students called, articles and books were reserved, lunch was eaten.

The entire time I had a counter ticking off in the back of my mind. With each passing hour my awareness of the time grew until I was certain that anyone standing close enough to me would be able to hear it. When Jasmine picked up her purse at ten to four, my body was quivering from the inside out with excitement.

"Are you heading out soon?" She pulled her mass of long black hair into a bun. "You still don't look quite yourself."

"Yeah, I'm leaving at four."

"Good. Make sure you get lots of rest. I'll see you tomorrow."

I stopped moving as she walked down the hallway, my gaze following her as she went past Eric's office and disappeared into the stairwell. The counter in my head ticked away. The flicker of shadows danced across the hallway from where Eric's door was open. He was moving around, probably cleaning up. I didn't need to see the clock to know the moment the minute hand hit the top.

Eric stepped out into the hall.

I straightened up in my chair and was about to stand when he walked down the hallway toward me. With each step closer my stomach did a weird flip and my pussy pulsed with desire. Olive-colored shirt today. Sleeves up and two buttons undone at his throat. His brown hair came down to his eyebrows and just past his ears. With his chin tilted down it looked as though he was intent on something, moving with purpose.

Coming for me.

He stopped in the doorway, his hands at his sides. "Hello, Glenna."

"Hello, Professor Morris."

He smiled softly. "I thought I asked you to call me Eric."

"Umm, of course. Eric."

"How are you feeling today? Better, I hope."

Oh, I'm so horny I could rub myself off against my desk and still come again just from the sound of your voice. "Much better, thank you. Just a twenty-four-hour flu thing."

"That's good." He stepped inside the office and stood in

front of my desk. I watched as he ran his fingertips around the lip of my R2-D2 penholder. "I was worried that my suggestion might have upset you. That you were trying to find a way to say no."

"No!" I was on my feet and staring into his startled gaze. "I mean I was really sick. Puking, actually."

He nodded. "You know that you can say no. I don't want you to feel pressured."

Eric was sweet. Clueless about how much I wanted to be with him, but sweet. "I'm not a shy virgin. I never meant for you to have overheard my conversation with Jasmine. And while I'm still a bit embarrassed by that, now that it's happened I can't say that I'm sorry." I stood up and retrieved my purse from the bottom drawer of my desk. He stepped back as I came around to join him. "Where would you like to go?"

He looked at me for a few seconds longer before placing his hand on the small of my back and allowing me to step past him. "I was hoping to take you for drinks. I know a nice patio bar that offers adequate privacy so we can discuss details."

My lips trembled from excitement as I smiled. "I don't have a car."

"I do."

"Lead the way."

10

I've had one-night stands before. I mean, I'm a twenty-eight-year-old, healthy woman who happens to like sex. I haven't always been a big fan of relationships, seeing as none of the ones I'd had in the past had worked out particularly well, but the sex part was awesome. So hookups were one thing that I'd done, but I hadn't done that with the same person more than twice. As I sat in Eric's car, trapped with him and his heavenly body, I couldn't help but worry that I might be getting into something that was bigger than I'd be able to handle.

As long as I'd spent lusting after him, I really didn't know much of anything about him. He was my one consistent fantasy and now that I was sitting next to the reality in his Lexus, my curiosity began to get the better of me.

"How old are you?" I rolled my head to the side so I could see his face.

His eyes were locked on the road and the car ahead of us. "Thirty-seven."

"Wow. You tenured young."

"I did." He arched an eyebrow and flicked his gaze toward me briefly. "You sound surprised."

"No, I didn't mean anything by it. I just realized that I don't actually know much about you."

"I'm thirty-seven. Never been married. Did my undergrad at Carleton, my master's and PhD at UBC. I moved back to Toronto after I finished my studies and started teaching at the University of Toronto. I was there for four years before I started here. Anything else you'd like to know?"

Huh. "Lots. Those are some details, but that doesn't tell me a lot about the type of person you are. What's your favorite color?"

"Green."

"Favorite food?"

"Steak."

"Musician?"

"Harry Connick Jr."

"Movie?"

"*Little Shop of Horrors.*"

I sat up and turned fully to face him. "What?"

"*Little Shop of Horrors.* I preferred the original ending where Audrey II and her spawn devour the entire city. It's a shame Frank Oz had to bow to studio pressure and make that change."

I totally wasn't expecting that.

He smiled as he turned into the parking lot. "You're still processing that, aren't you?"

"Yeah." My poor brain was shouting *does not compute.* "This is it?"

"Yes." With that he got out of the car and came around to my side. I was terrible at the waiting for a man thing, so I'd already pushed open my door by the time he'd come around. It didn't seem to bother him though and he held out his hand for me to take without comment.

There was a brass sign that read READING STREET PUB, framed with iron leaves. Walking in I realized that this was one of those gastropubs that were so popular in California, high-end food and craft beers in a pub-style environment. Exactly the type of place I'd always wanted to go but that was completely out of my pay grade.

There were only a few couples sitting inside eating. A quick look outside though told me that was where all the action was happening.

"Eric!"

I looked for the source of the voice and was surprised to see a man even taller than Eric come striding out from the kitchen. His blond hair was shaved on both sides, but the top was long enough to nearly cover his eyes. He had on a chef's outfit and was grinning as he made his way to us.

"Claude." They hugged with a loud mutual thump to the back. "How've you been?"

"Working my ass off. But what's new." Claude then turned his attention to me. If I thought I felt small beside Eric, I was downright dwarfed by the wall of muscle standing before me. "You must be Glenna. When Eric told me he was bringing a woman to my place, I didn't quite believe him. But here you are and now I owe him a beer."

"Yup, here I am." *Stuck in between two pantie-dropping-attractive men. Go me!* "It's nice to meet you."

"Likewise. Now, if you'll follow me. I have a special table reserved for you."

Eric had his hand pressed to my back again, and I was amazed at how reassuring that simple touch was. The patio was filled to near capacity. It was a beautiful fall day and this was clearly a popular attraction. Claude led us past the majority of people down a small path to a section that contained three tables for two.

"I have this area set aside for you two. Eric, I took the liberty of chilling that white you like, but I wasn't sure if Glenna had a different preference."

"White's perfect." Okay, so we had wine preferences in common. This was going well.

"If you need anything, just flag Connie down. I asked her to keep an eye on you, but she won't interrupt unless you want her to."

With a grin to us both, Claude strode away. And yes, he did have a lovely ass.

"I didn't even know if you drank, but I figured I couldn't do too badly bringing you here." He pulled a chair out for me and this time I didn't hesitate to sit. "If you do want something else—"

"Honestly, no. I do drink and while I'm not a wine connoisseur, I normally love whites. So this is awesome."

Eric took the chair that was opposite me and moved it so we were sitting closer. He filled my glass and I waited until he'd poured his own drink before lifting it to my lips. Our gazes locked, and I couldn't help but match his movements, drinking as he did. The wine was sweet, but not overpowering. I took another, deeper sip and hoped that I wouldn't lose my head before we got to the interesting part of our conversation.

He put his glass down, fingering the base for a moment before he sucked in a breath. "You're attracted to me."

"Yes." There was no sense in lying to him, in denying what we both knew to be true. I leaned forward, putting my weight on my elbow and bracing my chin on my hand. "Are you attracted to me?"

When he looked up, there wasn't a spark, but a blaze dancing in his gaze. "Yes."

I shifted my hand to the side of my throat. His gaze shifted, watching where I touched myself. "I didn't think you even knew who I was."

"You've walked by my office every day for the past year.

I've begun to recognize the sound of your gait. I know it's you and not someone else. Your laughter will sometimes reach my office and I can't help but wonder what had made you smile." He looked awkward with his admission.

I must have looked like some sort of deranged owl given the number of times I'd blinked. "You like my laugh?"

Eric reached down, pulled the cards from his pocket, and set them on the table between us. He'd taken a clip and attached them to the middle of the stack, ensuring that none of them would get lost. It partially obstructed the words printed beneath. There were thirty in total, a month's worth of pleasure waiting for us to reach out and take it.

There was something that had been bugging me all day, something that I wanted to get out there before things got serious. "I'm not good at relationships. It's not that I don't want one, or want to settle down, I'm just shitty at them. It's not that I'm selfish, but Jasmine says that I'm a bit oblivious to things around me sometimes that aren't related to my research. So you need to know that about me."

He nodded.

"And I'm pretty open about stuff, but I'm a stickler for condoms. I'm on the pill, so that will help keep the babies at bay."

He nodded again.

I took another large sip of wine. "Damn. That's really good."

"Is there anything else?" Again he somehow turned a question that I might find abrasive from anyone else into one of genuine concern.

"Not really. I don't think so."

Eric picked the cards up, leaned back, and tapped them on the table. "I'm not looking for a relationship either. I haven't seriously dated anyone in years and I wanted to be honest about that. I see these cards as an opportunity to relax and have a bit of fun. Does that make sense?"

Not back rubs? Or bubble baths? "Yes."

He looked away then, and an odd expression passed across his face. "I need you to understand that I'd be using you. That sounds horrible, but I don't want to lie."

That wasn't exactly what I was expecting. "Using me for what?"

"Sex. The reasons are a bit personal, and I honestly would prefer not to discuss them."

There was something about the way he spoke that didn't sit right with me. "Given what we are about to do, I think I should know at least something."

He nodded, but took his time considering his words. "Let's just say that the last relationship that I was in didn't end well. I . . . I need to prove something to myself. This gives me that opportunity with someone I can trust."

It was weird thinking about him as having this whole thing, this life beyond the little bit that I knew about him. Clearly, something had happened and it was not my business. "Okay then. I'll happily use you for sex."

That at least drew a small smile from him. "One other thing. I think for the time being that we keep this between us."

Maybe he didn't know me as well as he thought if he imagined that I'd be blabbing this around campus. "I wouldn't think of saying anything—"

"Even from your friend Jasmine. At least until we figure out if this is something that we really want to do."

Oh. Well, that was a bit different. "Ah."

"She seems nice enough, just enthusiastic. Also a bit protective of you. I'd rather not upset her if it can be avoided."

In the end it was a small price to pay for trying out some kinky fun with him. Plus, if things went sideways, I wouldn't have to handle Jasmine wanting to go over and kill him. "Deal. At least unless she finds us out. I'm not the best at hiding things from her."

"I guess that's fair enough."

With the particulars discussed, I wanted to start talking about the good parts. The actual sexy-fun times. "So, Professor, what now?"

He glanced around as though he was making sure no one was watching. If he'd been debating something he clearly made up his mind once I'd asked my question. "Leave your things and come with me."

Taking my hand in his, he led me along one of the side paths toward the building. Before we disappeared inside, he flagged Connie down. "I'm just showing Glenna the brewery. Could I get an order of bruschetta and some more wine?"

"Of course." Connie's smile was meant to seduce. "I'll place that right away."

Well, if she was interested in Eric, too bad for her. I'd finally gotten him to notice me and I'd be dammed if I'd let him go that easily. I squeezed his hand a bit tighter as he tugged me along.

The air in the building was cool and the smell coming from the room we'd entered was pungent to say the least. Thankfully, we didn't stay there long. Eric obviously knew the building and within a moment we were in what looked to be some sort of storage area. It was empty except for a few kegs. Not that I had much time to process my surroundings. One moment I was looking at the barren wall and the next I was pressed against it.

Eric's mouth was so close to mine that a strong breeze could have pushed the two of us together. He held back, his gaze darting across my face. "I want to seal our deal. Show you how much I appreciate what you're doing."

"You don't have to do that." *Kiss me! Oh please, God. Please kiss me.*

"I do. I want to." Rather than do what I'd silently begged, he tugged my skirt up with his hand. "I'm not going to fuck you. Or hurt you."

Stunned. Such a simple word and it barely began to capture

how I was feeling. When his fingers pressed against my clit through my panties, I gasped. He was tentative at first, probably waiting to see if I would turn around and hit him. When I pressed my hands to his chest and gave him a little nod, his touch grew firmer.

"I've been listening to your laugh for a year. I want to hear what your moan sounds like."

"You have?" My breath caught in my throat and I had to fight to keep my eyes open.

He began to rub small circles against my clit, making my pussy heavy with arousal. "Yes. Your giggles teased me. But I knew you were holding back with those. It was when I heard your full-out laugh that my cock would grow hard. If it weren't for the windows in my office I would have jerked off more than once."

I pressed my back hard against the wall, needing its stability to hold my weight. Eric braced his arm above my head, his breath washing across the side of my face and throat. "I didn't think—" I gasped.

Using his thumb and forefinger, he tugged my clit, milking my arousal. "Didn't think?"

"That you knew who I was."

He chuckled as he pulled my panties aside and slid a finger into my pussy. I could hear how wet I was as he moved his hand against me. "I knew, Glenna. I knew."

I shuddered as my body responded to the intensity in his voice, the skill with which he manipulated my body. My arousal unfurled, spreading through me, obliterating my ability to think beyond *yes* and *more* and *Eric*.

"Yes." His mouth was open and I felt his breath kiss my skin in sharp, short pants. Leaning in, he rubbed his nose along the side of my cheek as he increased the rhythm of his fingers fucking my body. "Don't hold it in. I want to hear everything."

I shivered, partially from the nearness of his voice, but mostly from the orgasm that was bolting forward like a sprinter in the

Olympics. His hand was so large it forced my legs farther apart, until I was practically rubbing myself off on him, fucking his hand as though there weren't anything left in the world. The change in my position forced me to reach up and cling to his shoulders so that I wouldn't fall.

We were close, so close now. With my eyes closed, I flexed my fingers against him, grabbing at his hair, his shoulders, everything I could. I didn't want this moment to end. I'd wished, dreamed for far too long to be with him, to feel his body against mine. Now that my wish had come true, I knew it would never be enough.

Eric crooked his fingers and increased the pressure on that magic spot deep inside me. My pussy felt warm, burning, as though my orgasm had a fuse that had been lit and it was only a matter of time before it exploded.

"Shit," I whispered. My attention focused on the places where our bodies met.

His cock was a rock against my side as he moved against me. I wished I could have reached over and grabbed him through his pants, but that would have meant removing my hold on his shoulders. Still, I nearly risked it. If he hadn't taken that moment to lower his head and mouth at my breast through my shirt, I might have.

With his teeth ensconced behind his lips, he worried at my nipple, rolling and teasing it. Pleasure fired my breasts. I wanted to strip naked and rub against him still fully clothed. It was crazy, he was *making* me crazy.

I cried out in frustration as my orgasm refused to come. Eric lifted his face, shifting his body so his hand was better positioned to rub my clit. "You have no idea how beautiful you are."

I no longer had the ability to speak. My mouth was open and the air barely reached my lungs, I was breathing so shallow.

Our gazes locked for a moment and I knew he was as shaken, as aroused as I was. "I can't wait to put my face between your legs and lick your pussy. I want to know what it feels like to have your thighs squeeze my face. What your come will taste like."

And that was it. Nothing was going to stop me from coming now. My body was too primed, my pent-up lust having gone on for far too long to ebb away now. It was full speed ahead, and Eric was going to carry me over the finish line. He pressed a bit harder as he leaned in and sucked my earlobe. He flicked the lobe in time with his hand on my pussy. The dual sensations connected and I felt my muscles begin to tighten.

I sucked in a breath and for a moment I didn't know if I would ever be able to let it out. My body tensed and tightened before that first burst of pleasure exploded. My eyes squeezed shut, my mouth opened, and I cried out.

"Fuck!"

Pleasure rolled through me at a lightning pace. It consumed me, chewed me up and spit me out. It was as though Eric had let something loose inside me that I'd never be able to stop. He continued to fuck my body with his hand, moaning softly in my ear. Whether intentionally or not, he pressed his cock hard against my side, and for a moment I thought he might come in his pants. He might have for all I was aware.

Finally, after what felt like an eternity, the intensity faded. My body slumped against his, and it took everything I had to simply catch my breath. With only his hands and his voice, he'd given me the best orgasm I'd had in ages. I couldn't imagine that I'd survive if we ever had skin-to-skin contact. Wow.

Eric held me as he removed his hand from my panties and righted my skirt. Never before had I had this sensation rolling through my body after sex of any kind. I was drained of energy, and yet my senses were heightened. And there was still a rock-hard cock pressed against me. He hadn't come, and so far hadn't made a move to do anything about it.

Once I started to move against him, clearly recovered, he

placed a kiss to my cheek and took a step back. "That was everything I could have wanted."

"But you haven't come?" Sure we didn't have a condom, but I was more than happy to repay his awesomeness with a hand job. Anything. "Let me do something for you."

"No, this wasn't about me. Besides, the bruschetta should be at our table." He held out his arm for me to take. "Shall we?"

My brain couldn't wrap itself around this. He'd whisked me away to a private room and given me the best orgasm ever, and was refusing any reciprocation? Was he even real? Was I a fool for not grabbing him and refusing to ever let him go again?

I took his arm. "Your erection is very obvious."

"We'll walk back to our table slowly then. I won't talk for a few moments so I can picture some horrible things in my head to make it go away."

"Guys really do that? Like imagine dead puppies and plane crashes and stuff?"

The air was just as pungent when we emerged from the storage room. Eric gave his head a shake as we walked through. "Yes, we do. That smell will also help."

He was right; by the time we made it back to the table our bread and wine were waiting. Unlike the first time he pulled out my chair, this time his fingers brushed along the back of my shoulders. When he sat down, I made sure to reach out and put my hand on his thigh.

"Why did you do that for me? Why not let me do the same for you?"

"I wanted you to be certain. This might just be about sex, but not everyone is compatible. Now we know that we are." He took a deep drink of his wine before turning his attention back to me. "And I wanted you to know that I'm doing this for you, too. I wouldn't want to take advantage of you. I couldn't do that."

"I know. Look, you seem really worried that I'm not a willing participant in this." I took a moment to collect my thoughts. "I'm twenty-eight years old. I'm happily single, but I do enjoy sex. I've played things safe my whole life. When I found these cards it was as though someone was trying to tell me to get out there and do something crazy, something beyond my normal, safe bubble. I'm not going to force you into marriage or blackmail you if that's what you're worried about. Honestly, I just want to have awesome sex. That's it."

"I can relate to that. Two normally solitary people seizing on an opportunity to have some fun."

"Yeah. There are only thirty cards. We can do a few and then stop. Or whatever."

Eric nodded and held out his hand. "Agreed then. Thirty cards, thirty nights. We can stop whenever."

"Deal." As we shook on it my heart raced. This was it. "So where do we go from here?"

There was no mistaking the wickedness behind his grin. He lowered his chin and narrowed his gaze. "Now we pick a time, a place, and a card. So what's it going to be, Glenna? Where do you want our thirty nights to start?"

Without breaking his gaze I reached into the deck and pulled out a card.

Part 2

An Experimental Phase

11

With my cell phone in hand, I stood in the hall outside the hotel room and debated going home. It was Saturday night, four days since Eric had gotten me off in a storage room and we'd made our plans to tackle the first card that I'd selected from the pile.

Day Ten
Play strip poker

I had to reassure Eric that yes, I did indeed know how to play poker. I was actually pretty good and had made a surprising amount of money when I was in grad school. Great Glenna had been the one to teach me when I was much younger. She was also the one who pointed out that I seemed to have a natural ability to count cards and recommended that I never go to Las Vegas. Ever.

There were a few times I'd been tempted, but so far I'd managed to keep out of the casinos. Still, it was cute that despite my assurances about my skill level, he was being all chivalrous about the game. *We can change it to something else. I don't mind.*

So cute. So misguided.

When he'd e-mailed me to tell me where he'd gotten us a room for the night, I was flattered. It couldn't have been cheap booking a suite at the Westin Harbour Castle, and yet he had. He'd let me know what time he was planning on arriving and the front desk told me that he had in fact already checked in. There was no reason I should be standing out in the hallway.

None whatsoever.

Just because I was about to use sex cards from a graveyard with a professor from my school—purely as a sexual research experiment, just to see what it would be like to engage in sex beyond the missionary position. Why should I be nervous? I'd agreed to this, I *wanted* to do this.

Not to mention that I'd been thinking about Eric and his amazing ability to give the best orgasms ever since our dinner. Every time I closed my eyes I could see him. I could hear his voice and feel his cock against me. I would be able to have the real things as soon as I used the card in my hand and opened the door.

"Chickenshit." I closed my eyes and counted to three before I slid the key into the reader. The electronic lock snapped its release and I stepped inside.

The room was huge. There were two love seats opposite each other in the living room, flanked by end tables. The wood flooring made my heels click as I walked across it to explore. The windows were large and the curtains pulled open revealing a gorgeous view of Lake Ontario. I didn't see a bed, but figured it was in the other room. This place was miles above my apartment in beauty and décor.

Eric stood in front of the windows, dressed in his typical dress pants—black—and shirt—light blue. Knowing what we had in store for our first . . . date? Experiment? Thing? . . .

whatever, I'd chosen to wear as many layers as I thought I could reasonably get away with. He could be a poker shark for all I knew. No reason to make things easy for him.

"Hi." I'd pulled my hair up into a bun, but had left several tendrils around my face. It was tempting to reach up and play with one, but I didn't want him to think I was nervous. Even though I was actually freaking the fuck out. I couldn't believe how stupid I was being, especially given what he'd already done with me back at the restaurant.

He didn't say anything immediately, instead giving me a once-over. I'd always laughed when I'd read a book and it would liken a look to a lover's caress. How could that even be a thing? Going forward, I would *never* make fun of that again. My skin seemed to know exactly where his gaze landed, tingling as though being caressed by invisible fingers. When he finally looked up again, I could have sworn I saw relief.

"I'm glad you came. Can I get you a drink?" He walked over to the ice bucket and pulled out the chilling bottle. "Claude reassured me that this is a good vintage. I'm not as familiar with this region, so I'll have to trust him on this one."

"Yes, please. I never did ask how you two met."

"Our mothers were friends for years. They ended up getting pregnant around the same time and we pretty much grew up together."

He handed me my glass and I quickly took a sip. "Were friends?"

"Claude's mom passed away a few years ago. It was hard on him. She was a single parent and he never had much of a relationship with his dad."

"That's awful. I can't imagine not having my parents in my life." Now that I'd started to relax, I noticed the wooden desk he'd pulled out, positioned by the window with a chair on either side. "So this is where our poker match is going down."

"I bought some cards in the gift shop. I didn't have any at home."

"You should have said something, I have a bunch." They were more than well loved and probably not ideal for poker, but would have served our purpose for tonight.

Without waiting for him I opened the card deck, pulled out the cards, and started shuffling. This was something that Great Glenna had also taught me at a young age. She claimed that it was because she had arthritis and that her hands hurt too much to do it. Mom told me later it had more to do with the fact that it kept me busy for ten minutes, which gave her time to enjoy her drink, a gin and tonic. She'd claimed that the staff at the nursing home where she lived never quite made them right the first time she asked for one, so she always had them make her a second.

God I missed her.

Lost in my thoughts I hadn't realized that Eric was still standing up. I smiled and nodded toward his seat. "Going to join me?"

"You play cards." His eyes were a bit wider than normal and he seemed to be holding his wineglass a bit tighter.

"I told you I did." *Wait a minute.* "Do I detect a note of fear in your voice, Professor?"

For the first time in the year that I'd been aware of Eric's existence, he looked uncomfortable. He took a sip of wine before joining me at the table. "I just hope I've brought enough clothing."

I couldn't help it, I got excited when I smelled blood in the water. *This is going to be so much fun.* "We'll start off simple then, just so we each get a feel for each other's skill level. Straight poker, nothing wild, one discard. Fair enough?"

"Fine."

I dealt the cards and turned my attention to my hand. *Oooh, a pair already.* "How many?"

Eric was staring at his hand with a narrow gaze. "Four."

"You have to put them into the discard pile before I can deal." He dithered for a moment before tossing the cards. "You've played poker before, right?"

"Yes." He drained his wineglass. "Once."

Oh dear. "Dealer takes three." I didn't improve on my pair of eights, but I wasn't worried. "So what do you have?"

He stared at the cards for a long time. "Can you tell me how the winning hands go again?"

"Sure. Straight flush, four of a kind, full house, flush, straight, three of a kind, two pair, pair, high card."

"Right." He stared at his cards a bit longer. "A flush is all the same suit, right."

"Yup." *Oh bless.* I was going to obliterate him.

He looked at me, then back down to his cards before he laid the pile between us. "Ten high." The way he said it, I knew he wasn't certain that was the right way to call the hand.

"Dealer wins with a lucky pair." I shouldn't have been this excited for a game. I'd come here to have sex with Eric, to finally sate the curiosity that had been burning inside me for so long now. And yet, I had a competitive streak a mile wide and couldn't help but be thrilled with my win.

"I guess that means I need to lose a piece of clothing."

I hadn't played strip poker before, preferring to play for money instead. But anytime I'd seen it in a movie or heard about it from a friend, most people who lost would remove the smallest article of clothing they had first, saving the bigger pieces for the end. Eric either hadn't watched the same movies that I had, or else he had a different strategy in mind. He stood and began to unbutton his shirt.

Starting at his sleeves, he undid the buttons and loosened the ends. He then went to work on the trail of white circles that held the well-tailored shirt together. Any smugness I'd felt from winning the game evaporated as each inch of firm, tanned chest was revealed.

An entire year of looking, of wondering, hadn't quite pre-
pared me for the awesomeness that was a half-naked Eric.

There was nothing soft or bookish about his body. Hair
covered his chest and trailed down to his stomach where it
stopped just above his belly button. His biceps and triceps were
balanced and well defined, as much as his pecs. He wouldn't
pass as a bodybuilder, but he clearly looked after himself.

Finally seeing what I'd wondered about for so long made
my libido take notice. My nipples tingled and I became uncom-
fortably aware of how full they felt. A burst of arousal spread
through my pussy and I had to fight the urge to press my hand
between my legs. This was going to be harder than I'd assumed.

Once he'd folded his shirt and set it on the bed, he sat back
down at the table. "Another hand?"

If he was nervous about losing, he didn't show it. Probably
because he knew that naked Eric was a surefire method to distract me. I dealt the cards again, but this time my excitement
about the game had been replaced with anticipation for what
would come after.

An annoying side effect of card counting is that it's not a
skill you can simply ignore. I didn't have to work to remember
what cards had been played and what the probabilities for the
other cards were. It meant that, given Eric's lack of experience,
I had a greater opportunity to direct who would win which
rounds. On the next hand I threw away an ace, king combination, ignoring my sobbing inner gambler. "Seven high."

"Pair of threes."

"My turn I guess." There were two ways I could go about
this. I could take off my sock and keep as much clothing on
until Eric was well and truly naked, increasing the tease. Or I
could lose my shirt, which would put us on even ground.

I stood and pulled it off over my head. I couldn't be bothered to fold it, so I dropped it on the floor by my chair. "Next."

While I might not be the flirtiest girl in the world, I still took pride in my appearance and appreciated it when a man noticed. In preparation for tonight, I'd gone out and bought a bra and pantie set that had little to do with comfort and support and everything to do with making my breasts and ass look spectacular.

And they really did.

Still, when Eric made a noise that for a second I thought sounded like a growl, I couldn't help but feel a mixture of relief and anticipation. "Pardon?"

"Deal."

I grinned and took another sip. "We can change the game up if you want."

"Deal."

"I'm good with Crazy Eights, or Go Fish."

"*Glenna—*"

"Okay, okay. Dealing."

I showed no mercy for the next three hands, winning each one. I think it was then that Eric realized that I clearly had the upper hand and he changed tactics. He took off both of his socks and his belt. The next round I'd been hoping that the pants would be the next thing to go, but he surprised me with a straight.

"Nicely played." I stood and unbuttoned my pants.

When I'd gotten dressed, I'd decided to go with my garters and stockings. If he'd turned out to be a good player, it gave me a few more bits and pieces to dole out. But I also knew the overall effect the lingerie would have.

Tossing my pants to the side, I paused for a moment before slinking out of my panties as well. I then sat down on the edge of the chair and crossed my legs. "Any more of that wine?"

Eric stood so quickly that his chair fell over and landed silently on the carpet. He stared at me for what felt like forever, when in reality it couldn't have been more than a few seconds.

He might not be a good poker player, but he had the smoldering glance down to a science. He came around to my side of the table. I turned in my seat, but kept my legs crossed, enjoying the added pressure on my clit.

"I concede." He spoke softly, but there was no weakness in his words.

"Winner takes all?"

He held my gaze as he pulled the front of his pants and freed the button. With a steady pull the zipper came down and with it, the last of my reservations. Gravity tugged the fabric to the floor, leaving him with one final article of clothing. Eric's erection was pressing hard against his briefs, straining to be freed. I wanted to reach out, to do the last bit of the work myself, but I couldn't move. Heat rolled from him that made my head swim. Or maybe that was the wine and the rush of excitement that flooded through me. Either way, I was more than ready for whatever was to come next.

He didn't leave me wanting for long. Slipping his thumbs beneath the waistband he held my gaze as he pulled them down over his hips and thighs, all the way to the floor. I watched the muscles in his arms and shoulders move as he did. The way his chest rose when he stood up again, taking a deep breath. I couldn't wait any longer. My gaze slipped down to the one part of his body I'd wanted to see more than anything.

Holy. Shit.

His cock was perfect. Well, perfect for me. I'm sure there might be other ones out there that would qualify, but none of them were attached to Eric. It was thick and straight and not too long. His balls were tight and he looked ready to rock and roll. I wanted to take him in my mouth, suck him until all I could hear were moans coming from him in that low rumble of a voice.

I would have done that if he hadn't taken that moment to drop to his knees in front of me. His gaze traveled up my leg, pausing briefly on my pussy, my stomach and breasts, before landing on my eyes. He took my foot in his hand, and my breath caught in my throat.

"May I?" There was no smile on his face, but I could hear the teasing in his voice. I might have won the poker game, but we were still in the middle of a very different competition. Who could arouse the other the most?

Eric was totally winning.

I didn't mind.

My voice took that moment to abandon me to my fate, so all I could do was nod my consent. He turned his attention to my legs. Lifting my foot, he placed it on the floor next to my other one. He slid his hands up either side of my left thigh, avoiding any accidental touch to my pussy, before he went to work undoing the clasp to free the stocking from the band.

When he slowly rolled the stocking down, his fingertips teased the sensitive skin of my inner thigh. I moaned, wishing for more, but not wanting to rush a single moment of this slow seduction. I'd earned this given how long I'd wanted him. And since his revelation the other day, I guess he'd earned this too.

Once he'd removed the first stocking, he went to work on the next garter. It joined its mate on the floor within moments, leaving me now bare legged. He rested both of his hands on my thighs and gave my legs one additional caress. Goose bumps rose on my skin and I shivered from my sudden heightened awareness.

"Stand up." He was already assisting me from my chair.

I could smell his arousal, could feel the heat coming off his body in waves. His cock stood proud between us and had I leaned in slightly, it would have pressed firmly against my stomach. Thankfully, the height difference between us didn't prove awkward and I couldn't wait to rub firmly against him.

"Turn around." His voice was growing rougher, as though

he'd been yelling instead of speaking in urgent whispers. "Please, Glenna."

Another wave of goose bumps rose, this time on my arms as I complied. Hot breath rolled across the back of my exposed neck. Eric leaned in and placed a kiss on my shoulder, then hooked his finger beneath my bra strap and pulled it down my arm. Each inch he moved it earned me another kiss, then a lick, and finally the gentle graze of his teeth. Once the strap fell limp to the side, he shifted his attention to the remaining one, repeating his actions.

With both the straps now dangling, the weight of my breasts wasn't supported by the bra cup. The lace slacked, slipping down to let the cool air lick at my hard nipples.

"I've wanted to see you like this for so long." He spoke the words with his lips just above my ear. "You fascinate me."

"Please." The moment I felt his fingers on my bra clasp I moaned. "Yes."

Two quick movements later and the bra joined my other discarded clothing. When Eric didn't reach around to cup my breasts, I leaned back against him, trapping his hard cock against me.

"If I do anything you don't like—"

"Eric."

"Anything at all—"

"Fuck me. Now."

The restraint he'd been showing was gone. His growl was primal as he took my breasts in his hands and pinched the nipples. I gasped, but the pain was more of a stimulant than a deterrent. His mouth descended on my shoulder as he ground his cock against me. "So beautiful."

"Please, dear God, tell me that you have a condom. Because if you don't have one and we can't fuck then I'm going to lose my mind."

"In my pants pocket." But he didn't let me go so I could go get it.

"Eric," I moaned, reaching back. I dug my fingers into his hip, encouraging him on. "Need you."

"Get on the—never mind."

He spun me around and lifted me up to carry me through to the bedroom. I didn't have time to take in the décor or the room, nor did I particularly care at that moment. He strode over to the mattress and threw me on top of the quilt. My legs fell open, exposing me fully. My pussy was wet and more than anything I needed to feel him thrust into me, to ease that ache that had grown inside me.

He dropped to his knees between my legs and ran his hands up the insides of my thighs. I wasn't a girl who shaved her pussy, so I knew my wet arousal would cling to the hairs. I reached between my legs and ran my fingers through the hair, forking out around my clit. Eric's gaze was locked on my movements. Yes, he'd touched me here a few days ago, but he'd been as much in the dark about what my body looked like as I'd been with him.

His tongue darted out across his lips. "I want to lick you."

I groaned and bucked my hips up in encouragement. He dropped forward, so his weight was held by his hands and his face hovered above my cunt.

I let gravity do the work of keeping my legs spread as I lifted up enough to watch him press his nose to my pubic bone. I felt him breathe in my scent before the first swipe of his tongue crossed my clit. My strength left me and I fell back against the bed. He licked again, softly in a wet circle that teased more than it aroused.

"You're going to make me come." With such little contact he'd somehow moved me to the precipice already. I didn't want that. I wanted his cock pressed deep inside me when I went over that edge. Being as primed as I was, I knew coming wouldn't be a problem.

"Next time then." He kissed my clit before pushing himself back to his knees. "Need to get the condom."

"Better hurry up. I'm so horny a strong breeze might get me off."

He smiled and kissed the top of my knee. My gaze followed Eric's bare ass as he walked to his pants and fished the condom out of his pocket. His fingers were steady as he pulled out the packet and tore it open. He was about to roll it down his shaft when I sat up. "Can I?"

His eyes slipped closed for a moment before he held it out for me to take. My fingers weren't as steady as his, but I wasn't worried about dropping the one thing that would allow me to finally enjoy some relief.

"Come closer." Given my position and his height, his cock was near perfectly lined up with my mouth. I shouldn't but the temptation was too much for me to resist. I leaned in and licked his head with just the tip of my tongue. Like a kitten, I lapped at his skin, teasing every inch of him that I could.

The taste of his arousal was strong in my mouth. I wanted to suck him down as far as I could manage, and yet I knew neither of us would last if I did that. Our mutual arousal was too present for either of us to resist for long. Still, I wasn't about to deny myself completely and took a moment to lick several long swipes from his root to his head. Eric groaned and his fingers found their way to my head.

With his urging, I pulled back and looked up at him until he opened his eyes once more. Only once I held his gaze did I slide the condom down his cock, making sure it was secured at the base of his shaft. The silicone shone in the dim light of the room as it sheathed him. I couldn't look away, even as I leaned back, spreading my legs once more.

In my fantasies I would have begged him to take me, to make me his. He would have teased me until he finally, graciously gave me what I wanted. But this wasn't a dream and Eric didn't seem to need my begging to take what he wanted. For the first time since this insanity had started between us, I ignored my fantasies and focused on what was real.

I thanked all the gods in existence when he reached down and took each of my feet in his hands and pushed until my knees were back and up by my ribs. It should have been uncomfortable, but it wasn't.

"Glenna?"

I bit down on my bottom lip and nodded. This wasn't what I'd imagined. No, it was way better.

He sighed and dropped his knees to the mattress before leaning in to press his cock to my pussy. The moment I felt the tip of his cock start to stretch me, I closed my eyes and savored the feeling.

Everything about this moment was perfect. As Eric filled me, he dipped his head down and caught my nipple with his mouth. His teeth grazed the swollen tip as his tongue tortured it with repeated flicks. It was what he'd done back at the bar, but a thousand times better. There was nothing between us, no lace, no cloth, just his mouth.

"Jesus." I pushed my hands into his hair, amazed at how soft the strands were between my fingers, and pressed his head down harder. I wanted to feel everything, remember each caress with acute intensity so that if we never did this again, I wouldn't forget how alive I felt.

Eric didn't push into me all at once. He teased his way in, filling me with small thrusts. My body stretched to accommodate his girth, my arousal rising the farther in he went. Once the base of his cock was finally pressed against my pubic bone, it was as though I finally felt complete. He held still and I took the opportunity to let my mind as well as my body adjust to him.

I opened my eyes and was shocked when I realized he'd been staring at me. It was strange, but for the first time since beginning our acquaintance it felt as though our connection was more than physical, something deeper. He was opened up,

if only briefly, and I couldn't help but be in awe of the surprised wonder I saw on his face.

"Eric?"

Rather than respond, he held still, waiting. One moment I
knew his thoughts, and in the next he seemed to close off again,
hidden away from me. I opened my mouth to say something,
but was cut short when he began to thrust at an agonizingly
slow pace that froze any ability I had to think.

His body was so much larger than mine that I should have
felt consumed by him. His weight pressed me into the mattress,
but it wasn't oppressive. Instead, I reveled in the comfort of his
mass. I ran my fingers up the length of his back, letting the flex
and release of his muscles dance beneath my touch.

He was careful not to hurt me as we slowly began to learn
each other. He twitched when I ran my nails along his sides,
thrust harder when I got too close to his armpits. I giggled
when he licked along the underside of my arm in retaliation,
which changed the angle of his thrusting again.

Somehow he shifted his body enough to the side that he was
able to lift my breast to his greedy mouth. Each time he pulled
back, he flicked the tip of my nipple with his tongue. I felt it,
each wet caress, down in my pussy. When he took my other breast
in his free hand and began to tweak my nipple in a counter
rhythm, my body threatened to fly apart. My clit throbbed in time
with his touch, only to then suffer the intoxicating slide of his
body against it.

"Shit." I buried my hands in his hair, hoping that I'd hold
on, hold back just a little bit longer.

"Are you close?"

I nodded frantically.

"Should I slow down?" He did so until his thrusts were ag-
onizing. Leaning in, he rubbed the tips of our noses together. "I
can drag this out. Keep going until you're begging me."

My mind couldn't process that. I wanted to come, wanted it to be hard and fast, but I wanted it to go on forever. "Yes."

Eric was apparently having none of that.

His grin was wicked. "Maybe I don't want that. Maybe I want to pound into you until I feel your pussy squeezing my cock. Would you like that?"

"Yes."

Pushing his weight up onto his forearms, he licked and kissed the side of my throat as he rolled his hip in such a way that each thrust hit my clit. It was already swollen, primed from our teasing and his mouth. I'd been ready to come since I'd walked into the room. There was no way I could hold out against this. Against him. I let my eyes fall closed and sucked in a deep breath. The scent of him, the feel and taste of him, everything Eric consumed me.

"Please." I didn't even know what I was begging for, but I hoped he'd figure it out.

His response was to lick around the shell of my ear before sucking hard on the lobe. That was apparently the right answer. I lifted my hips to meet him, every sensation in my body culminating in my pussy. I sucked in a deep breath, held it for a moment before my orgasm erupted.

I screamed.

Pleasure and pain from the intensity of the release seized my body. Eric groaned as I cried out, flailing and clutching at any part of him that I could. I wouldn't have been surprised if in that moment someone told me that my body had flown apart. The orgasm continued, and I was terrified that it would consume me.

Eric's grip on me tightened, bringing my awareness back to him. His thrusts became staccato, wild. His skin had grown slick with perspiration, and our bodies slapped as we writhed together. Finally, he pressed his face hard to the side of my neck and groaned as he came.

When his body finally stilled, he didn't let his full body weight descend on me, nor did he immediately pull out of me. It was nice, not to be immediately abandoned. I ran my fingers through his hair once more, enjoying the way the shorter strands caught beneath my fingernails. Sweat had beaded on his skin and pooled between us. It felt funny and a bit gross, but I wasn't about to say anything that would have him move.

I swallowed, my throat slowly remembering how to work. "Wow."

I don't know exactly what I'd been expecting from him, but the look of concern on his face when he pulled up to look at me wasn't it.

"What?" I brushed his bangs to the side.

"Nothing." He pushed himself to the side, but didn't move away immediately. "That was wonderful. Thank you."

Whoa, what? "You don't have to thank me. It was a mutual thing, right?"

"It was." He cupped my cheek and kissed my forehead. "Let me get you something to clean up."

And like a shot, he was gone to the bathroom.

So, that was weird. And a bit concerning. We'd danced around each other for weeks now; maybe he was disappointed in the reality of what happened.

Shit, maybe he doesn't want to hurt my feelings.

By the time he returned, I'd pulled the comforter down and had wrapped myself in it. It wasn't a blanket fort, but it was the best I could do under the circumstances.

"I got you a cloth." He held it out for me, but I didn't take it. "Glenna?"

"I'm sorry if I disappointed you. We don't have to do this again."

His hand fell to the side, but he didn't look away from me. "I'm not disappointed."

"Are you sure? Because you're not really acting like a person who just enjoyed what was, in my humble opinion, some great sex."

That look I couldn't name flashed across his face. "You're mistaken. I'm not disappointed. I'm concerned."

"About?" What the hell could he possibly be concerned about? "I told you I would keep this between us."

He shook his head and smiled softly. "I'm not worried about what we've done. I'm worried that I won't be able to stop."

12

Honestly, my brain was more than a little annoying at times. Given how crazy this time of year was at school and the fact I was trying to cover everything that Professor Mickelson was sending me via e-mail regarding his research, *and* handling the hiring process of our student assistant for the next term, the last thing I should be doing was setting up a sex board in my apartment.

And yet, here I was.

I'd had my old corkboard since high school. Dad bought it for me when he realized that I did better in school when I could visualize things. It helped me piece together threads that might have escaped me otherwise. Eventually I got good enough that I retired the old board to the back of my closet.

I'd hauled it out and set it up on the wall in my spare bedroom, which I used as an office. On one side I pinned a card at the top labeled **30 Nights**. Beneath it I pinned the Day Ten card at the top.

"Prehistoric Pinterest." I laughed.

The first card had been random and a whole shit-ton of fun.

Before we'd left the hotel room, Eric had asked if he could pick the next one. I wasn't about to say no, because sex. But given that he was using this as a means to get over . . . something, I wanted to try to track his choices so I could figure out what that something was.

Which brought me to the second half of my board.

Along the top I pinned a third card labeled **EM**. On the off chance someone unexpectedly stumbled into my bedroom and saw this, I wanted to make sure that I held up my end and did not reveal his identity. But it was a column and they needed titles and so this was my compromise.

I wanted to try to add everything that I could to that list, which was unsurprisingly not very much. In fact, everything I knew fit nice and neatly onto one card. Green, steak, Harry Connick Jr., *Little Shop of Horrors* (original ending), poker neophyte.

That was more than a little depressing.

There had to be something more.

I cocked my head to the side and stared at what was written there again. Nope, that didn't do much to change my perspective. Maybe if I got a drink it would loosen up the cogs in my brain.

"Drink!"

I started a new card and neatly printed *Claude*. There was at least one personal thing that I knew. His childhood friend whom he was obviously still close to. Proud of myself, I added the card to the board and took a step back. *Self high-five.*

The phone rang and I answered it without looking away from the board. "Hello?"

"Hello."

My breath caught in my throat at the sound of Eric's voice. Somehow I'd forgotten that I'd given him my number before leaving last night. "Hi there. How's your Sunday going so far?"

"Wonderful." There was a long pause, and I couldn't be sure but I thought I heard rustling on the other end. "How are you?"

My God, I thought I was the awkward one? "Are you freaking out? I didn't think guys freaked out about sex." In a way it was strangely reassuring that he wasn't all cocky and arrogant about this. Though it did change a few of my more consistent fantasies about him and a whole BDSM thing. He was dark and a bit broody, but didn't give off the dominant vibe.

I tucked the phone against my neck and grabbed another card. *Not a Dom.*

By the time I'd added the card to the list, I realized that he still hadn't said anything. "I had a great time last night. And I'm sorry I kicked your ass so badly at poker. I won't suggest that again."

"I might have to take you to Vegas. We could be rich."

This was better, a bit of teasing to break the ice. "I promised my Great Glenna that I'd never do that. Something about mobsters. I think she'd seen too many Scorsese movies."

"I have a question for you."

"Okay."

"You said you had a good evening."

"I did." My body hummed for hours afterward.

"Why didn't you stay the night?" There wasn't anything accusatory about the question, more curiosity.

I had wanted to stay. I really had wanted nothing more than to have stretched out on that bed and woken up to him and room service this morning. "I wanted to. I really did. But in a way it was probably best that I didn't."

"Why not?"

"Well . . ." *You just wanted this to be about sex and then you told me that you didn't think you'd be able to stop and me sleeping in your arms would have fucked with my brain too much and made this way harder.* "I guess I'm just trying to keep things . . . professional? No, umm, I'm trying to keep that boundary."

"We're going to have thirty sexual encounters. It stands to

reason that we will form a certain attachment to each other. Even if it's not romantic."

"Which you don't want?"

"No. Not the romantic one. But I realized after you left that I was giving some mixed signals. You don't deserve that."

Disappointment clawed at me. "It was all fine. I know something happened to you and this is just an unexpected way to help you get over things. I'm cool with that. It's helping me, too. I'm learning to be more adventurous. It's win-win."

"You're an amazing woman. I hope you realize that."

Thank God he couldn't see me blushing. "You're not so bad yourself."

"So we are both in agreement that we want to continue?"

"We are." Like I was going to be able to stop now.

"Good. I wanted to make sure that you didn't have any second thoughts about our arrangement."

"Second thoughts about having hot sex with an attractive, kind, and charming man? Hang on, let me think. Umm, no, no, I think I might be really fine with that. Especially if said man was calling to see if I had any plans tonight."

I hadn't heard Eric laugh very often, so hearing it now coming through my phone ignited a warm, fuzzy ball of joy inside me.

"I was hoping you might be free. I had a look at the cards and there was one that I thought might be fun for both of us."

My legs began to tremble and I sat down on the edge of the bed. "Oh?"

"Are you interested?"

"You haven't told me what it is yet."

"No, I haven't."

Dear God, if he had a playful side on top of everything else he was going to completely ruin me for all other men. "What time do you want to pick me up?"

"Seven. And I don't normally tell my dates what to wear,

but it would be . . . easier if you wore one of those beautiful skirts of yours."

So, this was me dying of lust. "I'll text you my address."

By the time seven o'clock rolled around, I was a mess of nerves. I'd chosen a different skirt, one that was a bit shorter than the previous ones I'd considered for the night. I might be short, but I do have nice legs and love showing them off whenever I have a chance.

Small but mighty. And sexy.

Eric had texted me to let me know that he was on his way. Rather than make him come all the way up to my apartment and run the risk of him seeing my crazy sex-and-Eric obsession board, I told him I'd wait for him outside.

Punctual as ever, he pulled up at six fifty-seven and I bolted for his car before anything strange could stop our evening. I still didn't have a clue what he had in mind, but I hoped it would be as unexpected as our first night. I hopped in, slammed the door shut, and turned in the seat to face him. "Hey."

Instead of his normal dress shirt and pants, dude was wearing a tight-fitting T-shirt and jeans. I totally might have drooled a bit at the unexpected casual look. Who could blame me? He was hot all dressed up and formal; like this he was lethal.

A not-quite smile tweaked at his lips. One of these days I was going to get him to grin.

"Hello. You look lovely."

"Thank you." I had told myself that I wasn't going to blush if he paid me any compliments. *Fail!* "You look great too."

Eric pulled his car into traffic and off we went. He didn't say anything about our destination, but I couldn't help but feel an undercurrent of excitement coming from him. Knowing that he was excited made my anticipation for what was to come even higher. So when we pulled into the parking lot of a movie theater, I was a bit let down.

"Is there something good playing? I haven't checked the listings in ages."

"Mind pulling your skirt up and taking your panties off?"

There were my owl eyes back again. "What?"

Eric reached into the backseat of the car and pulled out a small U-shaped vibrator. "It's clean, but if you'd like me to give it another once-over I brought some wipes."

"Day Twenty-six." I couldn't believe that this was the second card that he'd chosen for us. Especially after all of the teasing Jasmine had given me over it. This was very much one-sided—my side—and it would be more than a little challenging. I sucked on my bottom lip and counted backward from ten in my head.

"You can say no."

"No way." I let out a breathy little laugh. I'd been looking to do something that was adventurous, and this more than qualified. "I'm just wondering how long I'll last. Just looking at that thing and I'm ready to come. Honestly though, I'm not sure I could do that in public." Even if I really wanted to.

"It has a remote control. I'm going to keep it, run the controls." He took my hand and placed it on my palm. "I'm going to get out of the car. You can decide if you want to do this or not. I won't know until I press the remote and that won't be until after the movie starts. If you leave it in the car, all is fine. I just hope you don't mind horror movies."

And with that he got out, leaving me alone in his Lexus to make a decision.

My gaze was locked on the vibrator. It was a We-Vibe, which I'd seen at the Toronto Sex Show that Jasmine had dragged me to last fall. She'd tried to convince me to buy one, but I just couldn't afford it at the time. This one still had that new silicone smell—and wasn't that weird to realize that I could tell?

The silicone material was bright pink, not something that

would go missing easily and totally clashed with my bra and pantie set. It would easily slip inside me, one end to press against my clit while the other pressed against my G-spot. The experience would be one for the books, that much was certain.

The only problem was that this was a public place. We could get caught and that would put us both in a horrible position. Though it was remote controlled . . . and no one would be able to see it . . .

"Shit," I muttered as I spread my legs.

Was I really going to do this?

I looked out the window to see where Eric was. He'd stepped in front of the parked car, but had his back to the window. There was no way that he'd be able to see what I was doing. He wouldn't know until the moment he pressed the start button. I wondered if he'd be as surprised as me.

There was only one way to tell. I guess this was going to happen.

I didn't bother taking my panties off, instead pulling them to the side. The cotton was stretched hard against the side of my thigh while I slid the vibrator into place. The bulky part moved smoothly into my pussy and the other edge cradled my mound and rested perfectly on my clit. A long, shaky breath escaped me once everything settled into place. A quick adjustment of my panties and skirt and no one would be the wiser to what I had going on between my legs.

How the hell was I going to walk with this thing inside me without him noticing?

Acting wasn't my strong suit, but I wanted to make a concerted effort to keep him guessing. It turned out to not be as difficult as I'd assumed. The vibrator was held in place by my panties, so I wasn't worried about it slipping out of my pussy and falling onto the asphalt.

Because if that happened, I would die. Like on the spot, *oh my God dead!*

I fixed my skirt and took a few tentative steps forward, before I relaxed and enjoyed the foreign sensation. "Okay. I've made my decision."

Eric looked me over, but didn't ask the question I'm sure he was dying to know the answer to. Instead, he held out his arm for me to take. "Shall we?"

The movie theater was packed. A new family movie must have just released because the lobby was swarming with kids and their respective harried adult guardians. I generally loved children, but I could honestly say that I'd never been so self-conscious in my life.

Eric already had tickets, but led me over to the concession line. "I know it's not healthy, but I love the popcorn." He looked a bit sheepish with the admission. "Let me treat you to something."

He was seriously going to kill me with the cuteness. That in itself was weird given how I'd never once considered him *cute*. Handsome. Serious. Intelligent. Sexy.

But not this warm, fuzzy normalness that made me want to hug him to death. It was new and I kind of liked it.

I leaned in against his arm and took a moment to soak in the warmth of his body. "I've been trying to be good when it comes to my eating. But I wouldn't say no to a package of Twizzlers."

It was weird, but he actually relaxed as we stepped up to the counter. Like he too wasn't certain if this was a date or simply a weird sex thing. I was acting like a date, so that made it easier for him, too. "One large popcorn and a package of Twizzlers, please."

Not once had I considered that Eric might be nervous about our little outing. After all, he wasn't the one with a vibrator shoved inside him. But when I thought about it, it made sense. He couldn't know how I'd react to his proposal, if I'd go through with it or run out screaming. Despite him being the one with the remote, I was in charge. Hell, if I changed my mind at any time, all I would have to do would be to go to the bathroom and take the thing out. Pervy case closed.

In that moment the muscles in my back and neck relaxed. My anticipation also rose, as did my awareness of Eric's actions. He didn't have the remote in his hand yet, but it would only be a matter of time before the fun started.

We found our theater and managed to get seats that weren't too close to the front. Conversation was awkward at first as we started chatting off and on about work and the new semester. He asked me some questions about what I was working on for Mickelson, but my mind was too scattered to go much into detail.

The problem was the remote. Or the lack of remote sighting, as the case was. I knew I shouldn't focus on it, but I couldn't help but sneak glances at his hands to see if he was holding it or not.

He wasn't.

Not yet at least.

Dammit, why had I agreed to this?

When the lights finally went down, there were several loud whoops from a group of students who'd conglomerated in the middle rows behind us. I normally didn't bother seeing horror movies, not because they scared me, but just the opposite. I found them predictable and more annoying than anything. With a few notable exceptions, they just weren't my thing.

Depending on how things went tonight, I might have to reevaluate my opinion.

The trailers started and I settled into my seat. Our arms brushed as we shared an armrest, bare skin on skin. There was no way I'd be able to pay attention to what was on the screen, so I focused on relaxing so that he wasn't at least immediately aware that I'd used the vibrator. I let my mind wander and steadied my breathing.

The previews and commercials finished and the theater filled with ominous music. The opening sequence was typically my favorite part of all horror movies. They set the tone and told me if this was going to be one that I'd giggle through, or if I might have an opportunity to actually be scared. Within thirty seconds, I knew this was going to be the former. The acting wasn't bad, but the trope wasn't one that did it for me. Demonic possessions? Not so terrifying for an atheist.

Fifteen minutes into the movie with no sign of Eric going for the remote control, I started to wonder if *he* was the one who changed his mind. I was completely at his mercy and that was driving me a bit insane. I mean, I'm a puzzle solver who looks for logical connections. Point A to B ending at Q. There was nothing logical about the situation I currently found myself in. I couldn't demand that he turn it on and get this show on the road. I couldn't turn it on myself, at least not without drawing a whole shit-ton of attention.

All I could do was wait him out and see what was going to happen.

Well, shit.

That meant I had no choice but to watch this stupid movie.

Currently on the screen was a young man, maybe in his twenties, his eyes fully black and his face covered in black veins as he walked around a school. The dialogue was sparse to this point, so there wasn't much to concentrate on, but eventually I got into the atmosphere. The young man turned a corner and walked into a large, empty cafeteria. There was a group of students huddled in the corner crying and whimpering.

"No, Justin!" A girl stood, tears flowing down her face. "Don't do this!"

I snorted.

"Ashley, get away!" Another tearful girl called out as idiot-Ashley approached the poor, possessed Justin.

"I can reach him. I just know I can. Justin, please. I know you're in there, baby. Talk to me."

One minute Ashley was standing in front of Justin and in

the next Justin's mouth opened to epic proportions and he bit her face off. I opened my mouth to laugh—because it really was the most ridiculous thing ever—but instead a startled scream escaped me.

Eric—the asshole—had chosen that moment to turn on the vibrator. He let it run for a moment before turning it off.

The guys behind us laughed and I couldn't help but over-hear the snide, *scared the girl* and *girls are lame* remarks. If Jasmine were here, she would have thrown her popcorn at them and probably her drink.

Me? I was too preoccupied wondering when Eric would turn the vibrator on again. He reached over and wrapped an arm around me, pulling me a bit closer to his side. Then he shifted so his mouth was close to my ear.

"Scream as loud as you want."

I wanted to laugh, especially now that I knew what the game was. He really did have a devious mind.

Every time something happened on screen, someone died or there was a lame-ass jump scare, Eric would flick the vibrator on. Not only did it have an on-off function, but also variable speeds that he'd cycle through and sometimes leave on for an entire scene. When I didn't think I was going to be able to hold my orgasm at bay any longer, I pressed my face to the side of his chest.

Of course, that was the moment he turned the fucking thing off.

I looked up at him. "I'm going to kill you."

His smirk was visible from the light of the movie screen.

I'd never paid much attention to the length of horror movies before then. They had always seemed to go relatively quickly when I'd watched them in the past.

So this one was either the longest fucking movie *in the entire history of the world ever,* or having a vibrator inside you in public did strange things to the space-time continuum. The movie

was starting up its final crescendo to the inevitable battle between good and evil. My body was engaged in its own fight,
one that I was hoping would be over soon.

I pressed my thighs together, which increased the pressure
of the vibrator against my clit. I hoped that maybe I'd be able
to get myself off without Eric's evil finger on the controls. He
leaned in and nipped at the shell of my ear. "No cheating."

"I hate you."

"Want me to stop?"

"I'll kill you."

"Watch the movie."

The movie's heroine was now running through the school's
basement in search of a hammer, or a book, or something. I didn't
have a clue really what was going on because *vibrator in my pussy*.
Still, the music rose and the actress flew around a corner only to
come face-to-face with the now mutant Justin. She screamed as
she attacked him with a—where the hell did she get that?—
chainsaw.

The vibrator kicked in and on what must have been the high-
est level. I bit down hard on my bottom lip to keep from crying
out, but there was no way I could stop. As mutant-Justin bit
down on the heroine's shoulder, I screwed my eyes shut and
screamed.

Loudly.

Oh so very loudly.

My orgasm was the hardest I'd ever come in my life. Even
harder than at the hotel. I couldn't hear anything beyond the
blood pounding in my ears. I couldn't feel anything beyond Eric's
arm around my shoulders and the waves of pleasure as they
ripped through me. Even after he finally turned the vibrator off,
my body still buzzed and aftershocks rolled through me. My
breath came out in huge gasps that could be mistaken for sobs if
you weren't really listening.

The screaming died down on the screen shortly thereafter

and was quickly followed by the lights coming up and the credits starting. Not that I was completely aware of what was passing before my eyes. Shit, I could barely see, let alone process.

Eric placed a kiss to my temple. "How are you doing?"

"Sorry, Glenna's unavailable at the moment. Please find her a proverbial cigarette and she'll get back to you once her brain restarts."

I felt him smile against my temple.

It took a minute, but I was finally able to get to my feet. I turned and only then realized that the group of college guys was still sitting there, all ten of them. They weren't looking at the credits either, they were looking—no, gawking—at Eric and me.

I was too stunned to say anything. All of them looked from me to Eric and back, as though they were trying to figure out if what they thought happened, actually had. Eric hadn't noticed the extra attention we'd drawn until he'd finished picking up the garbage around our seats. It was only then that he realized that I was looking at the group.

"Gentlemen." He nodded toward them. "Are you ready to go, sweetheart?"

"Sure."

"I'm so glad you enjoyed the movie." He started to walk away. "We'll have to make sure that you come again for the sequel."

Somehow, there wasn't a sinkhole waiting for us when we reached the parking lot.

13

I'd had the most sexually adventurous weekend of my life. It was now Monday morning and I was lying in bed awake well ahead of my alarm. Every minute of the last two days with Eric played on a loop in my brain as I dissected every expression, word, and smile that he'd shared with me. It had been crazy sex and awesome, but there'd been something about Eric that I hadn't been able to put my finger on.

Even when he'd said good-bye last night, I couldn't shake the feeling that he'd been making amends for something. Eric had walked me up to my apartment after the movie and had placed a kiss on my cheek.

"Thank you for tonight." He gave my hand a squeeze. "Perhaps we can continue our project again Friday night?"

Jesus, I wasn't going to last a week seeing him every day and not want to do nasty sex things to him. "That would be great." Then we went our separate ways.

The minute I shut the door something niggled at me in the back of my head. I couldn't be certain, but I couldn't help feeling as though despite everything we'd done, he was still not okay with it.

Throwing the sheets back, I marched into the office and looked at my corkboard again.

I'd learned a lot about him this weekend. He was shitty at poker, but he had a clever mind and wasn't ashamed to use it. The whole thing at the movie theater had been about me, about making sure that I was getting as much pleasure as I could. I had no doubt he'd gone home and gotten himself off. When he'd kissed my cheek, I'd felt his erection against my hip. He'd gone before I'd even asked him if he wanted to come inside.

"So Professor Morris, what's up with you?"

I took another note card and wrote **Bad Breakup?** on it. He'd said he was trying to prove something to himself, which implied that something had happened in the past that made him question himself.

It seemed odd that someone who'd accomplished as much as he had in his life had any self-doubt.

I also took a moment to add Day Twenty-six to the sex side of the board. That had been unexpectedly awesome. Jasmine had only assumed that I'd last ten minutes; I wished I could have told her that I'd far surpassed her estimate. This was the first card that he'd selected, and I'd given him my blessing to pick the next one as well. I was hoping that a pattern would emerge.

Well, that didn't give me much, but it was something.

My weather app told me that today was going to suck. It was raining and would be colder than normal. Typical that the temperature would start to go crazy on us, but totally unfair given how warm it had been only last week. I hauled on my jeans and a shirt, grabbing my sweater before I made my lunch and headed out.

The hallway between the staircase and my office was clogged with students. I groaned, drawing the attention of several people before I headed forward through the throng. Today was the first day students could drop classes and switch to something else. That meant a lot of back and forth between offices and waiting for professors to finish classes and show up for office hours.

Any hope of having a private word with Eric today was officially out the window. I pushed my way past his office, but his door was completely blocked with some of the tallest freshmen I'd ever seen in my life. That dude must have been fed weed and feed as a child. Crazy. The second I made it into my office I shut the door and let out a sigh.

I really did hate the beginning of term.

Jasmine made it in fifteen minutes later, looking much the same way I must have. "They've fucking multiplied overnight, I swear."

"I saw at least three of them crying."

Jasmine snorted. "Poor things. How was your weekend?"

Oh, I had sex with Eric then got off in a movie theater. "Pretty quiet."

"I thought you were getting together with that guy of yours to have some fun?"

I had a screaming orgasm in front of a bunch of students! "I did. But it was . . . um, uneventful."

"That's too bad."

"How's Nell?"

Jasmine actually let out a purr. "She's wonderful. I took her out to supper and then I spent hours licking dessert off her body."

I know it was childish, but I pressed my hands to my ears. "Lalalalalalalalala."

"Baby." She looked too smug to actually care.

I chose that moment to open my e-mail. Now, I loved my job more than anything, loved the school and being able to have an office with my best friend. I even loved the work that Professor

Mickelson gave me. The man himself though, he sometimes drove me insane.

"What's wrong?" Jasmine was up and around my desk before I could respond. "Boss man?"

"He's coming back a week early to attend a lecture in Vancouver. He wants me to compile the last six months of his research into a fact sheet to hand out. I need to have it done in two days."

"You're kidding. Why can't he do this shit himself? He's the one with the PhD."

Professor Mickelson was many things, but when he had an opportunity to have me do the work for him, I ended up with the project. "It's fine. I can't bitch too much, it is my job."

"It's not your job to do weeks' worth of work that quickly. It's still not cool."

"It's fine."

"No it's not. You let him take advantage of you. Just because you work for him doesn't mean you have to let this happen."

"Jaz—"

"Don't Jaz me. You've done this since first year. You put your needs second and the job first. You won't do anything to rock the boat and he knows that. Never mind the fact you're fucking brilliant and could run academic circles around him. You need to start putting yourself first."

In all the years I'd known her, Jasmine had never talked to me quite that strongly. I'd never considered myself a pushover, not even a little. I knew what I wanted from life and I went out and got it. I didn't let myself get taken advantage of, did I?

"I better get working on this." I stood up quickly, forcing Jasmine to take a step back.

"Glenna—"

"No, you're right. But I still have a job to do. Better to get it out of the way before he comes back."

"Glenna, I'm sorry."

"For what?" I pulled my planner close to my chest. "For telling me the truth? That's nothing to be sorry for. But you said it yourself, I'm a chickenshit." I left before she could say anything else.

The hallway was still full with students, some looking more frantic than I currently felt. The group in front of Eric's office was even thicker than before. A quick look at the forms told me that these were people looking to sign up, not drop his class. He'd been popular with students last year, so it wasn't a surprise that his name had circulated as a good professor to take.

There weren't any living human-tree people in front of his door this time, so I was able to see him sitting at his desk when I got to his door. Our gazes met briefly before I ducked my head and kept going.

"Ms. O'Donald!"

I stopped and the students around us cleared a path for Eric to emerge. More than a few of the females in the crowd looked at him with adoration, while a few others looked between the two of us. Yeah, being the center of a scene was so not going to happen.

I smiled as brightly as I could. "Yes, Professor Morris?"

He didn't acknowledge the group around us, but he was obviously aware of all the eyes on us. "Are you heading to the library?"

"I am."

"I know this is a bit of an imposition, but would you mind returning something for me?"

"Of course." Jasmine's voice groaned in my head. Eric was yet another man taking advantage of me. At least he'd been up front about the whole thing.

He disappeared into his office for a moment, then returned with a thick volume. "I might have left a bookmark or two in it. Feel free to pull them out before you deposit this."

"No problem at all."

I took the book from him, shivering at the feel of his finger against mine. I looked into his eyes and the most astonishing thing happened.

He winked at me.

"Thank you, Ms. O'Donald." He turned and faced the students. "Introduction to Sociology 100 on Tuesdays and Thursdays is now full."

The collective groans chased me down the hallway as I went.

I didn't look at the book until I reached the library. I shouldn't have let Jasmine upset me the way she had, but a part of me knew that she was right. I did let Professor Mickelson push me around more than he should. I loved what I did, so I never really thought much about his requests. If it didn't bother me, then it wasn't really a bad thing, right?

When I finally got to the lobby, I walked immediately over to the return cart and set the book on top. I'd only gotten a few steps away when someone called out. "Excuse me."

I turned. "Yes?"

There was a young woman standing there, holding the volume I'd just set down. "This isn't a library book."

"What?" I came back and took it from her. There was nothing on the spine. "Sorry, he must have given me the wrong one to take back. Thanks."

It didn't seem like Eric to make that kind of mistake—

Oh wait. I was being an idiot here, wasn't I?

I headed over to one of the booths reserved for staff and graduate students to conduct research. There was one in the corner that I loved to take. It had a wall behind it, so I knew no one would be reading over my shoulder. It was thankfully available, and I quickly dumped the book in the middle of the table.

Bookmarks? Apparently I really was thick in the head.

The book fell open easily to the page with the paper sticking out of the end. Unlike the class notes I'd been expecting, my name was scrawled across the top of the paper.

Glenna.

My hands suddenly grew damp as I took the paper and unfolded it.

I'm intrigued by Day Sixteen. Thoughts on where that might happen?

Shit. I couldn't actually remember what that was. I folded the sheet back up and quickly scrolled through the days in my head. Cheap hotel room? No. Sixty-nine with your partner? No, but that would be awesome. Heat my mouth with hot liquid and give him a blow job? No, but I really wanted to work that one in somehow. Have sex blindfolded? Boring. Role-play? Oh wait! Day Sixteen was shower sex.

That was actually a bit normal. Wasn't it? All sorts of people had shower sex. I'd even done that one with one of my former boyfriends. It had been awkward and there'd been a near slip that could have ended with me getting my head bashed in. Not to mention that I'd nearly drowned when I'd gotten on my knees to give him a blow job.

This might actually be a problem.

I realized that there was another page bookmarked. When I shuffled the pages over and opened it up, I was surprised when I saw a brochure for what looked to be a high-end spa here in the city. I wasn't a spa type of person, and Eric didn't strike me as one either. Upon closer inspection though, I realized that Haven was a bit different from the norm.

Specializing in couples, Haven gives you and your partner the opportunity to connect body, mind, and spirit. Bathe in our essential oils. Rejuvenate in our salt caves. Relax in our waterfalls. Treat yourselves to the best natural foods nature offers.

That sounded like a whole lot of naked-sexy-fun times, accompanied by food. Really, he couldn't have gone wrong suggesting this place. I set the brochure down and flipped to the final bookmark. It was a printout of an online registration. It was a booking for two for this Friday night.

I mentally squealed as I did a seated happy dance.

A simple piece of paper shouldn't make me horny. It really shouldn't, but this was a confirmation of shower sex in a swanky spa for couples. I couldn't have asked for a more perfect outing.

Damn, Eric was good at this.

Which got me wondering yet again what the hell he thought he had to prove to himself. It was so bizarre that I couldn't wrap my head around it. He was smart, attentive, cared about my needs and my comfort level. Not to mention he was proving to be an amazing lover. Sure, not all relationships work out, but that shouldn't mean he needed to blame himself.

Unless he did something horrible.

No, not Eric. He didn't seem the doing-something-horrible type.

So far he'd been kind, thoughtful, put my concerns and my pleasure before his own. I couldn't even imagine what he thought he'd done to warrant needing to prove things to himself.

I removed all of the bookmarks and tucked them into my day planner. These were obviously meant for me and I wasn't about to return them, lest he think I wasn't interested. Because I totally was and wouldn't be able to think of anything else for the rest of the week.

The jerk.

I managed to find several original sources to support Professor Mickelson's latest idea before my brain officially disengaged. A glance at the clock told me that most of the students should be gone from our building now and taking up residence at the registrar's office to finalize their course changes. Someday our school would move into this century and do all this shit online.

Dear God, please.

I packed up my things and headed back. Eric's book was on top and I couldn't help my excitement. When I reached his office, I was relieved to see that his door was open and there didn't appear to be any students in sight. Before I had a chance to knock, he looked up from his desk and gave me a small smile. "Hello."

"I wanted to return your book. It didn't belong to the library after all."

"My mistake." Oh that smirk was far too cocky. I would have loved to have wiped it from his face. "Thank you for your efforts."

"I did take out your bookmarks though." I gave him a smirk of my own when I realized he was waiting for an answer. "I assume you don't want those back?"

"Only if I need to cancel the reservation."

"That's good to know." The papers were neatly tucked away in my planner and I had no intention of returning them. "Is there a dress code?"

When his smirk bloomed into a full-on smile, my heart did that weird flippy-turn thing again.

"Come as you are. They provide everything we need. The appointment is approximately two hours long."

Two hours mostly naked with Eric at a spa.

How *awful* my life had become.

I sighed. "Well, I guess that will be fine."

"I'm pleased to hear it."

"Glenna!" I turned to see Jasmine standing in the doorway of our office. She looked less than pleased.

"I better go." I took a step away, but it was far more difficult that I'd imagined. "Thank you for this."

"I should be the one thanking you. You've brought fun back into my life."

"Glenna! Professor Mickelson is on the phone for you."

"Shit. I have to—"

"Go."

I ran to get the phone, powered by the knowledge that somehow our strange little relationship was becoming something more than I ever could have imagined.

14

I really did love my job. I made a point of keeping up-to-date on all sorts of information, research tools, new theories in the field, the whole thing. Sometimes I'd get into these amazing conversations with my coworkers, other professors, and research students. We'd have in-depth debates about the significance of social media's impact on the communication styles of my generation. How it influenced children, supported social revolutions. It was awesome.

And then there was talking to my boss.

My head still pounded and my fingers were sore from the hour-long phone call I'd had with him. I'd never be so foolish to call it a conversation, because that would imply that I'd actually done some of the talking. I took notes, *extensive* notes of all the things he wanted me to do before he got back to school next week.

"I'll only be there one day before I leave for the conference. I won't have the luxury of time to fill in any holes, so make sure you complete the portfolio."

"It's mostly done—"

"Now, I want you to do me a favor and set up these meetings for me as well."

I wasn't his secretary. The department had a whole office staff that would do this sort of thing if the professor was somehow unable to do so. Not that they loved looking after Professor Mickelson any more than I did. If anything, it was easier for me to do this and they appreciated not having to waste their time doing something he could set up from his laptop. Still, a part of me always cringed when I had to do these things.

When I finally hung up the phone, my ear had gone numb from having been pressed to the receiver for so long. "I really need to get a headset."

"He's an asshole." Jasmine had given up trying to get her own work done fifteen minutes ago and had turned her attention to staring at me and making faces. "Why the hell can't he book his own appointments?"

"Something about not having access to Wi-Fi where he is."

"Bullshit. He's in England, not Mars. I'm confident they have Wi-Fi."

"It's my job—"

"No, it's really not. You need to put your foot down one of these days."

"I know."

Jasmine leaned forward, elbows on knees, and cupped her chin in her hand. "Maybe Eric can help you sort things out."

Aw, fuck. "What the hell's that supposed to mean?"

"Don't go all innocent on me. I saw you standing at his office looking all dopey at him. What's going on between you two?"

"Nothing." This wasn't going to be easy, but I had a promise to keep. As much as I'd step in front of a bus for Jasmine, I knew there was no way she'd be able to keep this to herself. If anything, she'd tell Nell and that would then be the start of the rumor mill.

"You couldn't lie to save your life."

"I know I can't. But really, there is nothing going on between Professor Morris and me." That was totally splitting hairs. There was nothing going on between *Professor Morris* and me. Eric was a completely different matter. "He'd asked me to return a book to the library for him, but he handed me one from his personal collection by mistake. I was just returning it."

Jasmine rolled her eyes. "I can't believe you're holding out on me."

"If I had something that I could share with you, I would." If I gave her even a crumb, she'd want all the gory details. There was something about sharing what we'd done with Jasmine that felt wrong. He was trying to make up for something, and I didn't want to throw a bump in the progress. "Honestly, it was a book. You can even ask at the library."

She gave me a good hard look before shaking her head. "Fine. I'll let this go *for now*. But I swear if I find out something awesome happened and you didn't tell me, I'll cry. Actual tears. With sobs and stuff."

"So dramatic." I really did love her.

It also meant that we'd have to be extra careful not to give off any signs that we were getting together in the evenings, if Eric wanted to keep this on the down-low. If Jasmine smelled blood in the water we wouldn't be able to take two steps without her coming after us. Even though she was nosy, I knew she didn't mean any harm. She'd been playing the part of my big sister since about five minutes after we met in college, and it had become second nature to her.

I had to admit, it was kind of awesome having this secret life going on and not even my best friend knew about it. Great Glenna wanted me to do something adventurous, something outside of my comfort zone, something that would make me feel alive. This was by far the most exciting thing I'd ever done.

I couldn't wait for the weekend.

* * *

I didn't see much of Eric over the remainder of the week. With the semester in full swing, he spent most of his time switching between teaching, marking, and meeting with his students. There were always a few students who stood out, even if I wasn't involved with them directly. You'd see them spending time with the professors and grad students, discussing topics and books.

I used to be like that. Excited to finally be in an environment where I didn't feel like a weirdo. It was cool to be smart, to want to reach beyond what was expected of you, to grab an idea that wasn't mandated by the curriculum and see where you could take it. High school had been hard and I'd spent as much time concealing my love of learning from my friends as I had studying. The freedom that came with taking those first few steps into a secondary education was thrilling.

I missed that feeling. The thrill. I loved my job and what it allowed me to do, but sometimes after having to deal with an overly demanding Professor Mickelson, I got a bit tired. And more than a little frustrated.

There were worse problems to have in life. At least, that's what I told myself.

I buried myself in documents, charts, and presentation folders, spending extra time to make sure that Professor Mickelson had everything he needed for the conference. Somehow my work hours extended past normal, to the point where I was saying hello to the cleaning staff most nights. When a shadow spilled across my desk, I didn't look up and instead reached for my recycling bin.

"Do you need me to dump that for you?"

I jumped and let out a yelp at the sound of Eric's voice. "Shit, you scared me. What are you doing here?"

He lifted an eyebrow. "It's four o'clock."

"Is it? I swear I just ate lunch half an hour ago." He didn't say anything else, which was a bit odd. Then it dawned on me. "Oh my God, it's Friday!"

"I can take a rain check if you need to finish this."

"It's fine. I still have most of next week to finish up before Professor Mickelson is back."

Eric frowned. "What does Phil have you doing?"

"Just some prep work for a conference he's presenting at. Let me get my things."

My normally clean and orderly filing system devolved into me shoving file folders into my desk drawer and hoping I'd be able to figure things out on Monday. I raced around the office, shutting off the printer, making sure the plants were watered and grabbing the recycling bins to put out in the hallway. I must have looked as frazzled as I felt, because Eric was trying to hold back a grin as he watched.

"What?" I tucked my hair behind my ear.

"You're cute when you're panicked."

"I am?" *Don't blush. Don't blush.* "Thanks. Okay, I'm all set."

We got out into the hallway and I locked the office before I stopped dead in my tracks. "Shit."

"Problem?"

"I don't know. Maybe. I don't have a car."

"I'm aware. And you know I'm happy to drive."

"But that means leaving together. You wanted to keep this a secret and me climbing into your car at school isn't very discreet." I would have happily taken a bus, if it was that important to him to keep his distance. Though I didn't know what bus route I'd need to take or where exactly this place was . . .

And I didn't want to go without him. I didn't want whatever this was between us to be nothing more than a dirty little secret. We didn't need to announce it to the world, but I was discovering that I didn't want to hide in the shadows either.

Eric must have had his own thought train. One minute he was nodding to himself and the next he reached for my coat. "It's gotten warm out. Let me carry this for you to the car."

And my heart melted to goo.

I wasn't sure what we would have said if anyone had stopped to talk to us on our way to the car. By the look of how empty the lot was, most people had headed out already. There were some students getting into a car a distance away, but they were too far for me to recognize any of them. Still, I didn't want to tempt fate any more than we already had. I got into the car as soon as Eric opened the door for me.

Haven was located in the entertainment district of the city. Not a location that I would have assumed would work for a spa like that, but who was I to argue their business decisions. There was a smallish parking lot behind the building, which was a treat unto itself. Eric pulled in and I got out as soon as the car stopped.

"I take it you're excited about this?" At some point, he'd lost his little half smiles and was full-on grinning.

It was a much better look on him.

"Dude, I've been hunched over a desk for the past four days compiling stats and organizing case studies that he might only reference in passing, but if they're not there I'll have my ass handed to me. Not to mention that I'm a girl and we're at a spa. Of course I'm excited."

"Well then, I better not keep you waiting." He held out his arm and I happily accepted it.

The warehouse was completely misleading as to what was hidden on the inside. The yellowing stone and black bars covering the tinted windows made me think that we were headed inside to some sort of kinky dungeon. As we crossed the threshold, the inside revealed not red paint and leather-clad attendants, but tall, lush tropical trees and an indoor waterfall that was easily twenty feet high.

The floor was made from polished wood, cork if my guess was right, and it shone in the dim lights from above. A soundtrack of tropical sounds filled the air. The front desk was long and took up most of the foyer. There were two women standing behind it, tall and slim, looking as though they'd just stepped out from between the glossy pages of a fashion magazine.

"Good afternoon." The woman who spoke looked to be ageless, her skin flawless and her hair coiffed into a perfect roll. "Welcome to Haven. I'm Kayla. How may I help you?"

"Eric Morris and Glenna O'Donald. We had an appointment for five thirty."

The woman's nails clicked as she brought up something on her computer. The second woman looked between Eric and me, smiling sweetly when she caught my gaze. I held a bit tighter onto Eric's arm, suddenly terrified that someone would deem me unworthy and steal him away.

"Wonderful, Mr. Morris. We have everything set up for you and Ms. O'Donald. If you would follow me and Ms. O'Donald follows Tori, we'll get you ready for your treatment."

Before we parted ways, Eric bent down and placed a kiss to my temple. "See you soon."

Tori whisked me away to a ladies-only section of the spa. I was presented with a locker and a bathrobe that was fluffy enough to swallow me whole. "I'll draw a bath for you and add some of our oils. You have twenty minutes to soak and get ready for your massage."

I was going to love Eric forever and ever. "Sounds awesome."

"I take it this is a bit of a surprise for you?" There was something about Tori's personality that put me immediately at ease. Maybe it was the easy way that she smiled, or she was simply really good at her job. Either way, I'd already begun to feel the tension in my body ebbing away.

"I knew he was bringing me here, but I didn't know exactly what he had planned." Well, except for the shower sex part. I still couldn't figure out how that was going to happen, especially if we were separated. Only time would tell.

Tori showed me where everything was and left so I could get changed. It was weird getting completely naked in a place that I didn't know, getting ready for something that I didn't have all the details of. But the bathrobe was warm and I stuffed my feet into the bamboo flip-flops and headed through the door that Tori had indicated.

The room held a floral scent tinged with the barest whiff of coconut. Unlike in the main room, there was no water feature. Instead a large fireplace was embedded in the wall, giving off both a comforting light and subtle heat. The tub was already filled with water and floating on the surface was a myriad of rose petals.

"Wow." I barely got the word out past the sudden tightness of my throat. It was strange to be overwhelmed by something as simple as a bath, yet I was. This was something that I would never have done for myself, even if someone had prompted me to. That Eric had wanted to treat me to this warmed my heart.

Tori knocked softly before coming in through the main door to the room. "I wanted to let you know that when you hear the chimes, the next part of your treatment will be ready. You can dry off, put your robe back on, and step into this room. I hope you enjoy your soak."

The second she was gone I took the robe off and slipped into the tub.

This thing was *huge*. Being shorter than a lot of women, there was no way my legs came close to reaching the end of the tub. Thankfully, they had a neck cradle that kept my body in place. It took a minute of adjusting myself into the right position before I was able to close my eyes and let myself float in the blissfully warm water.

I didn't exactly fall asleep, but I lost track of time. Before I knew it, the chimes pulled me from my near slumber. *I never want to leave.* With effort, I pulled myself from my watery cocoon, dried off, and climbed back into my robe.

The next room was different from the previous one. The fireplace was gone and replaced with another water feature. This one was half the height of the one in the lobby, but took up a generous portion of the sidewall. In the middle of the room were two massage tables. The heads of them were close enough to be able to have a conversation with the other person.

Which could only mean—

Eric came through the door on the opposite side of the room, dressed in a robe of his own. He held up his hand and gave me a little wave that was beyond cute. "Hey."

Not *hello,* or *Glenna* like he'd normally address me in his almost formal manner. This was a dopey, more relaxed Eric. It was an Eric I could picture waking up with Sunday morning after having been up late the night before reading—or whatever he normally did on Saturday nights when he wasn't inflicting remote vibrators on his dates at horror movies.

"You had the gigantic tub too?" I knew he did, because his hair was damp. I wanted to push my fingers into the strands and rearrange them. I took a step closer. "Did they put petals in yours, too?"

He took a step as well. "They did. Did they use the tropical oils in yours?"

"With the hint of coconut? Oh my God, yes. I want to buy a bucket of that and use it every day now."

We'd closed the distance between us and stood in the middle between the beds. I looked them over and touched the soft cotton sheets. "A massage?"

"I thought we could both use one. The freshmen this week were challenging."

"They were. And loud."

The smile we shared was comfortable. It was weird seeing him in this light, as a man and not simply as the professor whom I'd lusted after. I looked away, knowing my blush would still be visible, even in the dim light.

"Glenna?" He reached up and cupped my cheek. "Are you okay?"

I stepped back on impulse when I heard the door open. Tori stood there with two women whom I hadn't seen before. "This is Rachel and Marianne. They will be looking after you for the next hour. If you need anything at all, please ask."

So this was weird.

I pulled my bathrobe a bit tighter around me. "I've never done a couple's massage before."

"I promise it's easy." Rachel wasn't much taller than me, but I could see the muscles on her forearms from where I stood. *Holy crap, she might break me.* "We'll step out of the room for a moment to let you get on the table. Normally, I massage the male, but I'm happy to switch if there's a preference."

Eric looked at me and shrugged. "Whatever works for Glenna."

"I'm sure that's fine." What the hell was I going to say? It's not like we'd done this before. "So we just get under the blanket?"

"That's it. We take it from there."

The ladies left and it was once again me standing there staring at Eric. "Umm, do you have a preference for the table?"

He smiled. "How badly are you freaking out right now?"

Dear God, please kill me. "Oh, only a bit. It's just a massage, right? Not that I've actually had one before."

He froze. "You've never had a massage? Ever?"

"Nope. I never really thought about it."

"You're in for a treat." He made his way over to the bed closest to me. "Want some help?"

It wasn't as though Eric hadn't seen me naked before, so why I had this sudden onslaught of shyness was beyond me. Still, I wasn't the kind of fool to say no to a handsome man offering to help me strip. I stepped up to the table and undid the sash of my robe. Before I had the chance to pull it open, Eric stepped behind me and ran the back of his hand along the side of my neck.

His gentle caress lit my body on fire. My breath hitched and my nipples tightened as he reached around and pulled the robe down my shoulders. "You're beautiful. Your skin is all flushed and you smell like flowers."

I moaned and tipped my head back until it was pressed to his chest. "They'll be back soon."

"This will only take a minute." The robe fell, getting caught between our bodies. Eric reached up and cupped my breasts and tweaked my nipples until they were hard peaks. "Do you know what I'm looking forward to the most?"

When I spoke, it barely emerged as a whisper. "What?"

"The shower after the massage."

Dead.

I was dead. Or this was the best dream in the world.

"We better get you on the table before they come back." He pulled the sheets back and helped me get situated on my front. Before he pulled the sheet up to cover my body, he ran a finger down my spine. "My cock is so hard I'm going to punch a hole in the wood."

I laughed as I pressed my face into the weird open pillow. "They may charge you extra if you damage the table."

Eric didn't take any time at all to get into place and before I knew it, the masseuses were back. If I thought the soak in the tub was good, the massage was stellar. She found knots in my neck that I hadn't even realized were there. And when she put the hot stones on my back and then proceeded to coax away every ache hiding in my muscles, I knew I could die a happy woman.

The added bonus was having my head be next to Eric's. Every time his masseuse hit a knot, he'd hold his breath for a moment before letting it out. If I let out a soft moan of plea-sure, I knew he heard and would sometimes let out a little sigh of his own. It was arousing and relaxing and by the time she was finished, I was coated in oily goodness.

"We're all finished. Take your time getting up. Please don't rush. There's a shower in the back for you to use, clean towels set aside for you both, and some organic fruits for you to eat. We also have a selection of naturally flavored waters for you to drink. Whenever you're finished, feel free to dress. This room is yours for another half an hour."

I waited for them to leave before I let out a long moan. "I never want to leave."

"I think I might have fallen asleep if it weren't for all of your moans."

Lifting my head, I looked at him. We were just far enough away that a kiss would be dangerous, but close enough that I could see how wide his pupils had grown in the dim light. I couldn't see any of the rich brown that I'd grown fond of, but the intensity that I always associated with him was there in spades.

I swallowed. "I think I'd like to have that shower now."

And then I got the one thing I'd wanted for ages.

Eric laughed.

15

We started kissing the second our feet hit the floor. I wrapped my hands around his neck and let him hold me to his chest. This was different from our time at the hotel; there wasn't any awkwardness, any second-guessing what we were about to do.

It was just me and Eric, naked and willing in our escape from reality.

I wanted to keep my eyes closed as he kissed me long and deep, but I equally wanted to see his face. The Eric I'd known for over a year always appeared in tight control of his emotions. He was the consummate professional, kind and intelligent. Passion wasn't a descriptor I would have used for him before now. Even our previous nights didn't seem to have this powder keg feel to them.

He moved his mouth from mine and traveled down the side of my jaw to my throat. "You kept moaning and I was turned on so much." He spoke between nips and kisses. "I wanted to push them away from you. I wanted to lick your pussy until you screamed."

"Fuck." I pushed my hand into his hair, tugging on the strands. "Eric."

It was a comment on how lost to the moment I was when I didn't react at all when he picked me up and swung me into his arms. Instead of speaking, I began my own assault on his ear, licking the shell and teasing his lobe with my teeth until he growled.

"I need to turn the shower on."

I groaned in protest. The last thing I wanted was to break contact, to lose my hold on him in case this really was a dream and I would wake up at any moment.

"I promise I'll be quick."

He was a man of his word. It only took a few seconds for him to figure out how the controls worked and for the soft splatter of water to burst from the six showerheads. The stall itself was an open booth, tiled floor and walls that sloped perfectly toward the drain. There weren't any walls closing the stall in; rather, it seemed to be an open concept area, easily accessible to anyone.

The pressure from the water wasn't going to remove any skin, but it was perfect for getting rid of the oils that had been used. Eric moved me into position under the water, letting it hit my back first. For a moment I thought we were going to jump right to the main action, but he was a patient man. Using a squirt of scented soap, he massaged my skin on my shoulders and neck. He washed my throat and cheeks, pausing to kiss the spots before lathering them. He turned me around and washed my back. His hands traveled down my body, and he dipped his fingers into the top of the crack of my ass. I groaned and instinctively bucked my hips back.

"You like that?"

"Yes." My body was shaking from this contact, the persistent tenderness that he bestowed to every inch of my skin.

Eric cupped both my ass cheeks in his hands and squeezed.

"Not tonight, but if you want, I would love to fuck your ass. To tease you there. Maybe fuck you with that vibrator, using the remote so you wouldn't know what I was going to do next."

Hallelujah, yes! "Condom?"

He held a packet in my periphery. "I slipped it in my robe."

"So naughty, Professor."

He laughed and kissed the back of my neck. "How do you want to do this?"

I didn't hesitate. I moved to the wall to the side of one of the showerheads and braced my hands. We were close enough to the water to feel the spray, but not so much that we would drown. "Like this."

I felt his movements, rather than heard him put the condom on. Even then, he didn't immediately push his way into me. Eric reached around and once again cupped my breasts with his hands. He teased one nipple while he moved his other hand down until it covered my pubic mound. I squeezed my eyes shut and willed him to touch me. The moment I felt his cock press against my pussy, his fingers threaded through my pubic hair and forked around my clit.

"Oh God." My head fell forward as I savored the sensation of being filled.

He pushed all the way forward until he was filling me. I waited for him to move, even bucked my hips back against him to encourage him on, but he didn't. Without warning, he moved his hand away from my clit and reached for the showerhead. "I have an idea."

With the first burst of water against my clit, I was scrambling to hold on to something. Eric took my hand and placed it on the safety handle so I wouldn't slip. "Wouldn't want to end up in the emergency room."

Yeah, that would be a fun thing to explain.

"Hold this. Point it down on the top of your clit, not up." We shifted and I gripped the showerhead as hard as I could and

I held the handle. With both his hands free, Eric gripped my hips and began to fuck me.

Our mutual gasps were swallowed by the water and ambient music playing in the room. We didn't need to speak, to tease and beg each other for what we wanted. We said what we needed to through our actions.

The water was a continuous stream on my clit. Pleasure filled me, my pussy alive and sensitized in a way I'd never experienced before. I felt hard, swollen from the pleasure, engorged with desire and Eric's cock.

I knew there was no way I would be able to hold out long. Between the massage and Eric's touch, my nerve endings were alive and sparking. My pussy squeezed around his cock every time he filled me, and the tightness drove my sensitivity up another notch. Eric's arousal must have been as high. On every thrust he squeezed my hips harder, his fingertips digging into my skin. It didn't hurt, if anything it was a turn-on.

He was clearly as far gone as I was. Words slipped from him in soft gasps. I couldn't even be certain he was aware of the *mine* and *yes* and *fuck*s he muttered. With each syllable, my longing for him grew. We'd made no promises beyond this, beyond sex, but I knew I wouldn't be satisfied until I won his heart.

My orgasm didn't give me much in the way of notice before it rolled through me. I cried out briefly before I clamped my mouth shut, biting my lower lip in the process. My muscles tensed and I lost my grip on the showerhead, sending it to fall limply from its hose. My other hand was engaged in a death grip with the handle. It and the strength of Eric's hold on my hips were the only things keeping me from falling to my knees.

Eric flexed his grip on me, but continued with the same steady, firm pace until my orgasm subsided. I turned my head, catching only the briefest glance of his face—contorted, red, handsome—before he pulled back and slammed into me. He didn't make a sound as he came, but I felt every pulse of his body as he filled the condom with his come. With a final mighty thrust, his body stilled and he slowly bent forward and rested his head between my shoulder blades.

"Jesus." I barely heard him speak before he kissed my spine. "Are you okay?"

I couldn't help but laugh. "You're hilarious. And crazy if you think I'd be anything other than amazing after this."

Eric slowly pulled out of me and peeled off the condom. The water washed us both clean and he carefully disposed of the condom in some paper towel and hid it in the garbage can. I couldn't be certain, but I had a sneaking suspicion that we weren't the first couple to take advantage of this shower. Something the spa most likely counted on.

We were still well within our extra time, which wasn't all that surprising given how horny we both had been. It was weird, but as we dried off and put our robes back on, my shyness started to creep back. Here I'd been having these amazing nights with Eric and I still felt as though we didn't know each other. I pulled my hair out of the now disastrous bun and fixed it while trying to get a sense of where he was emotionally.

Pleased? He looked pleased. Or maybe that was simply his after-sex face. He also looked a bit relieved. His honesty about using me and these cards as a means to sort out something started playing a bit of havoc with my head.

"Where did you find this place? You don't strike me as a spa guy."

Eric still hadn't pulled on his robe, so I was able to see the muscles tighten in his back. "I've been here before. It's been a few years ago though."

"You've done this?" Okay, I shouldn't have been surprised by this particular revelation. I knew Eric had a past and, as Jasmine said, the man could have sex with anyone he wanted.

But this had felt . . . I don't know, special somehow. That

this was our thing, an event from the cards that no one knew about. If he was rehashing something he'd done with a previous lover, that was more fucked up than I could handle.

"Not exactly this, but yes. We'd been here before."

The warm fuzzies I'd been feeling vanished. "You and who?"

Eric straightened and turned to face me. "Grace. Her name is Grace."

"Are you seeing her anymore?"

"No."

"Is she the person you're using these cards to get over?" *The person you're using* me *to get over?*

The muscle in his jaw twitched. "Yes."

"I see."

In a way, I couldn't be mad at him. He'd never promised me love and roses when we started out, even if that's where my mind had jumped to recently. It had always been about sex, about fun. Shit, he'd *told me* that I was being used. This shouldn't hurt!

It was knowing her name that killed me. Knowing that they'd been a couple—Grace and Eric—and for whatever reason they'd broken up and he wasn't over her. Or it could be worse. "She's not dead, is she?"

"No. She's . . . fine. Lives here in Toronto. She used to teach with me at U of T."

"She's the reason you left there and came to our school. You were getting away from her?"

He looked away. "I don't want to discuss this."

"Right. I'm sorry." I wasn't sorry, not in the slightest. I was hurt and embarrassed for letting myself get emotionally attached to a man who was clearly unavailable.

I'd taken a step out into the land of adventure just like Great Glenna had wanted.

I didn't like what I found.

"We better get out of here and get dressed." I smiled, hoping that he couldn't tell how upset I was. "Do we go out the main

door? I'd hate to walk into the tub room and catch some unsuspecting person naked."

"Glenna—"

I held up my hand. "Seriously, it's fine. You've been nothing
but honest with me. And I'm still dopey from the massage and
the great sex. Let's just head out."

My mind was screaming for me to run, to get as far away
from him as I could so I wouldn't get hurt more. I didn't. I
slipped into my bamboo flip-flops, tucked my hands inside the
deep pockets of the robe, and made my way to the main door.
Eric was staring at me, but I couldn't look back at him. The
thought of seeing something there, on his face, hurt or confu-
sion, was more than I could handle.

I placed my hand on the doorknob and waited. "Ready?
Wouldn't want to give people a free shot."

"Ready." His voice wavered.

I ignored it.

"Okay, I'm heading to my dressing room. I'll meet you out
front."

I got dressed slowly. My fingers shook as I pulled on my
shirt and did up the buttons. My mind spun and I couldn't get
a single word out of my head.

Why?

Why did they break up? Why was Eric having such a hard
time getting over her? Why did he want to use me? Why had I
agreed to let myself be used?

Why couldn't I learn that adventures weren't meant for
someone like me?

Eric was waiting for me in the lobby when I finally got out.
He was smiling as he spoke to Tori, but the sparkle wasn't there
in his eyes.

"Sorry I'm slow. I never want to leave this place."

Tori tittered out a little laugh. "We hear that a lot. I hope the
two of you will come back again."

Yeah, no. "It's going on my list of things I want to do. And I'm totally going to tell all my friends."

Eric remained quiet as we left. Unlike our arrival, he didn't offer me his arm, nor would I have taken it if he had. We didn't speak as we got into the car and pulled into the busy street. It was Friday night and the students and young professionals were already hitting the clubs and restaurants in the area. Eric stopped at a red light and a sea of young, happy people passed.

I was one of them.

I was only in my twenties, single, self-sustaining, and generally happy. Hitting the clubs, meeting new people, those were the adventures I should be having. A call to Jasmine and I could be out there dancing and drinking like there was no tomorrow.

Sitting in a car feeling butt-hurt about the intentions of a man who'd proven to be more human and less fantasy wasn't logical. I kept my gaze fixed on the last group to cross the street. "I've had fun this past month."

Eric didn't say anything as he pulled the car forward when the light turned green.

"You've opened my eyes up to a lot of things. These cards were a bit crazy. I'm sure that's why Alyssa left them behind. There's only so much a person can do with them before reality kicks in."

"I know what you're going to say. Please don't." There was something in his voice—fear, hurt, longing—that I didn't want to label.

"It would be for the best."

"Give it the weekend. Think. I will too. We can talk Monday?"

This was stupid. I didn't need time to know that if we continued playing these little games things weren't going to end well for either of us. "Fine."

"Thank you." He reached over and gave my hand a squeeze.

"No problem." Only time would tell if that would be the case.

*   *   *

Monday morning came and went much the same way that my previous week had, with my head buried deep in research. I wasn't as frazzled as I could have been, but that was simply because I'd spent most of the weekend here.

I'd realized quickly on Saturday morning that there was no chance I'd be able to stay in my apartment, alone with my thoughts. Jasmine was busy, and I didn't want my bad mood to add grief to Mom and Dad's healing process. The only other option I had was work.

And that sucked on a level I couldn't begin to describe.

I was the oldest twenty-eight-year-old I knew.

Saturday bled into Sunday, which somehow morphed into Monday afternoon. I'd been so head-down that I had barely acknowledged Jasmine all day. Even her projectile jelly beans weren't going to distract me. I had my noise-canceling earbuds in and some electro swing music on replay to keep me focused on the task at hand.

Not thinking about Eric.

To this point, I'd only been moderately successful.

One of the things that I couldn't do anything about was my unfortunate need to visit the library. I'd been putting it off as long as I could, knowing that Eric had class in the afternoon so the chances of me running into him were slim. I could have taken the stairs by our office, but wanted to prove to both him and myself that I was fine. That I was stronger than my self-doubt. So rather than taking the easy way out, I picked up my books and ID and pulled my earbuds out.

"Heading to the library."

"Are you okay?" Jasmine was frowning, something she rarely did.

"Yeah, of course. There was just a ton more work that I had to do for this conference than I'd realized. I want to get it done so I can relax for a day or two before Mickelson is back."

I didn't wait to see if she believed me or not. Eric's office door was closed as I passed and he wasn't inside. Relief filled me. Stupid that I'd been tense at all. I *knew* he wasn't there; he never was in the afternoon. But it was a milestone, knowing that I could maintain my normal routine and not turn into a blubbering mess.

My trip to the library was short. Most of what I needed to do for the rest of the presentation could be accomplished online. Once I returned these last few books, it would be a while before I would have to come back. Of course, things like *an actual reason* wouldn't stop me from coming here. I loved the library; it always gave me a sense of history and calm.

Plus, they had a kick-ass coffee shop near the front.

Knowing I probably owed Jasmine at the very least a coffee for my behavior this morning, I got us two large double-doubles and headed back. It was strange how my brain went from high alert to stupid in a matter of minutes. It wasn't until I was almost at Eric's office that I realized he was there and was talking to someone. What the hell was he doing here and not in class? Unless something important came up and he needed to step out for a few minutes . . .

Even though I didn't want to draw any attention to myself, I couldn't help but slow down enough to hear his words.

"Yes, that's right. A dozen carnations. Delivery today, please. The address is a school. Hang on, I'll get that."

My heart pounded as I lowered my head and marched past his door not wanting to hear another word. He was buying me flowers. He was sorry for what happened on Friday and he was buying me flowers to make up for it. No one had ever done that for me before. The only time in my life I'd ever received flowers was from my dad when I turned eighteen. If anyone asked, I said it never bugged me that I didn't receive them.

It did.

Eric was getting me carnations.

"Well there's the Glenna that I know and love." Jasmine smiled when I bounced through the door. "And she comes bearing gifts of caffeine. I do love you so."

"I'm sorry. I was being a bear earlier. I'd been here most of the weekend, which made me grumpy."

"That sucks. You're done though? Can you head home early?"

"Mostly." Not that I was going to leave now, not with flowers on the way. "I'll tough it out today and come in late tomorrow."

If Eric was giving me peace offerings, then maybe he'd come to the conclusion that he really did want to continue on with our experiments. The question was, did I? I continued to ponder that very thing even as I saw him leave to head back down the hallway toward the stairs. I continued to ponder when the clock rolled around to four and there still hadn't been a flower delivery.

"When are you heading out?" Jasmine turned off her monitor. "I'm flying solo tonight. If you don't have plans maybe we can get some supper or something."

Nothing had come.

Eric had returned to his office fifteen minutes ago, hesitating briefly to look down my way before disappearing inside. I knew he was expecting me to have a chat with him. Maybe the flowers were actually in his office?

"Um, I have something I need to do first. Maybe we can do a movie or something tonight?"

Jasmine stared at me, frowning. "Are you sure you're okay? You're really not yourself."

I hadn't been myself for two weeks now. "I am. I promise. I'll give you a call and we can go see something. I'll let you pick."

"Oh goody. I heard there's a good horror movie playing. We'll be able to laugh at the characters dying."

Thank God she left before she saw my blush.

My nerves acted as fuel and had me up and marching down

the hall the second I knew Jasmine was gone. Eric was sitting at his desk like normal, but rather than reading or writing something down, he was simply staring at his bookcase.

There weren't any flowers in his office.

When the realization hit me, I felt instantly ill. "They weren't for me."

Eric jumped and his gaze locked onto me. "Hello. What wasn't for you?"

"I walked by earlier and overheard you ordering flowers for delivery at the school. I should have realized you were sending them to her. To Grace."

"Glenna, it's not what you—"

I held up my hand and took a step out of his office. "Stop. Please don't say anything that's even close to a lie. You are working on some closure with her. Or you're trying to win her back. Either way, this is turning out to be something that I wasn't expecting. I think I'm going to stop this."

"Stop what?"

"Everything. The cards. You and me. I guess I'm not as adventurous as I thought I could be."

"Glenna—"

"No. I'm done." I raced back to my office, grabbed my things, and went out the closest door.

This was wrong. Everything about what had happened, about how I was feeling. None of the excitement and passion that we'd shared was worth the pain of this heartbreak. From now on, I was going to stay true to myself. Someone else could have the adventures.

16

The pounding on my apartment door was getting to be more than a little annoying. I knew who it was, but I honestly didn't think I'd be able to deal with Jasmine, not right now. If I opened the door she would be able to see that I'd spent the last several hours crying. Then she'd want to know what had happened and who she needed to go kill in order to make things right. That would lead to a whole conversation about Eric and another round of tears.

Yeah no. I was more than happy to skip all of that and move on to the drinking-of-the-wine part of my cycle of misery.

When the knocking finally stopped, I hoped for a moment that perhaps Jasmine was going to give up for once and leave me in peace. Then my phone started ringing and I knew that, as always, I was going to have to give in to her. Rather than answer the phone I pushed myself off the couch and made my way to the door. When I opened it, she was standing with her cell phone pressed to her ear and a scowl on her face so deep, I had no doubt there would be permanent marks in her skin.

"What the absolute hell is going on with you?" Jasmine pushed her way into my apartment and I simply closed the door. "I've been worried sick about you. You didn't answer my e-mails, or texts or calls. Then this shit with the door when I could clearly hear you crying."

I didn't expect her to pull me into a hug, but that's what she did. Jasmine, my best friend and surrogate sister, the only other person who knew me better than I knew myself, crushed me in a hug and didn't let go until my sudden onslaught of tears finished.

"Better?" Jasmine wiped my face before she let me pull away. "I brought wine."

"Oh, that's the best thing ever."

"I'll get glasses. You sit and start talking. What's been going on with you? You've been off for at least the last few weeks."

I wanted so badly to tell her all of the details. Everything that was going on with Eric, the cards, Grace, but I couldn't. While I might be upset at how things ended between us, I'd made him a promise that I wouldn't identify him. He'd been honest with me, and the very least I could do was live up to my end of the bargain. That said, I knew I had to tell Jasmine something.

"You know those sex cards?"

She raced out of the kitchen, a wineglass in each hand. "Oh shit, you were using them? With whom? One of those online dating dudes? Do I need to smash kneecaps?"

Good old Jasmine. I could always count on her to make me laugh with threats of physical violence. "You're insane. You know that, right?"

"I'd do anything for you. Like get you drunk on a work night. Here." She filled my glass to the brim and handed it to me. "This is the cheap-ass shit too. Guaranteed to cure all ills, give you heartburn, and leave you with a nasty hangover."

"Cheers."

I swallowed down as much as I could stomach on the first pass, before letting out a sigh. "Yes, I used the cards with a man. No, it wasn't an online person. No, I'm not going to tell you his name. We'd agreed to keep this between us and I want to honor that."

"Okay." The humor of the moment passed as Jasmine tucked her feet up on the couch to sit on them. "Did he hurt you? Physically?"

"No." Shit, the thought of Eric doing anything to harm me was crazy. "No, he was a perfect gentleman."

"Good. Because I would have called the cops if that had gone down. So I take it he broke your heart?"

I groaned. "Yes, but that wasn't his fault either. He was up front with me when we started. He was interested in the cards when I showed them to him. He wanted the sex part of things and told me that's what it would be about. I was the one who let things go too far emotionally."

"Of course you did. You're kind and sensitive and despite having done the occasional hookup, you're not a sex-for-sex's-sake kind of woman."

"I wanted to be. I wanted to do what Great Glenna suggested and find a man to go out and have an adventure with. These cards and her letter to me seemed like fate lining up to say, 'Here's your shot, go for it!'"

Jasmine cocked her head to the side and hummed as she took a sip. "Did you get along okay?"

"We did. I even managed to make him laugh."

"So you had sex with him."

"Yup."

"More than once?"

"Oh yeah."

"Good sex?"

"He took me to a fancy spa for a luxury massage and we fucked in their shower."

Jasmine's eyes bugged out. "Holy shit. So what the hell happened? You were compatible, were good in the sack, and he was treating you well."

"I found out that he still had feelings for his ex-girlfriend. I overheard him ordering flowers and I thought they might be for me. They weren't."

The thought of it, of knowing Eric still wanted Grace, ripped at my heart. I was many things, but delusional wasn't one.

"It sounds like there is a lot more to this than I realized." Jasmine set her glass down. "I'm going to use your bathroom and then we can talk some more."

When she left, I did the best I could to clear my mind of everything Eric. I knew I was blowing things up, making them bigger than they should have been. Tomorrow, I'd get rid of the sex cards, I'd take them to the Social Club and leave them there for the students to find and have some fun with. Then, I'd get ready for Professor Mickelson's return and life would go back to normal.

That would be that.

After a solid ten minutes of no Jasmine, I got up and refilled my wineglass. If I had much more of this I really would end up with a sore head tomorrow. "Oh well."

Finally I heard the toilet flush and Jasmine bounced out, a grin on her face. "Sorry about that."

"I hope you turned the fan on." Lord, she was gross. "You want some more?"

"No. I'm going to leave the rest with you."

"You're going? You just got here." There was something on her face, something that probably should have me freaking out if the wine hadn't already taken hold. "Well fine then."

"I needed to see you, to make sure that you were okay. But now I think I need to go check out something."

"Oh. Okay then." Damn this wine worked fast.

"I'll stay if you want me to, but I get the feeling after that glass you're going to crash and fall asleep. And no offense, but your spare bed sucks ass."

"It does." I did love her, but now that I had my wine, I knew it would be better if Jasmine left me alone to wallow. "I'm sorry I worried you and you came all this way."

"Please. It's fine. Will I see you tomorrow?"

I didn't want to face Eric, but unless he quit his job or Professor Mickelson suddenly replaced me, there would be no avoiding it. *And this is why you don't date a coworker, asshat.* "I'll be there. I can't promise I'll be with it, but I'll be there."

As quickly as she swept in, Jasmine gave me a hug and was gone.

Well then.

That was interesting.

At least she left the bottle. Which I took and went to bed to watch television.

I did make it into the office on Tuesday, but it was closer to noon than nine. My head pounded in a way that it hadn't since my first year of college when I'd made the unfortunate mistake of doing triple shots of tequila followed by margarita-beer chasers.

That had not ended well.

Somehow I'd managed to down a liter of water before leaving. Food was so not happening, which was one less thing I had to worry about, again good because of how late I was. It was so weird coming in this time of day, especially seeing that Jasmine had arrived long before me. She looked my way as I walked in and didn't bother to hide her smirk.

"You drank the whole thing, didn't you?"

"Yup." My stomach flipped and not in the happy, fun way. "I hate you."

"You loved me last night."

"Can you talk a bit lower?"

"This is my normal voice."

"Did you know that you're loud? Like your voice could break rocks."

"Sit down and pretend to work."

I didn't have the strength to argue more. I fell into my chair and turned on my monitor. There were five messages from Professor Mickelson waiting for me, the subject heading each more frantic than the previous. "Shit."

"What?"

"Just more work. Mickelson is coming in tomorrow and flying out Thursday night. He wants to meet with me to go over everything." I let my head fall to the desk and gave myself several long moments to collect myself. At least I'd done most of the work last week.

"He'll be out West on Friday though?"

"Yeah. I'm not sure yet what that's going to mean for him and office hours. He's technically still on sabbatical until the end of December."

"Mmmhmm." And like that Jasmine was typing away on her computer, distracted by something else.

The day crept on slowly. As the hours went on, my head began to ease and my brain functioned once again. *I will never drink on a work night again.* I made it to four o'clock when Jasmine stood up suddenly and marched to my desk.

"Yes?"

"I need you to come with me."

"Why?" She looked to be on a mission. This wouldn't end well for me.

"Because I'm taking you somewhere. Come on, get up."

She pulled me out of my chair and led me down to the kitchen. Oh, a coffee would go down really well right now. Maybe she wasn't being normal Jasmine, getting all up in my business and dragging me along into hell.

We turned the corner to the kitchen and she swung me into the room. Eric was standing there, dressed immaculately as always, hands in his pockets and looking like someone had kicked his puppy. "Hello, Glenna."

I turned to glare at Jasmine, but she was already backing out of the kitchen. "I'm going to shut this door and make sure no one bothers the two of you. You can't leave until you work this out. Understand?"

The second she was gone, I marched over to Eric and poked him hard in the middle of the chest. "How the hell does she know about you? I didn't say a thing."

Clearly, he didn't realize the danger he was in because the bastard was smirking. "She told me you were hung over, but I didn't believe her."

"How?" *Poke.* "Does?" *Poke.* "She?" *Poke.* "Know?"

"I was going to ask you the same thing. I arrived at work this morning and she was standing outside my door waiting for me. I had to endure a lecture and more than a few threats to my person before she let me get a word in. She went to your apartment last night and said she saw something that let her figure it out."

My memory of what I'd said was a bit hazy in the aftermath of the wine. I know for a fact I hadn't used his name, nor given any indication that he worked here with us. Had I? "I promised you I wouldn't tell her your name and I didn't." That much I knew for certain.

"It's fine. I realized halfway through her lecture that you'd been hurt far more than I'd even realized. For that I'm sorry."

Memory of the flowers that weren't mine rushed back. "I

am too. But it doesn't change anything. We're done . . . whatever this thing was."

"Can I say something first, before we end things?" He waited for me to nod before taking my hand in his. "I haven't talked to anyone about Grace in a long time. Our relationship, Jesus, to say it ended badly is a horrible understatement. I was angry for a long time afterward, to the point where I had no interest in dating anyone ever again. Then I heard you and Jasmine talking about those cards of yours and something changed. You woke something up in me that I hadn't realized had been asleep. If nothing else, I wanted to thank you for giving that to me."

My anger at Eric melted into concern. I turned my hand so our fingers were entwined. "It was the flowers."

"What flowers?" The look of realization crossed his face. "You heard me placing the order."

"I thought they were for me. When they didn't come, I realized you were sending them to Grace, to *her* school. You'd told me you were using me for sex, and when I heard that I realized I couldn't be a Grace replacement. I wanted adventure, but not that."

"Never that." He reached up and cupped my face. "The flowers weren't what you think they were."

"What were they then?" I could tell he still didn't want to talk about what had happened between them, but I needed something. I needed to know if there was even a chance for us. "Eric?"

"They were a good-bye." His eyes glistened and I was shocked by his near tears. "I don't want things to end between us."

"Me either." I swallowed hard.

He lowered his face to mine. "Unless you stop me, I'm going to kiss you now."

"So not stopping you."

The remnant of my hangover was no match for the rush of lust and adrenaline that surged through me as his lips covered mine. Everything about him was warm, strong, enticing enough to pull my body against his without my noticing. I couldn't help but remember Jasmine's words the day he'd overheard us talking about him here.

For a second I thought he was going to throw you over the table and fuck you. . . .

I groaned. "Okay, change of plans. I'm not ending things. Is that cool with you?"

He leaned in and sucked my bottom lip into his mouth. "I don't want you to feel pressured. Not by me or by your friend."

"I'm not. I want this."

Great Glenna was right. The more I went on with this little adventure, the more I came to know the kind of man I wanted in my life.

Someone who was kind, honest, and willing to admit when he was wrong.

In other words, Eric.

But it was going to take more than some hot sex in a spa or hotel room to convince him that he was ready to move on from his past. It was going to take time and patience, and quite possibly some creativity on my part.

Reaching around his neck, I pulled him down and kissed him with every ounce of passion I had burning inside. I willed him to know, to see how much joy he'd given me. It wasn't until I felt the press of his hard cock against my stomach that I knew it was time to move this party along.

"Please tell me you're done for the day?" I licked my lips, savoring the taste of him on my skin.

"I am."

"Good. If you don't have any other plans, I have some cards that might prove for an interesting night."

Eric's smile made my heart dance. "Lead the way."

With his hand in mine, we left the safety of the kitchen. My adventure was back on and I was more determined than ever to see things through. After all, we'd started out being honest with each other, and we'd worked through a bump with little effort. Together we'd be able to handle anything that came our way.

Anything at all.

Part 3

An In-depth Examination

17

If someone had told me even a month ago that I'd have talked to Eric, let alone had sex with him on multiple occasions, I would have died from laughter. It wasn't that I thought so little of myself as a person, but rather thought little enough of my ability to keep a lover satisfied. I'd had sex and for the most part it had been good. But it had always been a bit . . . I don't know, bland? Yeah, that was the word. Bland. I never knew if my previous boyfriends simply weren't into crazy fun between the sheets, or if I didn't inspire passion from them.

That was a doubt I no longer possessed.

After our reconciliation, I came to the decision that I didn't want us to keep meeting in hotels and fancy spas. There were certain things that I would be far more comfortable engaging in at home. My sheets, my kitchen utensils, and my produce.

Was that even on a card? I couldn't remember anymore.

Eric had agreed to come over Saturday and we'd take some time going through the deck and picking out what cards we were interested in trying out. It had been difficult not to jump ahead and plan things out. I had to remind myself that this wasn't all about me. Instead I spent most of the morning cleaning, a thing that I didn't excel at. I dusted, vacuumed, and even went so far as to gather up the collection of old *Cosmo* magazines that I'd stuffed under my couch.

There were certain things about me that I wasn't ready to share with him yet—my *Cosmo* addiction being one of them.

It was just after noon when I heard the knock at my door. I'd spent so much time cleaning that I hadn't left myself long enough to primp properly. It was probably for the best, as I would have simply changed five more times and made more of a mess than I'd started with. With a final look around to make sure everything was in place, I ran my hands down my capris, fixed my shirt, and opened the door with a smile.

"Hi there."

Eric stood half a foot away, smiling. "Hi back. These are for you."

I could have cried when he pulled the bouquet of lilies from behind his back and held them out for me. "These are my favorite."

"I have to be honest, I asked Jasmine for suggestions. After your disappointment the other day I wanted to make it up to you with flowers of your own."

Taking the bouquet, I invited him in. "Thank you so much. Let me put these in water. I know it's a bit early in the day, but can I get you anything? Coffee? Beer?"

"Water, thanks."

Eric hadn't moved very far into my place, which really wasn't all that big. It was strange seeing this large man standing awkwardly, looking at my bookshelf without getting closer. He couldn't be nervous, not after everything we'd been though to this point. Given how things had almost ended, maybe I shouldn't have been surprised. My nerves had sent me running to the bathroom more than once already.

Or that could have been the three coffees I'd downed.

Focus, girl!

"Most of my academic texts are out here. I keep my reading-for-fun books in the bedroom."

"I love noir mysteries. Big fan of Alan Bradley and James Ellroy."

"Really? You don't strike me as a mystery guy. More literary bent."

Eric shrugged. "I read a variety of authors. Grew up on Stephen King and Dean Koontz."

"That explains the horror movie last week." I set our waters on the coffee table and scooted into the corner of my couch. "And I guess *Little Shop of Horrors.*"

There was something that changed in his entire body when he smiled. The tension bled out of him and it he seemed to let his guard relax. I couldn't imagine exactly what happened between him and Grace, but whatever it was had burned him badly.

"I'm glad you came. That we're still doing this." I looked down at my hands and tried not to pick at my nail. "I . . . I feel like this is something I need to do. To learn exactly what I'm capable of as a woman. With you I actually feel safe enough to take chances."

Eric sat down on the couch opposite me. His legs were long and stretched to the point where his knees nearly touched mine. "I understand. And I was being honest when I told you that I needed to prove something to myself as well."

If I ever met this Grace, I swore I'd punch her in the nose.

"Well then, we both have a sex agenda." Sexgenda? I needed to put that on the board.

Oh shit!

"Don't move. Just sit right there and don't move."

I'd been so busy cleaning up that I'd forgotten to hide the most damning and embarrassing thing in my house. I ran into my spare room so quickly I stubbed my baby toe on the door-jamb. "Ouch."

"You okay?"

"Yup. Stay there."

"Are you hiding your underwear? I don't mind seeing that."

Pantie fetish, good to know. "Nope. Ass on chair, please."

Limping through the pain, I snatched up the board, which had considerably more information on it now. Looking at the board it finally hit me: This was what Jasmine saw the other night. She hadn't gone to the bathroom so much as decided to snoop. It wouldn't have taken much for her to connect the **EM** heading to Eric given everything she'd seen the last few weeks.

I was going to have to thank her . . . before I smacked her for going through my things.

Carefully, I shoved the board in the closet, face first. There, even if he opened the door he wouldn't see what was on it. And if he picked it up to look then I'd have ample reason to kick his ass.

When I got back to the living room, Eric was leaning forward looking at something on the coffee table. Tremors of excitement tickled through from my core out to my fingers when I realized what he had.

The cards.

"I didn't know if you wanted to jump right into that discussion." I sat down beside him, careful to keep my body from pressing up against his. I had to show a certain level of restraint.

"There are a few missing." He laid them out on the table, much the same way I had the first night I'd brought them home.

"I took out the ones we've already done." And pinned them to a board where I could coo and sigh over the memories. So mature.

Eric hummed his acknowledgment, but it was clear to see that his attention was on the cards. Spread out this way, it was awesome to see the wide array of fantasy material. The author of the cards must have had a lot of fun coming up with this list. I picked up the one that had been the most intriguing to me.

Eric looked at what I'd picked up and read it much the same way he must say *the weather is fair* or *hand in your papers.* "Day Twenty-three. Have sex on a balcony." He looked up. "And I see you happen to have a balcony."

My face heated, but if I was going to do this, I had to trust that Eric would take my fantasies seriously. "Okay, here's the thing. I've lived in this building for three years now. This is my first place after moving out from my parents' house. The fourth night after I'd moved in, I was sitting here on the floor unpacking my things. The lights were off so no one could really see me. I had the window open and that was probably the only reason I heard my neighbors."

"They were having sex on their balcony." Eric adjusted himself in the seat. "That must have been . . . interesting to witness."

"Honestly, it was probably the first time sex fantasies became a thing for me."

Eric took the card from me and placed it to the side. "We'll make this the To Try pile."

My inner sex vixen sat up and took notice, bringing along with her an ample supply of lust. "Okay then." I found it suddenly very difficult to sit still. "Are there any that are of interest to you?"

He started to reach for Day Twenty-four—anal sex—but veered over and instead picked up Day Twenty-nine. "Let your partner tie you up and have sex with you." He handed the card to me.

"You want to tie me up and have sex with me?" I trusted Eric for sure, but being restrained was something I'd never considered before. I didn't know how I'd react.

"No. I'd like you to tie me up."

I blinked a few times before I looked back down at the card. "I didn't see that coming."

"I can tell." He chuckled. "You have your fantasies and I've had mine."

I quickly added it to our To Try pile and picked up Day Twenty-four while I was at it. It was Eric's turn to look shocked. "What?" I shrugged. "You're interested. I'm interested. Let's put that puppy on the list."

He closed his eyes and bowed his head. "I have such a raging hard-on right now." That little sentence was all it took for me to burst into a fit of laughter. He glared at me. "Trust me when I say that it isn't funny."

"You said *hard-on*." I did my best to stem my giggles, but was failing miserably.

"What would you prefer I say?" He leaned in so his face was close. "Boner?"

And that set me off again.

He shook his head. "You're weird."

I calmed down long enough to speak. "You're a professor and half the time you're all serious and brooding and have all the female students swooning over you and you ignore them. Then you said *hard-on*." My cheeks hurt from smiling so wide.

Eric tried to fight his own smile, but within a few moments he was chuckling along with me. "I'm not a prude."

"Chubby. Tentpole." I leaned in so our noses touched and whispered, "Popped a stiffy."

He pushed me and I let the momentum carry me back until I was lying on the cushions. Tears formed at the corners of my eyes and I couldn't stop the giggles. "I don't know why I'm laughing so much. This is stupid."

Eric dropped the cards and shifted so he was hovering over me, his body fully covering mine. "Maybe it's been too long since you last let yourself go."

When he leaned down and brushed his lips against mine, I

was still overcome with silliness. That dissipated the moment he deepened the kiss. It was passionate, without being frantic. While our bodies touched, pressed against each other, this wasn't about sex. Not yet. Eric was warm and as I slid my hands around his neck, I soaked in as much of that as I could.

I'd never kissed someone and had it be this fun before. I nipped and licked, let my tongue explore his mouth. I took advantage of my position and wrapped my legs around his thighs. The shift put his erection against my stomach, and I was able to wiggle against it.

"You seem excited about my hard-on." He pressed his nose to my throat and licked at the skin of my shoulder.

"Maybe I should give it a bit of attention. It seems that a few times we got together you missed out on some of the fun."

"I got mine as soon as I got home." Eric slid his hand down my side to my thigh. He gripped it and lifted me up even higher. "I want to make sure you're feeling good."

There was no way I was going to let this be a one-sided sexual relationship. I might be shy, but I was far from being selfish. "We need to do Day Twelve."

"What's that?"

Rather than simply tell him, I shoved at his chest. "Up."

He groaned, but complied. "I was just getting comfortable."

"You'll like this." I took his hand and led him down the hall to my bedroom. "We'll have more room down here."

When I'd moved out on my own, the first thing I'd splurged on was a queen-size bed. Not that I necessarily needed a lot of space, but it felt luxurious to be able to stretch all the way out and not touch an edge. Plus, I'd had high hopes that I wouldn't be sleeping alone forever.

"Your room is very purple." He gave it a once-over before turning his attention back to me.

"What's wrong with purple?"

"So Day Twelve?"

I pulled my shirt off and went to work on my capris. "Is to sixty-nine with your partner."

He looked skeptical.

"I know we have the height difference going on, but I don't think it will be an issue."

"Never let it be said that I wasn't willing to give things the effort they deserved." Within a moment he'd removed his shirt and tossed it to the floor.

Once I'd slid my capris off, I reached over and began to help him with his jeans. That led to me becoming fascinated with his chest—he had just the right amount of hair and oh, his nipples were hard—as I leaned in to kiss his warm skin. Eric groaned, stopped what he was doing, and cupped my face.

Our kiss this time was anything but soft and slow. Frantic would be a closer description. My head spun from the lack of oxygen as I panted between kisses. I wanted to feel everything, touch every square inch of his skin, play with his hair. His muscles in his arms and shoulders flexed beneath my hands as he lifted me up by my ass and carried me the short distance to my bed.

I wasn't even completely aware of him putting me down. Not until he pulled back and took my bra with him.

"How did you—"

"Not my first rodeo." He tossed the bra over his shoulder and bent his head to capture my nipple in his mouth.

My breasts had always been super sensitive. When I pleasured myself, I always made sure to pinch and flick the tips, as it always amped up my arousal. Having a lover pay them particular attention drew me close to the edge of release far faster than I liked. I only lasted a few moments before I had to push his head away. "Too much."

Dear God, he pouted.

"I promise I'll make it up to you. Take off your jeans. I want to suck your cock."

His face was flushed and with my words it spread down his

throat to his chest. I'd never known a guy to blush like that. I was totally going to have fun with him.

When he freed himself from his jeans and briefs, he leaned down and ran his hands along the tops of my thighs. "I think for this to work, I'm going to have to get on the bed with you on top. Otherwise I'll smother you."

Sorry, officer, I smothered her with my massive body during sex. Yes, I can confirm she died happy. No charges? Thank you.

"I'll scooch over. Lie down."

It's funny how a person's perception about a thing can change when another person is added into the equation. My big bed looked far smaller when he climbed on and stretched out. His feet dangled off the side even with his head near the edge.

"We should turn the other way." I pushed myself onto my elbow. "I don't want you to get a cramp."

"You are thinking way too much. I need to fix that."

Eric reached over and pulled me on top of him. His hair tickled my bare breasts as I squirmed and shifted into place. I wanted to keep kissing him, but I couldn't deny how much I wanted to turn around and suck the tip of his cock, which was currently digging into my stomach.

It could wait.

I covered his mouth with mine and used my position to explore his body more. He had a scar on his side, too ragged to be surgical. His biceps were hard, but not so large as to make him look like a bodybuilder. His hair covered his pecs and trailed down his stomach to his pubic mound. When he wrapped his arms around me, he held firm, but not so much that I thought he would hurt me. More like he cherished this moment.

Cherished me.

I pulled back and pressed my head to his shoulder. "Shit. I could come right now."

"Then do it."

"No! I want to suck you. I want to taste your come."

"Can you come more than once?"

"I . . . don't know. I've never really tried."

Eric pushed me so I was sitting up. "Let's see. Turn around. Put your pussy on my face."

Shit, he was going to be the death of me.

Despite what I've seen in the few porn movies I've watched, it's hard to be graceful getting into position for something like this. Eric was long and broad and I had to be careful not to put my elbows or knees in inconvenient places. I was about to swing my leg around when I got shy about what we were about to do. It's a rather intimate thing in the first place, oral sex. To then take it to the next step and basically grind my pussy on his face, well, it wasn't something I had done before.

Eric didn't give me much room for embarrassment though. He grabbed at my calf and pulled. "I want to taste you."

My pussy pulsed in response. Who was I to deny the man? Carefully, I lifted my leg and settled down so my clit was pressed to his chest. Eric did the rest. He slid his arms under my thighs, lifted my lower body, and positioned my pussy on his mouth.

"Fuck." I lowered my head as he sucked hard on my clit.

His tongue teased the swollen bud, he lapped at my labia, and he kneaded my ass with his fingers. It was intense, too much too soon. My body actually zoomed past my orgasm, unable to simply let the pleasure flow.

"Too much." I clutched his thighs. "Slow down."

Thankfully, he listened. He let up on the suction on my clit and I was able to relax. What I needed was a distraction. The long, thick cock bouncing in front of my face was the perfect way to slow him down and give my body a chance to adjust. I was just the right length to be able to suck the head of his cock into my mouth without needing to bend at an awkward angle. Sweat and the taste of his arousal burst across my tongue as I lapped at his cock. I licked from the base of his shaft all the way to his head, loving the way he stiffened beneath me.

When Eric moaned, the vibrations rocked my pussy, tickling the over-sensitized skin with his hot breath. We then began this back and forth of licking and sucking, teasing each other with our mouths and hands. I reached down and cupped his balls, grazing the skin with my nails. He retaliated by pressing a finger into my pussy, pumping it in and out of my body in time with his lapping tongue.

This time when I felt my orgasm begin to build, I knew there was no chance that it would fizzle. I continued to suck Eric's cock as long as I could without hurting him. The higher my pleasure rose, the more my body shook, the tighter he gripped my ass. He wasn't going to let me pull away, to give me the chance to run away from my release. I took his cock as deep as I could manage and held it in my mouth as I came.

I screamed around his shaft. My pussy heated as I came hard and he held me to him. Normally, I'd squirm when I'd orgasm, but I couldn't move and was forced still as the intense pleasure burned through me. When Eric finally pulled back, I continued to hold his cock in my mouth, breathing in and out from my nose as I regained control. He didn't say anything, simply continued to caress my body with his hands.

After a moment, I was finally able to continue. Slower than I had when he was licking me, I began to bob up and down, teasing his head with my tongue. Eric's mouth was still below my pussy and after a few minutes, he began once more licking my clit. It was nearly too much for me to handle. The skin was sensitive, my body still vibrating from the strength of my orgasm. I didn't think I'd be able to come again, but that wasn't exactly my priority.

I wanted to taste Eric's come.

It was strange and wonderful giving him a blow job from this angle. I was comfortable with my body resting on his. No awkward angles or having to push myself into a position that would inevitably lead to sleeping limbs. Both of my hands were free to torment him. I tugged on his balls with one, while teasing his inner thighs and ass with my other. I didn't know if he was into that sort of thing, but he didn't complain.

It didn't take long for me to notice his cock swell in my mouth. His shaft somehow grew stiffer, and I knew it wouldn't be much longer before I'd finally get what I wanted. He tapped my ass lightly with his hand, a warning that he was about to come, giving me a chance to pull off if that's what I wanted.

Ohhhhh no. I'd worked hard for this prize and I wasn't about to give it up.

Using my hand, I pumped his shaft in time with my mouth. I wanted to milk every drop of his come and swallow it down. What I didn't expect was for him to latch onto my clit again and suck me in earnest. Even less, I didn't think I'd be able to respond. So I was completely caught off guard when a second, less powerful orgasm rolled through me seconds before Eric's hot come spurted across my tongue and filled my mouth.

I managed to wait until I pulled the last of his come from him before I swallowed and collapsed forward, resting my cheek to his thigh. I tried to move my legs so I wasn't smothering him with my pussy, but he held me still. We stayed that way quite some time before my body began to protest the position.

"I need to shift." I kissed his thigh. "Don't move. I don't want to knee you in the face by mistake."

He helped me slide off and then pulled me up so my head rested on his chest. I was chilly and would have killed for a blanket, but that would have required moving. Being next to him, naked and satisfied, was too precious a thing to disturb. So I burrowed as close as I could into his side and let my mind go.

18

I woke up with a start and realized that there was an empty Eric-shaped spot beside me. When he'd gotten up, he'd taken the time to pick my blanket that had fallen from the foot of my bed off the floor and spread it across me. I was warm, but missed his presence.

Using the blanket as a robe, I tucked it around my body and went to see if he'd left completely or was simply stretching his legs. I'd made it down the hallway and most of the way to the kitchen when he turned the corner. Wearing only his briefs, Eric held a tray with an assortment of food and two bottles of beer. He actually looked a bit disappointed when he saw me standing there.

"Hey." I waved with one hand as I clung to my blanket with the other.

"You're awake. I was hoping to surprise you."

"I'm surprised . . . that you were actually able to find anything in my kitchen."

He shrugged. "It took a bit longer than I'd anticipated. You didn't have things where I'd assumed they'd go."

I walked out into the living room and went over to pull the curtains wide open. "My mom has the same complaint whenever she comes over. She says for being such a logical person, my organizational skills make no sense." They did to me, and in the end that's all that mattered.

He set the tray on the coffee table and handed me a beer. "I wasn't sure if you'd want one."

"Are you kidding? I could drink a case right now. You sucked the life out of me."

We sat down on the couch side by side and looked out the window to the city below. The light bounced off the building opposite mine and reflected in to spill reds, yellows, and orange light across the room. We drank our beer in near silence. Our bodies touched and we took turns placing soft caresses on each other. I reached out and traced the scar I'd noticed earlier.

"How'd you get this?"

He stiffened and drank from his beer before answering. "I was in a car accident."

"Shit. Was that the worst you were hurt? What happened?"

He took my hand in his free one, pulling my fingers away from the healed wound. "Do you mind if we don't talk about it? It wasn't pleasant and I don't want to spoil the mood."

If the incident at the spa taught me anything, it was that I needed to give Eric his space and respect his wishes. As much as my curiosity was killing me, the last thing I wanted was to ruin this moment. "Of course. I can't believe you found fresh fruit in my fridge. I had no idea I even had grapes."

And just like that I changed the topic like a frigging adult. *Boo-ya!*

Having the chance to refuel gave my body and mind time to recover. As much as I wanted to believe that I might have a future with Eric, there was a very real possibility that whatever had happened between him and Grace was too much for him to get past. I hated to think that I wouldn't be enough for him—

that, despite our mutual attraction, there would always be this specter of a thing looming behind him that prevented us from moving forward.

I basically had two choices. I could either do my best to woo him and run the risk of him pushing me away, or I could simply take the sex cards and enjoy the opportunity that had come my way. I knew that I'd run the risk of getting emotionally involved. Anyone but him and I might have had a chance to walk away. Still, he didn't need to know and I could deal with the consequences if it came to that. I was a big girl.

Eric was a kind man and I was actually comfortable enacting these cards with him. If it led to something more, then great. If not?

Well, then I had some sex for the memory book.

The sun had moved and the light didn't fill my place the way it had a short time ago. My apartment faced an office building. Normally, there were people there quite late into the evening. Even on the weekends it wasn't unusual for me to see people passing through the offices, sometimes cleaning staff. It wasn't busy though, not like it would be through the week.

The thought of having sex on my balcony was enough to make me nervous again. I honestly didn't think I had the proverbial balls to act on the fantasy. It would probably be better to do something like that at night with no lights on so the risk of anyone seeing us would be minimized. That's what a rational, sane human being would do.

Clearly, something had snapped inside my head because I found myself standing and the blanket falling to the couch beside Eric.

"Glenna?"

I bent over at the waist, giving him what I hoped was a nice view of my ass. "I'm just fishing out Day Twelve and moving it to the completed pile."

I felt the heat from his hand a moment before he caressed my hip. "You seem to be looking for something else?"

"I know what I want. I was just hoping you brought some condoms along when you came. If not, I'm pretty certain I have an unopened box in my bathroom somewhere."

Eric got to his feet and strode off to the bedroom. I heard the rattle of his belt buckle before he came back out, a string of condoms in hand. "I wasn't sure how many we'd need."

"I like a man who thinks of all the possibilities." I faced him and started to back up toward the balcony. "I've never thought of myself as wild."

With each step I took, he matched it until we were almost outside. "Me either."

"I've always played things safe, not wanting to rock the boat, do anything that would jeopardize my job at the college. Or upset my family if they heard."

Eric held my gaze as he cupped my breasts. I fought to keep my eyes open, but couldn't quite manage it. He ran his thumbs across my nipples repeatedly, teasing them until they were standing up hard.

"You want me to fuck you?" His voice was soft, but had an edge of excitement.

"Yes." Despite having come twice already today, it hadn't been enough. I wanted to feel him fill me, to thrust into me so hard I would feel it well into tomorrow.

"You want me to do that while you look outside, where anyone walking by could see?" He turned me around so that I was now fully naked to the world. We were still far enough inside the apartment that unless someone was looking directly across at us, it would be difficult for them to see me.

My legs shook, though from nerves or arousal I wasn't certain. "Yes."

He pressed his body against mine and with a step forward we drew up to the closed sliding door. "Do you want me to press you against this door? Fuck you with your hands on the glass?"

I could see that in my mind's eye. We'd still be safe, visible if anyone was to look, but easily hidden, ignored as a passionate couple who didn't realize they could be seen. There was no risk involved, not really.

I opened the door. The breeze blew against my skin and my already hard nipples responded to the invisible caress. Eric reached around and bracketed my waist with his hands. He kissed the side of my neck as he thrust his erection against my ass. "Are you sure? We can wait until dark."

Was I? It was risky, even though there was little foot traffic on the street on this side of the building. The cops could easily be called. We could both be at risk, even if it was easy enough to step back inside and close the door so no one would know it was us.

I stepped out fully onto the balcony, leaned forward, and gripped the ledge with both hands. My breasts swayed forward and the wind wrapped around my naked skin. My pussy was damp and the breeze made the sensitive skin tingle with awareness.

Eric made a noise, but I couldn't be sure what he was thinking without looking. I couldn't move to do that, needing all of my nerve to keep myself in place and not run back inside like the coward I'd always though I was. It was comforting to have him step behind me and hear the sound of a condom wrapper being opened. For better or worse, this was happening.

"Hard and fast." I spread my legs, giving him room to position himself.

He gripped my hip with one hand and guided his cock to my pussy with the other. Unlike the careful ease of our first coupling, Eric filled me quickly and set a fast, steady pace. With each thrust my body moved, my breasts swung, and my arousal spiked.

"Everyone can see you." He punctuated his sentence with a firm thrust forward. "See you naked. See me fucking you."

I let my gaze travel across the windows of the office building in front of us. There could be some poor worker there now, stuck on a project late on a Saturday afternoon. They didn't want to be there, would rather be home. Tired, they'd look out the window, maybe wanting to see if the sun was starting to set yet. Instead of the sun, they'd see me, naked. Eric, tall, powerful, behind me. They'd see the flex of his muscles, see my body accepting his cock as he pounded into me.

I moaned, then bit down hard on my bottom lip. The neighbors might not be able to see us, but they certainly could hear—I remembered that very well. They'd be curious; maybe they'd open their window a bit wider, straining to hear if there were any more sex sounds coming.

With each thrust I grew more aware of not only him, but also my body's reactions. The skin of my back tingled the closer he got to me. When he'd run his fingers down my back, I'd arch up into his touch. I hadn't realized how much of an erogenous zone that was for me before him. He moved his hand lower, his thumb pressing the base of my spine just above my ass.

He wanted to fuck me there. I imagined how full I'd feel when his cock would stretch me wide. I began to buck back, meeting his thrusts and silently encouraging him to move his hand lower. He didn't, instead sliding his fingers around to press my clit. I was so sensitive there, sore from our previous lovemaking. His caress was gentle and enough to pull my orgasm closer.

"Shit." I clamped my mouth shut, even as he began to fuck me harder.

"No. Let me hear you." Eric bent his knees and the next time he thrust, I nearly lifted off my feet. It was frantic, rough, everything I never realized I'd wanted from sex.

This time when I moaned, I let it go into the air. My palms

had grown sweaty and were starting to slip on the railing. My body shook from pleasure and the strain of holding myself in this position. I didn't want the moment to end, even as I felt it slipping toward its conclusion.

"Glenna. Come for me."

I shouldn't have been able to come again. Three times in one day wasn't something I thought myself capable of. No lover I'd ever been with had managed something like that. Then again, I'd never been with anyone remotely like Eric.

I didn't try to hold anything back. My sighs turned into low, steady groans as my body drew closer to orgasm. I felt Eric's body shaking against me, either from the position or perhaps he was struggling to hold back himself. It didn't matter, because my previously unknown exhibitionist was at the end of her restraint. I squeezed my eyes shut and let go of the railing with one of my hands. I swatted Eric's hand away and took over. I fingered my clit hard and fast until I came.

My inner muscles clenched down hard on Eric's cock as my pleasure pulsed through me. It seemed to be what he needed to push him over the edge. Another thrust and he stiffened, his fingers digging hard into my sides. He didn't make a noise, though his body shook until finally he stopped moving, his breathing coming out in large, ragged gasps.

We stayed that way for only a moment before he pulled out of me. "Better not tempt fate."

"I'm not sure I can move." I laughed, letting my head fall for a moment before forcing my body to stand. "Oh look, I'm not broken."

He wrapped an arm around me, kissing my temple as he did. "I'd never do that."

"Liar."

"Come on. Let's get a blanket for you."

As we stepped back inside, I could have sworn I saw a blind flick shut in a window in the building across the street. My face flamed at the idea that there really had been an audience watching. Well, if that was the case then I hoped they enjoyed the show.

We got dressed after that, both of us sated and I think more than a little dopey. Together we finished off the last beer I had in my fridge and I used an old premade pizza shell to bake us some supper.

Eric had pulled my kitchen stool around and sat watching me get the veggies and chicken ready for the pizza. When I caught him staring, he looked away.

"What?" This was the second or third time I'd caught him looking at me this way.

"You're amazing."

I wasn't exactly ready for compliments, so I did what I normally do in these situations and deflected. "Please make sure to tell Professor Mickelson that. Despite working my ass off my last performance review sucked balls."

"That could be because he wants you to suck his."

I stopped chopping and stared at him. "*What?*"

He held up his hands. "Sorry. I'm not the biggest fan of your boss. He's an asshole."

That was actually a pretty generous description of him. And Jasmine had always been vocal about her opinion of Mickelson, but I'd never heard anyone else say anything negative about him. It was weird. "Not that I'm disagreeing, but why do you say that?"

He opened his mouth and then quickly closed it before shaking his head. "Let's just say we have a difference of opinion on how to do our jobs."

"Yeah, well, having worked for him for three years now, I totally get that. He's very old school for someone only in his fifties."

"I've always been curious, why haven't you ever applied to

do your PhD? You're up on all of the latest research, have great opinions, and clearly are intelligent. Any school would be fortunate to have someone like you on staff."

Mom and Dad had asked me something similar when I'd finished my master's degree and then never followed through with my PhD application. What I hadn't told them was that Professor Mickelson, who'd served as my adviser for my master's, had told me that I probably wasn't a strong enough candidate at that time to continue on.

Get some practical experience first. Work with me for a few years, mature. You'll be the better for it later on.

After giving it some thought I had realized that he was probably right. I'd spent so much time in school that I needed a chance to be out on my own, to live my life a little before jumping back into the books. It wasn't that I would never do it; I knew I would eventually.

It had been the safe thing to do, the one that made the most sense at the time. I was in my mid twenties with a pile of student loans to pay off. Passing up an opportunity to pay that off and work with someone in my field had seemed too good to be true at the time.

Too bad the reality hadn't quite matched up.

"I might go and do it sometime. Right now I'm still mostly enjoying my job. As you said, I'm good at what I do. Eventually I'll get tired of working with Mickelson and I'll want to spread my wings again. For now, the pay is good and I get to work with my best friend."

"Fair enough." But there was something in his tone that told me he wasn't exactly convinced. At least he didn't browbeat me the way Jasmine did.

I dumped the ingredients onto the pizza shell and shoved it in the oven. "There. That shouldn't take long to heat up." I put my elbows on the counter and leaned forward, giving off what I hoped was a nice shot of my cleavage. "Whatever shall we do now?"

"Plan." His gaze circled from my breasts to my throat and back. "For our next night."

"I love how you think, Professor."

"What we did today was"—he flicked his gaze to mine—"the most arousing thing I've ever done. I know I'll get hard from now until I die every time I think about it."

For a moment, I forgot to breathe.

"Maybe we could do something else like that. If you think you're up for it."

There were more than a few cards in that pile that had great exhibitionist possibilities. And while I wasn't interested in doing anything that would get either of us in trouble, the excitement might be worth some risk.

"Maybe we could." I looked over to the cards, still sitting in a haphazard pile on my coffee table. "Maybe we could even combine a few of them. Kill two or three birds with one stone?"

The smile he gave me should have been illegal. "I'm all ears."

19

Sometimes the curveballs life throws your way can be a real pain in the ass.

We'd spent some time going through the cards as we ate pizza. Our planning didn't happen quite the way I'd hoped. It's funny how two rather intelligent people can have their conversation dissolve into juvenile jokes. That in turn led to us watching standup comedy on Netflix while we finished off a bottle of wine that I'd tucked away for a special occasion.

It was actually a lot of fun.

I'd invited Eric to spend the night, but he said that he wasn't ready for that. "There are a lot of things I'm still trying to figure out. Staying at your house feels . . . too much. I hope you understand."

I didn't think it was a big deal, especially when it meant we could have sleepy morning sex, but I wasn't going to push matters. Instead I took a long bath and crawled into my bed to sleep with the sheets that still held his scent.

Sunday morning I rescued my corkboard from the gremlins that live in my spare closet. I'd learned a lot about him in the last few days and I wanted to make sure I had my board as up-to-date as possible. I printed the details neatly and rearranged them as best as I could.

Big appetite.

Car accident—doesn't want to discuss.

Not a fan of purple.

Wants to have anal sex. Didn't want to ask.

Tries to hold in his giggles when he sees something funny.

Has the best laugh.

Goes to Blue Jays home games.

That last bit I found out Sunday afternoon when he texted me a picture of him and Claude in the stands with a beer. I stood in my spare room staring at it. There was something in his expression—a joy that I didn't normally see when he was working—that pulled hard on my heartstrings. Eric's recent past had taken some of the happiness from him. It was nice to see him having a good time, even if I wasn't there with him.

Maybe I should send him some naughty texts in return. Not that we'd done much in the way of that yet, but sexting *was* on the list.

I'd save that for another day.

I returned my attention to my task at hand.

After reviewing everything I had about him, I knew there was one important thing still missing. Reluctantly, I pulled out my pen and wrote *Grace* on a card and added it to the board as well. While I might have a bit of a jealous streak, and still wanted to punch her in the nose if I saw her, I couldn't deny that she'd been important in his life.

On a happier note, I added our completed cards to the proper side and then stood back to proudly survey our accomplishments. We'd certainly been busy in such a short time. Great Glenna might be mortified to know what I'd done, but she would have appreciated the chances that I'd taken in the name of having some fun.

Eric did text me once he got home from the ball game and we continued to chat well into the early hours. I'd drifted off to sleep at some point during our conversation and woke to the buzzing of my phone sometime around six in the morning:

How do you take your coffee?

Oh. Oh, he was totally a keeper. *Double, double.*

It will be on your desk when you get in.

Bless you!

I wanted to thank you for this weekend. It was the happiest I've been in a while.

I needed to learn how to take a compliment. *I'm sure Claude and the Jays actually winning their game helped.*

Eric didn't respond immediately, though I saw that he'd read the message. He went fifteen minutes before texting a simple *Not as much as you.*

I sighed. Then squealed loudly. Then panicked because I realized the time and had to haul ass or else I was going to miss my bus. I dressed quickly and made it all the way outside before turning around to go back and grab a sweater. I really hated September some years.

Walking from the bus stop to my building wasn't normally something that I paid attention to. I simply walked, my mind focused on my upcoming workday. This particular morning I seemed to notice things that I normally wouldn't. Eric's car was parked much the same place it always was, near the back of the lot. The air was far cooler than it had been up to this point in the year. The leaves were already starting to change. Students had made the switch from T-shirts and shorts to leggings, jeans, and sweaters. Soon, happily, the aroma of pumpkin-spiced everything would fill the air.

Eric said he was going to put the coffee on my desk, which meant he'd probably be sitting at his desk. I wanted to stop and chat with him, but I decided to play that by ear. While it wasn't a huge deal that we were sleeping together, he clearly still wanted to keep things on the down-low.

Which I could totally do if it meant more balcony sex.

The second I emerged from the staircase I knew there was something different from previous weeks. Eric wasn't in his office. No, he was standing in the doorway of *my* office and he was speaking to someone. Jasmine rarely came in this early, which meant she was probably swamped with something. If she caught Eric trying to sneak a coffee in, she would most definitely give him the third degree. Poor guy. *I'd better go rescue him.*

It was strange but my hackles went up before I even realized that I was walking into a problem. Eric stood directly in the doorway, blocking any sight of the person he was speaking to. The closer I got the more I realized that he was completely tense. He heard the click of my heels and turned as I got close, revealing Professor Mickelson standing in the office.

And he had my coffee.

Shit.

"Professor Mickelson, you're here." I nodded to Eric and gave him my politest smile. "Good morning, Professor Morris."

"Glenna." Now that I'd gotten to know him, I recognized that tone as him being more than a little ticked off. "Let me get out of your way."

Professor Mickelson isn't much taller than me, with a slight frame and sinewy muscles from being a marathon runner. He had this way of looking at me when he spoke that made me feel as though I was always being evaluated. I always felt as though I had failed. "Good to see you still arrive on time. I came back early to make sure we had a few days before my conference. I want to make sure you didn't have any errors in the presentation. Not that I could find anything on this desk of yours."

"I wasn't expecting you here today so I hadn't printed it off yet. Let me get organized and I'll pull it up for you to take a look at."

It was weird, knowing both Eric and my boss were watching me without watching, both drawing conclusions about what they saw. I knew Eric thought I was a pushover for jumping whenever Mickelson wanted me to do something. I also knew my boss didn't think I was ready to take the next step in my career. He, too, thought I was too meek, too inexperienced.

As far as I was concerned they were both wrong. I was still learning from Mickelson. Yes, he could be a pompous ass and took advantage of my skills when maybe he shouldn't, but he was my boss. He'd been working in this field for years longer than I had and had a breadth of experience I could learn from. Lots that I *had* learned. It would only be a matter of a few more years before I knew I'd want to take the next step.

I just wasn't quite ready.

"So when do you fly out, Phil?" Eric sipped his coffee and had taken to standing in the doorway again.

"Thursday. I'll be spending the weekend with some colleagues before the conference begins on Monday."

"And then are you back to England after?"

"I'm not certain. When I was at Oxford, I'd discovered a program that allows for Inuit students to complete education via mobile devices. I might change direction and go north for a while. Observe their program in action before I return."

I stopped moving and stared up at Mickelson. In all the e-mails he'd sent to me over the last few weeks, he hadn't mentioned that to me at all. "That sounds fascinating. I would love to see—"

"Yes, well, it should be." He made the small clicking sound in the back of his throat that he always did when he got annoyed. "Print off the presentation notes. You know I need to see them on paper and not on a screen."

I'd been dismissed by him so much over the years that it didn't bother me. Maybe it was the way Eric flinched or the fact that his research was also essentially *my* research and to be cut out of the conversation hurt. Either way, I ignored the rising tightness of my throat and hit the print button. "Of course."

"You two have a lot of work. I'll leave you to it."

"Thank you for the coffee." Mickelson held up the cup in a salute. "Much needed."

"Anytime." Eric's gaze flicked to me briefly before he turned and left.

So not fair.

"Well, my girl. Bring those papers into my office when they're done. And your pen so we can make corrections as we go. I want to maximize our time together."

"Yes, Professor."

He sipped his coffee as he left for his office upstairs.

Heartbroken would be a bit of an exaggeration, but something akin to that was how I felt. With Mickelson back, any daytime chats with Eric would have to be put on hold, or at least reduced to expected interactions. If I had any free moments at all. When my boss was in conference mode, he tended to be all consuming of my time.

Dammit, this sucked.

The printing didn't take long for me to finish and gather, so I had little reason to procrastinate. I stepped out into the hall and headed for the stairs. I didn't get far when Eric emerged from his office. "Hey."

"Hey." Mickelson could wait at least for a moment. I hugged the printouts to my chest and made my way to him. "So that sucked."

"I ran into him coming into the building. He asked who the coffee was for and I told him it was a thank-you for you helping me with something last week. He offered to give it to you and then started drinking it."

Yeah, that was typical Mickelson. "He probably forgot it was for me a minute after you told him and drank it on impulse. He's done stuff like that before. I've gotten used to it."

"I wanted to punch him. Repeatedly."

Never in my life have I had a man get protective of me like that. Seeing Eric, knowing that he'd been seething the whole time he'd been talking to Mickelson, did strange things to my libido. "That's hot."

"Hey, lovebirds." We both stepped back as Jasmine marched down the hall directly for us. "How was the weekend?"

"I'll let you go." He gave me a little smile before he turned away and waved at Jasmine. "Have fun. Don't let him ride you too hard."

"What's that supposed to mean?" She took one look at what I was holding and groaned. "Shit, Mickelson's back early."

"Because of course he is. I was just heading up to the office now to go over the presentation."

"I'll say a prayer for you."

"Does that work for atheists?"

"We'll find out."

At least I had two people in my life who had my back if I needed it. "Well, thanks in advance. If you don't hear from me by lunch, send out the search party."

"Damn right I will. I need to know how your weekend went." Her grin was downright maniacal. "Details. I want them."

"Later." I walked away to the sound of her groans.

"I just can't accept this. We need to change the entire template."

I wanted to cry. Not little tears either. No, I wanted to engage in full-out sobs. He'd rejected all of the work I'd done over the past few weeks. The terrifying thing was that the mistakes he'd pointed out were actual, honest-to-God errors and not him being picky. I'd been so distracted by Great Glenna's passing, Eric, and the sex cards that I'd screwed up.

"I'm sorry. It's been a rough few weeks."

"Not an excuse. Can you imagine the reaction had I gone on with the presentation in this state? Unacceptable."

"The file is on my computer. I'll clear my plate and have it finished by the end of the day."

I stood and wasn't at all surprised when he followed me out to the stairs. "I need to make a call and then I'll be down to check the status. I'm very disappointed in you."

Those five little words were enough to break my heart. "It won't happen again."

For the first time since I'd accepted my position with him, I wanted to give up. It didn't seem to matter how hard I worked, my work was never good enough. I was never going to be ready to do my PhD at this rate.

I didn't even have the pleasure of seeing Eric. His office door was closed and I knew he was off teaching for the rest of the afternoon. That was probably a good thing, giving me one less distraction. The moment I walked into the office, Jasmine was on me. "Tell me about the sex. Was he good? Did you do the cards? What days? You hid that stupid board of yours that you had in the office, right?"

I fell into my chair. "I can't do that now, Jaz."

"You promised." She was actually pouting.

"I promised before I had my work put under a microscope and found severely lacking."

"Bullshit. You're brilliant."

I held up the printouts that were now covered in bright red ink. "I used the wrong template, I mislabeled a diagram, I forgot to reference his new research study, and I misquoted him. That's just on the first five pages."

Jasmine frowned. "You don't make mistakes like that."

"I also don't normally lose a loved one and then start having kinky sex with my fantasy man. It's been a weird few weeks."

"I'm sorry. Can I help with anything?"

"No. It will be fine. He'll be down in a minute so I better get started."

The next person to walk through the door was Nell, not Professor Mickelson. "Hello, gorgeous. And hi, Jasmine."

"No flirting with my coworker. I'll get jealous." Jasmine stood and grabbed her purse. "We're heading out for lunch. Want me to bring you back something?"

"Chocolate." If I was going to be stuck here, then I was going to need the boost. "And a coffee. I lost out on mine this morning."

"I'll get it for you." Nell took Jasmine's hand. "This one can't tell good coffee from bad."

"If it has caffeine then that's all that's required." Jasmine tugged Nell in close and kissed her. What started out as a soft peck quickly deepened into something more. I'd already lost interest because *oh shit my work sucks ass* so I didn't notice him standing in the door until he cleared his throat.

Nell turned beet red while Jasmine simply cleared her throat and waved. "Hello, Professor Mickelson. Glenna mentioned that you were back at the school this week."

"Young lady, this is a place of work and learning." He braced his hands on his hips and glared at them. "You both should respect this as a place of employment and refrain from such displays until you're home."

"You're right." Nell stepped away from Jasmine. "I'll wait for you outside." Professor Mickelson let her by without another look.

Jasmine on the other hand looked ready to get into it right then and there. While she didn't work for him, the last thing I wanted to deal with was tension between the two of them, especially now. I stood and talked over Jasmine. "Sir, I managed to get the material switched over to the new template. Do you want to begin your review now?"

"Yes. I expect that you've not made any further errors."

Jasmine's hands were balled at her sides. "I'll be sure to bring you back that coffee."

"Thank you." *Just go, Jaz. Run away and cool off.* "Enjoy your lunch."

Professor Mickelson took Jasmine's seat and rolled it over to my desk once she'd gone. "Your friend needs to understand that employees of this school are held to high standards. She should know better than to behave like a student their first time away from home. Unacceptable."

"I'm sure it won't happen again. Now, I've brought up the diagram and I've started to relabel everything. Would you mind taking another look?"

First Eric, then Jasmine. Today was turning into something out of my nightmares. At least Mickelson wasn't going to be around for long. Only a few days and he'd be off again for the rest of the semester. Then things would get back to normal.

20

By the time we'd finished making all the changes to his presentation, I'd barely had enough energy to drag myself to the bus stop. Jasmine came back after lunch and tried to engage me a few times before she had to leave for her own curriculum development meeting. Eric came back after his classes and I caught sight of him leaving after he'd dropped a few things off.

My phone had buzzed a few times after that, but Mickelson had me completely focused on getting everything ready for him to go away. By the time I made it home, it was seven thirty and I was starving.

I grabbed a frozen dinner and threw it in the microwave while I finally remembered to check my messages. Eric had pinged me, and the simple act of seeing his name was enough to chase away some of the tension from the day. As I read his messages, my smile exploded into a grin.

Sorry about the coffee. I'll make it up to you.

I hope your day got better.

I ran into Jasmine and she filled me in. Phil is such an asshole.

Was going to come say hi, but saw he was still with you. Call me when you're free.

I pressed his number just as the microwave beeped. "Hey."

"You sound exhausted."

"It was a long day redoing my work. And before you say anything, yeah, I *had* actually screwed up."

"Given what you've been through in the last few weeks, that's understandable. How are you doing?"

"Good. Tired. Work keeps my mind off thinking about her. Missing her."

"Just work?" It was cute the way his voice went up.

"Oh and maybe the awesome sex I've been having recently with a really hot professor. That's helped. A bit. I guess."

"Would it help if I came over?"

I wanted nothing more than to see him then, I really did. But I was tired and it would take time for him to get here. "That would be awesome, but I'm not sure how much I have left in me."

"Do you want me to let you go?"

"No. It's nice having a friendly voice. Besides, I missed out on seeing you today. The least we can do it talk."

There was shuffling on the other end of the phone. "I have an idea, but I'm not sure you're up for it."

"Does it involve me leaving my apartment?"

"No."

"Then I'm game."

"Okay then. I want you to go to your bedroom and get on your bed."

I shoved the last of my measly meal into my mouth, pitched the container in the recycling bin, and shuffled as quickly as my feet could take me. "One minute."

Had Eric been here, I would have been embarrassed about him seeing the blanket that had his scent balled up in place of my pillow. I moved it over and stretched out in the middle of the bed. "Okay, I'm here."

"I'm also in my bedroom."

It was strange, but I hadn't really thought about his place, what it would look like, the types of things he'd have. "What color is it?"

"The walls are navy. My bedding is brown."

"Very manly."

"Thank you."

"And dark."

"Yes."

"Sounds depressing."

"Can we not discuss my walls?" Lord, he sounded cute when he was annoyed.

"Sure. What do you want to discuss?" There was more rustling on the other end, but I couldn't quite make the noises out. "What are you doing?"

"Getting naked."

Yes! *Naked Eric was naked.* "Should I do that too?"

"Not yet."

He might not have been able to see my pout, but I did it anyway. "Fine. What are we doing anyway?"

"Day Fifteen."

Shit, I knew I should have grabbed the cards on my way by. "Have sex blindfolded?"

"Role-play."

"And what are we going to be role-playing?"

"I was going to leave that up to you. We have many options."

My initial reaction was to say phone sex operator and client, but that was the safe and easy road. Going the whole professor and student road was a little too close to home. To be honest, I'd had more than my fair share of fantasies about Eric and there was one that I kept coming back to.

"You're going to think I'm weird when I suggest this, but

I'd love for you to be an evil villain that I'm trying to catch."
There was a muffled noise. "Eric?"

The muffles cleared up, but it was clear he'd been laughing.
"A super villain? Me?"

"Yeah. You'd be Professor Cyborg, hell-bent on taking over
the city of Toronto. You've been subverting all mechanical devices for your evil purposes."

"And what shall I call you?"

"I don't know. What do you suggest?"

"How about Super Vixen?"

"That's a bit sexist."

"Okay, do you want to change it?"

"Naw, it's fine." I'd never been considered a vixen by anyone before. Turns out I liked it.

"So how do you want to start this?" I heard him shifting
around on his bed. "I can hang up and call you back?"

Sex shouldn't be this fun. "Okay. Give me a minute to get
naked, then call."

"Leave your bra and panties on. The evil Professor Cyborg
might have an idea."

We hung up and I burst out laughing. This wasn't going to
turn into something sexy if I couldn't get ahold of myself. The
giggles didn't stop even as I stripped down to my unmention-
ables. I closed my eyes and took several long, deep breaths,
calming myself enough that when my phone rang again, I was
ready.

"Who is this?" I might not be the best actress, but I could
make this work. Glenna was gone and Super Vixen was here to
save the day. "How did you get this number?"

"I would think nothing I did surprised you by now, Super
Vixen."

There was a low purr to his voice, just smarmy enough for
me to buy the villain thing, but not too over the top. Eric had
hidden talents.

"Professor Cyborg." I growled, well, I tried to growl. I might have accidentally purred. "You're not going to escape me this time."

"How do you propose to stop me? You don't even know where I am."

It took me a moment to get my giggles under control. "I'm tracking this call as we speak. Within seconds I'll have all the information I'll need to finally find your secret lair."

"Not unless I do something to stop you first."

"Nothing can prevent me from bringing you in."

"Oh no?" He lowered his voice and lost the smugness. "You've forgotten the key thing about me, my dear."

"What's that?"

"That I have control over all machines. Including your cell phone. Right this moment I've activated a program that will force you to do anything I want."

Yes, this little scenario was going to work out just fine. "You bastard. I don't believe you."

"I'll prove it. Super Vixen, I want you to slide your hand across your breast and tease your nipple through your bra."

My hand shook as I complied. Maybe it was because I'd let myself get into the game, but I swore I could feel Eric's control being exerted on me. "No!"

"Oh yes, Vixen. You're completely under my control. I can make you do anything. Use anything. Pinch your nipple."

I did and gasped at the sudden rush of excitement that rippled through me. "This is wrong."

"No, wrong would be if I made you use something else."

"You wouldn't." *Oh please, Eric, do all the naughty things to me.*

He cleared his throat. "I want you to reach into your nightstand and take out the vibrator that's there. The bright pink one."

"How could you know that?" I was already reaching for it.

I'd kept the vibrator from the movie theater. I'd had so much fun with it that there was no way he was ever getting it back.

"I have cameras everywhere. I can see you night and day. Sleeping and awake." I froze and he paused to clear his throat. "Wait, was that too weird?"

"A little, but just move past it. You're doing great."

"Okay. Do you have it in your hand, Vixen?"

"I'm trying to resist you." I really wasn't. "Dammit, I've lost control."

"I want you to put your phone on speaker so you have use of both your hands. By the time I'm through with you, Super Vixen, you won't be in any condition to come after me."

If all went well, I hoped that I'd be coming *before* him.

I turned on my speaker and set the phone down by my head. "I can't resist you, Professor Cyborg."

"You have the vibrator?"

"Yes."

"I want you to turn it on. Press it to your nipple through the bra."

The buzz of the vibrator was louder than I'd remembered, and it would be easy for Eric to hear. I gasped at the first touch against my nipple. It was amazing how much I could feel even through the fabric. The vibrator's U-shape made it easy enough for me to hold, even though the entire thing shook in my hand.

"Now the other one. Nice and slow."

I lifted the vibrator up and moved it to my other breast. I held it just above my nipple for a moment before slowly lowering it down. "You bastard."

"I'm a super villain after all."

"You're making me horny." I'd been a raging ball of lust from the moment he'd suggested we use one of the cards.

"I've only just begun."

It was hard to hear much of anything with him on the speaker, but I thought I detected him moving around on his bed. I pictured him stretched out, cock jutting out proudly from his body. His neck and chest would be flushed as he reached out and grabbed his shaft.

It was even easier to imagine this once I heard the harsh edge that his voice had taken on. "Take off your bra."

There was no gentle teasing now. Eric was either really horny or getting fully into his role. I arched my back long enough to unclasp and toss my bra to the floor. My nipples tightened in the cool air and I wanted nothing more than to feel his mouth lick and tease them.

"I wish you were here. I want to feel you touching me." I rolled my head toward the phone and moaned. If he could tease, then so could L

"Vixen."

"That's Super Vixen to you."

"While I might not be there, my machines are. And you can't stop them."

And really, why would I even want to try? This was the most fun I'd ever had with sex. "You'll pay for this."

"Not before you do. Take my vibrator and slide it nice and slowly into your pussy."

"I still have my panties on."

"I'm sure you can work around that. I believe you have some practice."

Memories of the movie theater threatened to distract me. Groaning, I pulled my panties to the side and slipped the vibrator into my pussy. With it now inside me, it was easier to hear Eric's ragged breathing on the other end of the phone. Hearing how excited he was made my own desire that much keener.

"Eric."

"That's Professor Cyborg to you."

"Are you touching yourself? Are you stroking your cock thinking about me getting off on your machine?"

"Yes."

"Are you using lots of lube? Are you stroking fast or slow?"

"Yes to lube. Slow right now."

"The vibrator is on the lowest setting."

"Good. I want to torture you for all the pain you've caused me. I want to drag this out until you're begging me to let you come. I want to picture you stretched out on your bed, wishing that the silicone in your pussy was my cock."

"Jesus, Eric." My body tensed and I had to breathe through the unexpected spike in my arousal.

"I'm so fucking hard right now. I want to get in my car and drive over there to be with you."

"That would take too long. Make me come. Tell me what to do." I couldn't be certain, but it sounded as though he'd started stroking his cock faster. "Eric?"

"Professor Cyborg to you, Vixen."

I laughed. "Evil villain. Making me think that my friend was there."

"And you fell for it. Increase the speed on the vibrator."

I'd set the remote control somewhere on the bed, so of course now that he wanted me to use it, I couldn't find the damn thing. "It's not here."

"There's a button on the end of the vibrator itself. The part near your clit. Press it."

I moaned as the speed increased and set to an oscillating pattern. "That's handy."

"Pinch your nipples. Use both hands." He wasn't teasing anymore. "Match the rhythm of your pinches with the pulse of the vibrator."

The last remaining snarky thoughts I had fled and all I was left with was the rising tide of my pleasure. The vibrator was pushing me past any remaining resistance I had and I knew it wasn't going to be much longer before I came. "Good."

"Close?"

"Yeah."

"When you come, I want to hear you. Be loud. Scream. I need to . . . just be loud."

I imagined it was Eric's hands on my breasts, his mouth on my clit licking, his hand in my pussy fucking me. I abandoned one of my breasts and pushed the vibrator firmly against my clit. The added pressure was all I needed to take me over the edge. I cried out as I ground down on the vibrator. I pinched my nipple so hard pain threatened to override the pleasure. I yelled far louder than I normally would, wanting to give to Eric what he gave to me.

I was still milking out the last of my orgasm when I heard him roar on the other end of the phone. That desperate cry of pleasure and something primal sent another bolt of pleasure through me. We'd both been carried away on the ride and crashed together, sated.

Once I pulled the vibrator from my body and turned it off, I set it on the bed beside me and tried to get my breathing under control. It was a solid minute before I heard Eric chuckling on the phone.

"What?"

"I'm lying here naked on my bed, come covering my stomach and my dick limp and the only thing I can think about is how gorgeous you must look in that very purple room of yours."

I reached out and ran my finger along the side of the phone.

"I also realized that I haven't invited you over to my place yet."

Sitting up, I took the phone off speaker and pressed it to my ear. "I didn't think that was something you would be interested in. Too personal."

Sure, I'd dreamed that maybe things between us would eventually go to the next level, but I also knew that he was still dealing with his Grace problem. If he was serious about this, then maybe there was hope that we might actually become a proper couple.

There was a chance that he might come to love me.

"Well, it is. But somehow I think I need to do that. Make things a bit more personal." This was most obviously Eric and not Professor Cyborg I was speaking to. Gone was the cocky edge, to be replaced with a note of uncertainty that grabbed at my heart.

As much as I wanted to jump on this idea, I knew it wouldn't do either of us any good if I did. "Maybe right now isn't the best time to make this decision. Think on it and we can talk tomorrow?"

"You're right. Plus, I do owe you a coffee."

"Double-double."

"I won't forget."

"Good. Good night, Professor Cyborg."

"Good night, Super Vixen. Sweet dreams."

The line clicked and I was alone once more. Tomorrow, once I finished everything that Professor Mickelson needed and saw him off for his conference, then I'd pop in and see Eric. Visiting his place was a big step, but so was acknowledging our status in front of our peers.

Tomorrow, big things would happen.

21

The next morning started the same as most others. Up late, dressed, eating on the bus, bolting up the stairs to the office. Eric's door was open but he was on the phone. Seeing him like that, the receiver pressed to his ear, had me blushing. I hesitated long enough to give him a wave and watch him smile.

Then he winked at me and it felt as though the sun exploded in my heart.

If someone had told me that I'd skipped to my office after that, I wouldn't have been the least bit surprised. I was greeted by the smell of glorious coffee and an apple fritter waiting for me on my desk. There was a Post-it note attached to the cup.

I'll get you next time!
P.C.

That was precious. Taking the note as I sat down, I tucked it in my purse before swallowing down that first glorious sip of coffee. It was exactly what I needed to start my day off—caffeine, a treat, and a note from Eric.

I was humming when Jasmine came into the office. She stopped short and turned to stare at me. "You got laid."

"Nope."

"Liar. You only hum when you've gotten laid."

"Nope, nope."

She snorted. "Yeah right."

"There was absolutely no penetration."

"That's . . . interesting. Oral?"

"He wasn't even in the same building."

"How? Because if this boy has a way of getting you off without being present then we need to find a way to sell this ability. I want to be rich. He could make us rich!"

Laughter bubbled from me. How could I stop it when I was so damn happy? "I promised him I would keep all pertinent details to myself."

"No. That's not happening." She dumped her stuff on her desk and stuck her head out the door. "Eric!"

"Jaz, no! Get in here."

"If you won't tell me then I'll have to go to the source."

I threw myself across my desk and managed to snag her arm. "Shut up. I'll tell you, just stop yelling."

Women in their late twenties shouldn't squeal like a preteen, but that's totally what Jasmine did. "What did you do? Was there phone sex? Is that a card? It must be a card."

"It's a card, sort of. We did Day Fifteen."

"You say that like I had them all memorized."

"Role-playing."

Jasmine's chair was all the way around my desk. If anyone were to see us they'd think we were working on a project together. Fools.

"What were you role-playing? Like doctor and nurse?"

Yeah, I was never going to hear the end of this. "Not exactly."

"Then exactly what?" She started laughing the moment my blush kicked in. "Oh my God, what did you do?"

I didn't have the heart to say it above a mumble. She pinched my arm hard and I yelped. "Shit, okay. We played superhero and villain."

Jasmine froze and I got to a count of four in my head before she burst into maniacal laughter. "You didn't?"

"Maybe. Kind of."

I waited for her to catch her breath. "Was he the hero?"

Closing my eyes, I braced myself. "No, I was."

"Did you have names?" She grabbed my arm and jiggled me. "Please, dear God, tell me that you had names."

"Umm—"

"Glenna—"

"Super Vixen and Professor Cyborg." And there was another rousing fit of giggles from Jasmine. "It was hot."

"Only you would think someone with the name Professor Cyborg was hot."

No, I loved her but I totally wasn't going to let her ruin this memory for me. I turned and grabbed her by the shoulders. "He had the ability to control me through the use of anything electronic, including my phone. He laughed at me and then demanded that I use a vibrator on myself. He was the one in charge, telling me how fast or slow I could make it go. He was the one telling me to touch myself until I couldn't hold out any longer and I came hard. I screamed so loud that my throat is still sore this morning. Still. Sore."

The longer I spoke the wider her eyes got. "Whoa."

"It was amazing. And you'd think it was stupid and silly, and maybe it was a bit, but after a short time it was hot and he sounded so dark and tortured and commanding that I nearly came just from the sound of his voice." Jasmine's mouth had slipped open and I pushed it shut with my finger. "Catching flies."

"I can't believe you did that. No way."

At the sound of someone clearing his throat, we both looked up to see Eric standing in the doorway, his arms crossed as he leaned against the jamb. "I can verify that yes, we in fact did."

Even last week I would have wanted to die knowing Eric had overheard even a part of our conversation. But the look on his face, the smile and sparkle in his eyes were enough to tell me that he was in fact quite amused by everything.

I leaned back and nodded his way. "Professor. I hope the rest of your evening was enjoyable."

"It was. I had a bit of a run-in with a remote control, but I eventually bent it to my will."

It was in that moment that Jasmine lost her mind. Her face turned red as she fell from her chair in laughter. "You two. Killing me."

Eric and I looked at each other and burst out laughing as well. I pulled Jasmine back up into her chair. "We're consenting adults with sex cards. What do you want us to do?"

"I don't want to know!" It took her a minute to get herself under control. She wiped her eyes and caught her breath. "I'm going to have to redo my makeup."

"Please, you're beautiful no matter what." I gave her arm a squeeze. "Eric, why are you even here? You never stop by."

"I heard Jasmine call my name. And I wanted to make sure you got your coffee this morning." It was weird, but I could tell from the way he spoke that he was looking for a bit of praise. Strange, given how confident he normally was.

"I did, thank you. And thank you for the treat."

Jasmine pulled back. "Is this another sex thing?"

"No! He bought me an apple fritter."

"Any good?" He stepped farther into the room. "I bought it at the little bakery near my house."

"It was delicious." Yeah, I probably had a dopey grin on my face, but he'd made me so happy in such a short period of time, I couldn't help it.

"I wish you'd found these cards years ago." Jasmine reached out and draped her arm around my shoulders. "I haven't seen you this happy ever."

"Jaz—"

"Hush. If Professor Cyborg over here is the reason that you're smiling and happy then I'll forever be grateful. You're my best friend in the whole wide world, and I want nothing more than for you to have the life you deserve."

It could have been a result of the utter sincerity coming from my friend who normally teased me within an inch of my life, or I was simply going loopy from all this unexpected attention. Either way, I couldn't stop from tearing up. "Thanks, Jaz."

Eric cleared his throat. "I should leave you two—"

"Oh no you don't!" Jasmine pointed her finger at him. "You go nowhere until I know your intentions with my best friend. If you do anything to hurt her I'll be forced to beat you until you beg for forgiveness."

"Never." He pressed his hand to his heart. "I swear."

"Good. Because I actually like you and I'd hate to have to mess you up. So what are your plans now?" She bumped her shoulder against mine.

"Nothing. Well, we haven't had a chance to talk about anything yet."

"Are you still using the cards? Because if there was anything that I could help you out with, I'm more than happy to."

"You're terrible. What one could you possibly help with?"

"Day Twenty-seven."

Now, I had to admit that I didn't remember off the top of my head what was written on that particular card. Even as Jasmine stood up, pulling me along beside her, I was clueless as to what was about to happen. I looked at Eric, who looked both surprised and confused, before Jasmine turned my face toward hers.

I've had more than a few fantasies about kissing another

woman. I'm not gay, not by any stretch, but wanting to kiss a woman didn't necessarily have anything to do with sexual desire.

Okay, it did, but I wasn't in the mental space to fully examine that given what was happening.

Jasmine's lips were soft as she pressed her mouth to mine. Unlike when Eric kissed me, there was nothing hard, no rough edges. I knew Jasmine's scent, recognized it was her that I was holding as I opened my lips. It felt strange, but good strange as the tip of her tongue brushed against mine. She didn't go deep into my mouth, nor did I want her to.

The gentle kiss was wonderful and drew to a natural conclusion before I grew uncomfortable. When we pulled away, Jasmine grinned and I couldn't help but suck on my bottom lip.

"You're so straight." Thankfully, she didn't laugh at me, even though I knew she thought it was hilarious.

Well then, that was another card I'd have to add to the corkboard.

We both turned and looked at Eric, who was clearly fascinated with the entire thing that had played out in front of him. He swallowed hard and looked between us. "So that happened."

What none of us were immediately aware of was that Eric wasn't the only the only one who'd witnessed the kiss. Jasmine stiffened and bolted away from me before I clued in to what had happened. "Nell!"

"Don't talk to me."

The joy I'd been feeling only moments ago soured in my stomach. "Oh, no."

Jasmine ignored both Eric and me as she chased after Nell. Eric looked as sickened as I felt and came farther into the office. We both tried not to watch as Jasmine caught her at the end of the hallway. It didn't take a genius to see that they were fighting.

Eric reached out for my hand and gave it a squeeze. "Think they will be okay?"

"I hope so. They've had issues in the past. I think Nell is a bit jealous about how free Jaz tends to be with her affections."

"And seeing her kissing her friend would be enough to solidify her concerns."

"Oh yeah." I cringed when I heard Nell's voice rise to a screech, before Jasmine hauled her into the stairwell. "Today just went from awesome to shit."

"I'm sure everything will work out for them." He turned and placed a kiss on my forehead. "We can delay our conversation until tonight. Say around six o'clock? I'll pick you up and take you out to supper. Then we can figure out what we want to do next."

As much as my heart ached for what Jasmine was going through right now, for once I had a chance to take some happiness for myself. Getting up on my tiptoes, I placed a kiss on his cheek. "That sounds amazing."

"I better go. I have to grade assignments. I should have finished them last night, but I got distracted."

"I can't imagine why." Not only had we had great non-touching sex, but I'd distracted my super-serious professor from his job. I was fucking awesome! "Go. I'll talk to you later."

As Eric walked away, I couldn't help but wish the rest of the day away so we could have our time alone. Oh well, I'd have to deal with the rest of the crap that was inevitably coming my way. First, I'd help reassure Jasmine that she and Nell would be fine. It might require a bit of groveling on her part, but it would work out. Then, I'd tackle the rest of Professor Mickelson's report. He'd be on a plane tomorrow and out of the office for the rest of the term. That would give me plenty of time to have my fun with Eric.

I couldn't wait!

* * *

Jasmine barely spoke to me the rest of the morning. Once she'd come back from her fight with Nell, her face was lined with tear streaks and her hair was no longer hanging straight down her back. She only pulled it up into a bun when she was annoyed or upset and didn't want it to be a distraction. Clearly, she was both.

After three hours of uncomfortable silence, I couldn't take any more. "Jaz, are you okay?"

"No."

"Do you want to talk about it?"

"No."

"Do you want a coffee? I'd be more than happy to get you one from the kitchen."

"No."

I sighed. "I'm sorry about what happened."

"It wasn't your fault. You didn't kiss me, I kissed you. And despite what some people think, I don't have unrequited lust for you. You're straight and my best friend. It was just a kiss and nothing more than that."

That made me cringe. "Would it help if I spoke to Nell? Tell her about what was going on?"

"I told her. She doesn't seem to care."

I wanted to do something to help, but I'd learned from past situations that it was better if I just kept my nose out of things. Jasmine and Nell had been down this road more than once, and always seemed to bounce back. With some time, I hoped this wouldn't be any different.

"Well, let me know if you need anything. I have a feeling I'll be here most of the day again to get this presentation the way Mickelson wants it."

Jasmine nodded and put her earbuds in.

Okay, then that was the end of that.

It was nearly noon and I hadn't seen hide nor hair of my

boss. Given how hard he'd been riding me yesterday, it was strange and more than a little unsettling. Still, there was no sense in courting his tense presence on top of everything else that had happened this morning. Especially as I was nearly done with all his requested changes. If things went my way, I'd be done, get his approval, and send him out the door early and I'd have the rest of the week to tease Eric.

I'd finished up the slideshow and was moving on to the handout corrections when my e-mail dinged.

> **To:** O'Donald, Glenna
> **From:** Mickelson, Phil
> **Subject:** My Office
> **Message:** E-mail me all files related to
> my workshop, old and new. Once
> that is done, come to my office.

I sat there staring at the screen. In the three years I'd worked for Mickelson, he never wanted me to e-mail presentations that we were working on. He preferred to see things in print, claiming that he was better able to see any mistakes that way. It was only after we were done that he'd want the electronic version. I'd always thought that was a bit backward, but to each his own.

It only took a minute to pull all the files together and send them off to him. Unfortunately, that meant I didn't have much in the way to delay the office visit. I grabbed my notebook and walked over to Jasmine. I tapped on her shoulder and pointed upstairs so she knew where I was. At the very least, having some alone time might help her calm down and sort a few things out.

Clearly, my time with Eric had done strange things to my brain. A week ago, I would have marched right up to Mickelson's office and got to work. But I couldn't help but risk a small delay and popped my head in to wave at Eric.

"Hey." I smiled. "Heading to class?"

"Not for thirty minutes or so." He looked up at me and frowned. "How's Jasmine?"

"Not good. She and Nell had a fight. Apparently Nell thinks that Jaz is carrying a bit of a torch for me or something. Crazy."

"You mean she isn't? I was watching, remember. While I could tell you were enjoying it, there was something in the way she was kissing you." He shook his head. "If I were your partner and walked in to see that, I'd have some concerns."

That was crazy. Jasmine didn't have a thing for me. Did she? "Well, I'm sure she and Nell will work things out. Right now I have to go see the professor. He flies out tonight and probably wants to make sure I didn't screw anything else up." I took a step away before swinging back around. "We're still on for dinner tonight, right?"

Eric cocked his head to the side, his gaze slipping to the floor for a moment before he smiled. "Of course. I'll see if Claude can get us a table."

"God, yes. I've been dreaming about that bruschetta since the last time we were there."

He picked up his phone. "I'll book it for six then."

"I better go. He'll be upstairs waiting. I'll probably catch hell for being a bit late."

For the first time in years, I didn't dread the inevitable glare of my boss. Eric was taking me out to a wonderful restaurant where we'd get personalized service. With a few kind words and an intense look he managed to make me feel like the most special woman in the world.

Why would anyone ever want to break up with someone like him?

I knocked on Professor Mickelson's half-open door before I came in. "Hello. Sorry for the delay. I got stopped in the—"

"Sit down." He glared, actually glared at me. "Close the door."

I blinked. In all the years I'd worked with him, both as a student and an employee, I'd never heard him angry. Annoyed, frustrated, uppity, but not angry. My hand shook as I reached out and closed the door behind me, before taking my normal seat.

He didn't say anything at first, simply stared at me, breathing heavily through his nose. It made a small whistling sound that I wanted to laugh at, but knew that would be the worst possible thing in the world I could do.

Mickelson cleared his throat. His hands were balled tight in the middle of his desk. "Did you send the files?"

"Yes, as soon as you'd e-mailed me."

"Did you make the necessary changes?" He wasn't looking away, giving me no reprieve from his bright blue eyes.

I swallowed hard and adjusted my position in the chair. "To the presentation. I hadn't quite finished everything on the handout. It will only take me another hour at most to get everything the way you'd requested it."

"That's no longer your concern."

My stomach flipped and I squeezed the edge of my notebook. "I don't understand."

"I had a rather upsetting phone call from the administration. Apparently, you are engaging in sex games here on campus. You've involved your coworker and even a professor here. Though the name of the professor wasn't provided, you can be certain that there will be an investigation."

I wanted to throw up. "But—"

"Not a word. There is no sense in trying to deny it. A witness has come forward and provided all of the details." He leaned forward, the muscles in his neck and jaw tensed as he moved. "I want to hear it from you. Tell me the truth."

I wanted nothing more than to scream and cry my innocence. That this wasn't against the rules, that we hadn't done anything wrong. But I knew I couldn't. "I found the cards after my great-grandmother's funeral. I brought them to show Jasmine and the whole thing took on a bit of a life of its own."

Mickelson fell back into his seat. "You idiot."

"I'm really sorry. Honestly, nothing happened—"

"Something *did* happen and you were caught. I told both you and your friend that sort of behavior was unacceptable. Do you know what kind of damage the school's reputation could take if this sort of thing got out to the news? If the students saw and started talking about it on social media? You of all people should understand how quickly this sort of rumor spreads. I can't stand by and approve of this. Not by someone who works for me."

"But—"

"You're fired."

Tears immediately sprung from my eyes. If he'd slapped me it would have stunned me less than hearing those words. "What?"

"I'll follow you to your office so you can collect your purse, but then you have to leave. Someone will box up your personal effects and deliver them to you." He stood then and made his way around the desk. "Leave your notebook here. Any of that information is relevant to my studies and doesn't belong to you."

My head felt as though someone had hit me with a brick. I slid the book on the desk, not entirely thinking clearly. I then stood and followed him down the stairs to my office.

What used to be my office.

We came down the stairs just as Eric was coming out of his office and locking his door. His smile dropped as soon as our gazes met. "Hi, Phil. What's going on?"

"Dealing with a staffing issue. No concern of yours."

I followed lamely behind him, acutely aware of Eric watching us. When I came into the office, Jasmine was at the printer. She started to say something, but I quickly shook my head. Professor Mickelson crossed his arms and narrowed his gaze at her. "You're fortunate that it's not my funding that pays for your services or else you'd be out the door as well. I expect you'll be getting a call from HR later to discuss this situation."

"What's going on?" Jasmine dropped her papers on her desk. "Glenna?"

I couldn't stay there any longer. I grabbed my purse and sweater and at the last second took my R2-D2 penholder, dumping all the contents on the desk. "Bye, Jaz."

"What the hell?" Jasmine looked frantic. "Where are you going?"

"She's fired. And if I have anything to say about it you will be as well."

"No." I spun around and marched over to get right in Professor Mickelson's face. "Jasmine had absolutely nothing to do with this. I brought the cards in. I instigated the kiss. I'll confess to everything, but she is completely innocent."

"Glenna, don't."

"No, it's fine. This is all on me, not you. Now excuse me, I'm going to leave before I start to cry." I pushed past Jasmine out into the hall.

Eric hadn't moved from where he'd been standing. Clearly, he'd heard everything that had transpired. As far as Mickelson knew, the professor involved wasn't Eric. The least I could do was keep this shit-show from touching him as well. I didn't stop.

"Glenna?"

I took the far stairs for the last time and held myself together until I got home.

22

_____

I wanted nothing more than to spend the rest of the night locked up in my apartment feeling sorry for myself. Never in my life would I have ever thought that I'd get fired from my job. I worked hard and played by the rules. Sure, bringing the cards to work might have been a stupid idea, but it wasn't as though I'd really done anything.

It didn't take a genius to realize that Nell had been the person to lodge the complaint against me. No doubt she'd gotten the details from Jasmine while she was trying to explain the situation. Nell had always been a bit jealous, but I'd never realized quite how deeply that ran.

Maybe there was more to this than I'd first thought. Eric had said there was something in Jasmine's body language that told him the kiss meant more than simply fulfilling one of the cards. But Jasmine and I had talked about that years ago. I was straight. I wasn't her type. She was like my sister.

None of this made any sense.

The only thing that got me through the day was my upcoming supper with Eric at the Reading Street Pub. It forced me to wipe my tears and pull myself off my couch. After having a shower and picking out something nice to wear, I lay back down on my bed to air dry. It was only when my phone buzzed that I got myself going enough to read it. I even managed a smile when I saw Eric's name.

Would you like me to pick you up?

No, I'll take a cab. Faster.

I'll see you at six.

I only had forty-five minutes to finish getting ready and get downtown. Even with my world coming to a bit of an end, life continued. I pushed myself up and ordered a cab.

The restaurant was far busier than it had been the last time we'd come. The bar area inside was packed, the waitstaff dancing around the tables delivering drinks and mouthwatering food. I was greeted at the door by someone who wasn't Claude and gave her my name.

"Yes, Mr. Morris is here already. Let me take you back to your table."

The evening air was cool, so I wasn't surprised when she didn't take me to one of the outside tables. Instead, we made our way to a back corner of the restaurant next to a fireplace. It was on, but unlike the one at the spa, there was very little heat coming from it. Eric stood when we came into sight, but he wasn't smiling.

I had no doubt that he and Jasmine had discussed the details of my termination.

Eric came around the table and kissed me gently on the cheek before pulling my chair out for me. "Hi."

"Hi." The tension that had pressed down on me subsided a bit at his touch. "Thanks."

"I'd ask if you were okay, but I can't imagine you are."

Of all the people I could be meeting with, Eric was the one with whom I felt I could be the most honest. "September is turning out to be a really shitty month."

"I ordered some wine. I figured you wouldn't mind."

There was something strange about him, something in the way he didn't quite meet my gaze as he filled my glass. Maybe he was feeling guilty for me taking the fall for something that he was a part of as well. It wasn't his fault. "Today I will say yes to all of the wine." I took a generous sip as soon as he finished pouring. It was sweet heaven after the day I'd had. "Thank you."

We ordered our meal and Eric did an excellent job talking about everything except the gigantic elephant in the room. He even tried to make a few jokes, though as funny as he'd been pretending to be Professor Cyborg, humor when he was trying to be funny wasn't his strong suit. Still, he was making an effort to cheer me up and for that I was thankful.

It wasn't until we'd finished dessert that his entire demeanor changed. The eye contact I'd come to associate with him began to happen less the more we chatted. It was when he poured the last of the wine into our glasses that I realized he wasn't looking at me at all.

"I think we need to talk."

If there were more ominous words in the English language, I certainly didn't know what they were. I set my glass down and ran my hands across my thighs. "We have been talking. For over an hour now."

He winced. "You know what I mean."

"Talk about what?"

"Today."

"There's not much to say. Nell was upset over Jasmine kissing me. She found out about the cards and told the administration. They told Mickelson and I'm out the door." Dammit, I wasn't going to cry again. I wouldn't give the situation that power over me. I cleared my throat and smiled. "I'm going to have to pick a bottle of this up on the way home."

"We were both a part of this."

"I know. But you're not to blame for what happened."

"That kiss wouldn't have happened if I hadn't pushed Jasmine into it."

"You didn't—"

"I did and you know it." He closed his eyes and let out a sigh. "I'm to blame for this. For your life getting ruined."

Setting my glass down, I reached out and took his hand in mine. "You're not."

"Would you have acted on those cards if I hadn't pressed you about them? Would you have brought them to the barbecue and nearly had them seen? Would you have ever kissed Jasmine anywhere, let alone at work?"

My body felt as though someone had been punching me all day long. Hearing Eric speak, all I could feel was a giant wave of exhaustion wash over me. I pulled my hand away and reclaimed my glass. "What are you saying?"

"Would you?" There was something almost desperate about his tone. Pleading.

"No. You know I wouldn't have."

I couldn't imagine he thought I was going to say anything different, but the look on his face mirrored my own when I'd gotten home this afternoon—broken. "That's the problem. Whether I'd intended it or not, I'm the reason you lost your job."

"No, Nell is—"

"I don't think we should see each other again."

The air in my lungs froze. My head swam and my vision darkened around the edges before I forced another breath. "What?" I could barely get the word out past my lips. This couldn't be happening. Not on top of everything else.

This wasn't fair.

Eric's face was blank, his gaze fixed on the candle on the table.

"This is just like . . . I can't go through this again. I thought I was ready, that what had happened in the past was a onetime thing. But after today, I can't do this again."

I didn't have any fight left in me. I didn't even really understand what he was trying to say. "Is this about Grace?"

He looked at me, his fingers flexing on the glass. "I don't want to talk about her."

"So you're breaking up with me because of something that wasn't really your fault because it was similar to something that happened to you in the past but you won't talk to me about it? How the hell am I supposed to process this?"

"Glenna, you're a wonderful, sweet woman—"

"I don't want to be wonderful or sweet. I want to be with you."

He leaned in, started to reach for my hand, but stopped short. "I was told once that sometimes the best decisions for you are the ones that hurt the most when you make them. You might not think so right now, but it's better for you if we break things off." He sighed and his head slipped forward as though it suddenly became too heavy for him to hold. "I'm not good for you. For anyone."

What the hell could I say to that? "I disagree. You're kind and funny and sexy. Any woman would want you. *I* want you."

"You say that now. But what happens a week from now, or a month. What happens if you can't find another job and you're not sure how you're going to pay for your rent?" He leaned back and looked away. "Sooner or later you'll start to resent me. You'll hate that you did something out of character, something that you wouldn't have if I hadn't been the one to encourage you. There are many things I can handle, but having you grow to hate me isn't one of them."

If he was trying to keep me from hating him then he was doing a piss-poor job of it. "Eric, please."

"I wanted to give you this supper. A sort of thank-you. I'd been traveling down a dark road for a long time and you brought me some light. I wish it could have lasted, that I could have been the man you deserve to have. You're a wonderful woman and despite all the crap that you've been through, I know you'll come out on top."

"Stop." If he kept talking I knew there was no way I'd be able to keep from crying. As it was, my body ached from keeping the tears bottled inside. "Don't say anything else."

His lips pressed together so hard the skin changed color.

"This isn't fair." I finished my wine. "All my life I've played things safe. I've done what I was supposed to do, said all the right things. I bent over backward to help Mickelson. I never chased after men because that wasn't what nice girls did. It wasn't until Great Glenna's letter that I even thought that having this sort of adventure was possible. Girls like me didn't get guys like you. Smart and funny and sexy. But I thought, hey, maybe Great Glenna was right. Maybe Jasmine was right. I couldn't play things safe and have the life that I fantasized about."

Standing, I gently set my napkin on the table. "I did try and my life fell apart. It's not fair and I don't like this."

"I'm sorry," he whispered.

"Can you drive me home?" When he winced, I held up my hand. "On second thought, never mind. I'd rather take a cab. Thanks for dinner. I hope you find what you're looking for someday."

I walked away, from the last good thing I had left in my life.

Part 4

An End's New Beginning

23

Being unemployed was a strange state of affairs. The first day after I was let go, I got up the same time I always did. I had a shower and raced around trying to pull together something to eat so I could make the bus on time. It wasn't until I was about to pour some cereal that I realized what I was doing. There was in fact no rush, because I had nowhere to go.

So I made oatmeal.

After I finished my hot treat—I nearly drowned it in maple syrup and added chocolate chips for good measure—I called Mom.

"Hi, baby. What's going on?"

"Hey. It's been a bad week."

"What happened?"

"Oh you know. I got fired."

"*What?*"

There were many things I could talk to Mom about, but telling her about sex cards that I'd found after Great Glenna's funeral was something I didn't have the ability to do. I left that bit out but told her most of what had happened.

"After I read Great Glenna's letter, I figured I should take a chance with Eric. None of this was his fault, but he certainly felt like it was."

"I never did like that professor you worked for. Your father and I thought he was taking advantage of you from day one."

"He wasn't that bad."

"He was. You just didn't want to admit it because he gave you a job before you even graduated."

"There aren't a lot of positions for communication researchers. It was a great opportunity." Despite how things turned out, I didn't regret my decision. Not really.

"So what are you going to do now?"

"I'm going to pull together a résumé and check out some job postings on Monster. If I can't find anything then I might reach out to a placement agency or something."

"That's a good place to start. And you know if you need anything, your dad and I are here to help."

"Thanks, Mom."

"Why don't you come for supper tonight? We can talk and help you come up with a plan."

"Maybe. I'll let you know."

"Okay. I love you, sweetie."

"I love you, too."

After I hung up with Mom, I got a text from Jasmine. She was still furious, wanting to reassure me that there was nothing Nell could ever do to make things up to her or me. They were done, kaput forever. That didn't help me feel any better because I knew how much Jasmine cared for Nell. While she'd been involved with the kiss, she didn't deserve any of this either.

After I read Jasmine's rant, I swiped over to Eric's last text. It still hurt my heart to even think about him, about how things had ended between us. I knew there was more to what he'd said, but he'd yet again refused to talk about it. Whatever had happened between him and Grace was getting dumped on me.

No matter how awesome things had been between us, I refused to pine after someone who wouldn't give me the benefit of the doubt. It pissed me off. Screw him for being such an asshole about things. I should text him, tell him exactly how I felt and what I thought about him.

Jerk. Asshole. Evil villain.

Damn you, Professor Cyborg.

I'll get you next time, Super Vixen.

I tossed my phone on the couch and stomped over to my shoes and purse. I needed to get out of here. Résumés and angry text messages could wait.

The air was crisp, fresh in a way that it could only be in the fall. I walked through Toronto, enjoying the bustle without the stress of needing to be anyplace in particular. I made my way to the subway and without realizing where I was going, ended up in the part of the city where Great Glenna was buried. One short bus ride and I could be there.

It was strange how different a graveyard is when it's empty. The wind blew a bit stronger and the air felt cooler as I walked amongst the rows to where Great Glenna rested. Her letter was still folded neatly in the side pouch of my purse. When I got to her grave, I knelt down and pressed my hand to the fresh sod that had been laid since the last time I'd been here.

I took out her letter and sat with my back pressed to her gravestone. It only took a moment to read it again, but instead of sadness, all I felt was anger.

"Your letter sucked, Great Glenna. It made me do something that was so not what I would normally do. I went after adventure and it fucked everything. Why couldn't I simply have my fantasies and be happy? Have my job with my shitty-ass boss who may have been stealing my ideas and passing them off as his own. It might not have been perfect, but I was happy."

Had I been? I enjoyed what I did, and I loved working with Jasmine, but had I actually been happy?

I thought back over the previous three years of my life. I went to work every day, but I rarely felt excited about what I was doing. I tended to eat the same things, walk the same routes, follow the same routine day after day. It wasn't so much that I'd been in a rut, but I had grown complacent with my life.

Even the men in my life hadn't been all that exciting. I'd mentally blamed the not-so-exciting sex on my partners, wishing they would have taken things to the next level. But I seemed drawn to men who I knew weren't the right ones, who could never give me that passion that I'd wanted. It wasn't their fault we weren't a good fit.

Without consciously realizing it, I'd been sabotaging my happiness for years.

That was, until I'd found the cards. The last three weeks with Eric . . . shit, I couldn't imagine being happier. The times I'd spent with him, the crazy sex we had, the laughter we'd shared. None of that would have been possible if I hadn't found those cards, hadn't followed Great Glenna's advice and taken a chance to find the man who was right for me.

Eric.

I wiped at the tears as they rolled down my cheek.

He really was so very good for me. It was strange, but I felt more like myself when I was around him. I could relax and not worry about having to say the right thing all the time. Eric respected me as a person and as a professional, something that I hadn't realized was as important to me as it was. Mickelson had ground me so far down, I'd forgotten what my life looked like standing up. Eric helped me see that, even if he didn't come out and say it overtly.

And I'd let him go.

Shit.

I let the weight of my thoughts pull my head down until my forehead rested against my knees. Things were far too confusing for me, too heavy. No. I had to get my act together. Life would continue on regardless of if I chose to keep going or not. I needed to pick myself up and figure out how to move forward without Eric, my job, or Great Glenna. Standing, I brushed myself off and kissed my fingertips before I pressed them to the gravestone.

"I'm sorry. Love you, Great Glenna. Don't worry about me. I'll figure this out and get on with my life."

On my way back I noticed a woman standing at a stone. She looked to be a bit older than me, and far taller. She'd placed a bouquet on top of the grave and started to walk down the path at the same time.

When we were side by side, she turned her head and smiled. "Beautiful day."

"It is. We won't get too many more of these before the cold comes."

She reached into her pocket and pulled out a tissue. "You look like you need this."

"Thanks. I wasn't expecting to come here. Not exactly sure why I did."

"When my husband, Rob, passed a few years ago, I showed up here at the most random of times. Usually when I was trying to figure something out and I wanted to talk to him."

"I'm sorry for your loss." I swallowed. It was hard enough losing Great Glenna, I couldn't picture how I'd survive if I'd lost a man I loved. *You would probably feel like you did when Eric told you to go.*

"I'm sorry for yours."

"Great Glenna was ninety-eight and lived a full life. She wanted me to do the same, but I've somehow screwed mine up instead."

"I know that feeling. Like no matter what you do the opposite happens and you're all, you idiot, why the hell did you do that." Her voice rose an octave and she waved her hand around her head. "It took a while, but if I can figure things out, I'm sure you can too."

"Well, my track record has been pretty crappy recently. Lost my job and the guy who I think I could have fallen in love with dumped me for my own good."

"Ouch." The woman pushed her hands deep in her pockets. "I had something similar happen to me. My guy walked away and I actually let him go."

"It hurts."

"Yeah. But then do you know what I did?" She stopped walking as we reached the parking lot and faced me. "I realized that life is short and sometimes the things that get in the way are really just a means to prove to yourself that you can get what you want."

"So you got your guy?"

She smiled and I knew that this was a woman who was in a good place in her life. "There was groveling involved, and some... things that I probably shouldn't share with a stranger. But yeah, I got him."

If this woman who'd lost her husband could move on and find happiness with someone else, then there was no reason why I couldn't do the same. "Thank you. That actually helps."

"No problem. I'm not normally the advice person, that's my sister. It's good to know that I don't completely suck at it." She nodded and then got into her car.

It wasn't until she drove out of sight that I realized I hadn't asked her name.

Oh well. Mystery Woman was right, I could let what happened consume me, or I could overcome it. I could let Eric get away without a fight, or I could go down swinging. I needed a plan if I was going to do this. I needed to get home and take a look at my board and figure out the next step.

I wasn't doing this for Great Glenna, my parents, Jasmine, or even the mystery woman. Hell, I wasn't even doing this for

Eric. The only person who could make me happy was me. The time I'd shared with Eric had been what I wanted; I was the person I wanted to be when I was with him. If I let him drift away without even making an attempt to get him back, I would regret it for the rest of my life. No, I wouldn't be that person. I was going to go after him. I was going to make things right.

I drank a beer as I stood in front of my corkboard. Seeing as I didn't have anywhere to be, or any standards that I felt I had to meet, there was no reason *not* to have a beer. Plus it was after three, so that was like not even remotely bad. Not really. Just because I was drinking alone and unemployed . . .

Anyway. Eric!

I set my beer down and took a look at the board. I hadn't added Day Twenty-seven to the sexy fun time, even though that had totally happened. A part of me felt guilty for having enjoyed it, regardless of what the fallout had been. I debated with myself for a moment before I fished it out and put it on the board. There. I also added Day Fifteen for our role-playing adventure, smiling as I remembered how awesome the night had been.

It was hard to believe that had only been a few days ago.

With that done, I turned my attention to my primary focus: learning about Eric.

I hadn't added much on that side of the board recently. It was apparent that knowing he preferred the original ending to *Little Shop of Horrors* wasn't going to help me solve my current dilemma. The one card that I'd been avoiding was the one I knew would give me the most answers.

I pulled Grace's name from the board and held it up. I didn't have a last name or a school to go on, which would make tracking her down a bit difficult. A quick check of the faculty directory told me that she wasn't at U of T any longer. There was only one avenue that might give me what I needed to know.

It only took a second to look up the number for the Reading Street Pub online. The restaurant was closed, but thankfully someone still picked up. "Reading Street, how may I help you?"

"Hi." So this was a bit weird. "I was wondering if Claude is available?"

"Ah, maybe. I'll have to check. He was out in the brewery. Who's calling?"

"Glenna. You can tell him that I'm a friend of Eric's."

Vivaldi's "Spring" came over the line as I was put on hold. It was bright and warm, the complete opposite to how I currently felt. I couldn't be certain that Claude even remembered who I was. Maybe he'd been a big fan of Grace and the last thing he wanted was to see Eric off with some other woman. Or he could simply be busy and I'd have to delay my pursuit of Eric for another day.

The problem was, if I put this off I was terrified that I'd suddenly lose my momentum and Eric would drift away.

Vivaldi disappeared in a blink to be replaced with a cheerful male voice. "Glenna! Eric's little pixie friend. How are you doing?"

He thought I looked like a pixie? So wasn't sure how to feel about that. "Hi. Yes, that's me."

"Don't tell me he's done something to upset you already?"

"Not exactly. Well, sort of."

"Clear as mud." He laughed. "What did the little asshole do now?"

Ah, so they were *that* sort of friends. "He broke up with me."

"I'm sorry to hear that. But he's my friend and I'm not going to do anything to hurt him."

"I wouldn't ask you to. Honestly, I'm trying to figure things out."

I rattled off the entire story, not wanting to pause too long in the event Claude tried to stop me. I didn't need to worry. When

I finished, there was a brief pause. "I told you he was an ass-hole."

Okay, I liked this guy. "No he's not. Clearly, Grace hurt him and that's between the two of them. But it's impacting my rela-tionship with him. If I've screwed up and he wants to break things off, fine. But I don't want to be punished for someone else's crimes."

There was another pause. I heard tapping on the other end and a mutter that sounded suspiciously like *fuck it*. "I can't tell you what happened. That's their story. But I can tell you that Grace's last name is Bilodeau and she works at York. If she won't tell you anything, then I'm sorry."

"Thank you, so much. A chance, that's all I wanted."

"You have to promise me that you won't harass Grace. She's not the person you think she is."

"What do you mean?"

"Grace and Eric had a complicated relationship. In the end they wanted different things, which was neither's fault. Just . . . be kind. She did love Eric. I never doubted that."

My nerves jumped again. "I will. Promise."

"I have to go, Glenna. I hope I'll see you again."

"I hope so too."

Armed with a name and a location, it didn't take me long to call the school and find out Grace's timetable. If I caught the bus in the next five minutes, I'd be able to make it before her next class. Finally, things were starting to come together.

24

I stood in the doorway of a classroom as the remainder of the students trickled out. In typical fashion, there were always some stragglers lingering behind to speak with the professor. I'd been here for fifteen minutes, and from the minute I'd laid eyes on Grace Bilodeau I'd been trying to figure out what to say.

Claude was right that she wasn't exactly what I'd been expecting.

Grace sat in a sport-style wheelchair. Her black curly hair was piled on top of her head like a mountain about to avalanche. Her frame was small, but she looked to have a long torso. She spoke to her students in an animated fashion that had her arms flying around as though they were sentient beings of their own. She looked glorious.

The last student finally left and Grace caught sight of me. "I'm sorry, this class is full and I can't accept any more transfers."

I blinked. "Oh, I'm not a student."

She rolled her chair with ease around her desk at the front of the room, collecting her things. "I'm sorry. How may I help you?"

In all of my musings on the way over here, I hadn't come up with a good way to introduce myself. I stepped into the room and locked my hands behind my back. "Umm, this is a bit awkward. My name is Glenna O'Donald. You're Professor Bilodeau?"

"I am." She stopped moving and motioned for me to have a seat. "This is my last class of the day, but I believe there is a study group that meets here in thirty minutes."

"I don't think this will take long." I sat down in the desk and gave myself a moment to collect my thoughts. "I'm a friend of Eric's."

She looked at me, her gaze narrowing slightly. "How is he doing?"

"Until yesterday I would have said great."

"What happened yesterday?"

"I got fired. He's blaming himself."

"Ah." I could tell from the look on her face that she wasn't even a little surprised.

"He broke up with me. Told me that this was history repeating itself and that he didn't want to do to me what he did to you. Except he never told me what happened between you. I don't mean to pry, but I'm not willing to give him up without a fight and I can't fight what I don't understand. I was hoping you could help me with that."

"So he talked about me?" She ran her hand along the seat of her wheelchair. "I'm surprised."

"Not really. He mentioned you, but he didn't say much. I didn't want to push, so I didn't ask more."

Grace looked at me again, and I couldn't help but feel I was being assessed for my worthiness. "Tell me what happened."

It was strange giving her the details of the last few weeks of my life. There were many things I could have left out, but the last thing I wanted was for her to call me out for lying and not help.

"So my friend, whom I love, but is a complete jackass at

times, took the opportunity to kiss me in front of Eric. Her girlfriend saw and happily informed my boss about everything. The next thing I know, I'm being let go and Eric dumps me saying it was all his fault for me doing something that was out of character."

Grace actually laughed. "It's nice to know some things never change. Eric was always a bit of a martyr. That's actually the reason I broke up with him."

Okay, I wasn't expecting that. "May I ask what happened?"

"You were honest with me, so the least I can do is repay the favor. I'm eight years older than Eric. We met when he first started working here and hit it off. He was quiet, still feeling his way around the world of academia and I'd offered to help. One thing led to another and we started sleeping together."

There wasn't any reason to be jealous of Grace. Her relationship with Eric was well in the past, and she clearly had no interest in getting back with him. Still, I had to squash the evil part of myself that wanted to hiss at her. Shit, I was a child at times.

She turned her attention to the back of the classroom. "We were together for over a year. The sex was great, but it didn't take long to realize that we were at different stages in our lives. I knew he wanted to eventually have children, buy a house, get a dog. I didn't want any of that. I prefer books to toys and you couldn't pay me to have a pet. Just a little over two years ago I invited him out to supper and I broke up with him."

She'd done to him what he'd done to me. I wondered if he'd even realized the similarity.

Grace sucked in a breath and shook herself out of the haze she'd slipped under. "We fought. Eric was adamant that we could work things out. We didn't have to have children if I didn't want. The dog wasn't a must have, etcetera. I said no, I was done. I stormed out demanding he take me home. I could do that back then." She patted the wheel.

"What happened?" A part of me didn't want to hear the rest of the story, dreaded hearing my fears vocalized, but I knew I had no choice. I came here looking for answers and I wasn't leaving until I had them all.

"We kept fighting. I should have let it go, but I knew he wouldn't back down and once I get going, it's hard for me to stop. We fought as he drove. It's my fault that he wasn't paying attention when the deer ran out in front of us. He swerved, but it was too late and we ended up over an embankment and hitting a tree. He was hurt quite badly with a nasty gash to his side. The impact left me paralyzed."

Jesus. "I'm so sorry."

"So was Eric. He blamed himself for what happened. Once I got out of the hospital he promised me that he'd look after me, that he'd make sure I never wanted for anything. I loved him for the offer, but I didn't *love* him any longer. I couldn't make him commit to me, paying eternal penance for something he wasn't to blame for. So I was cruel to him. He ended up leaving the school."

I sighed. "That explains so much. He didn't socialize much at all last year. It was only in the past month that I even discovered he knew my name."

"Typical. I bet he was brooding. He had that nailed before he left U of T."

We shared a smile and all the jealousy I'd felt melted away. I liked this woman, admired her for what she'd gone through and come out the other side the stronger for. "So what should I do?"

"Go kick his ass. Tell him Grace said he was being a dick and to stop. He's not evil incarnate. Bad things sometimes happen to good people. It's what we do in the aftermath that's key."

I stood and held out my hand. "Thank you."

"You're welcome. It gives me peace to know that Eric has found someone who will make him happy."

"Do you think?"

"I have no doubt. I was surprised when he sent me a bouquet of flowers the other week. His note was simple. He said thank you, that I was right, and that he'd finally moved on. I suspected he'd finally met the right woman and I couldn't have been happier."

"Oh." The flowers were a good-bye, that's what he'd said. My heart fluttered and I jumped to my feet. "I better head out."

"Go get him."

I left the school with a plan. Poor Eric wasn't going to know what hit him.

I didn't put my plan into action immediately. There were things that I wanted to set up, arrangements to be made if I was going to make an impact. I talked to Jasmine after my meeting with Grace. It didn't feel right sharing what I'd learned with her, especially how bad he still felt about everything. But I needed her help if my plan was going to work, and that meant convincing her that he was still worth the risk.

I shouldn't have had any doubt that she'd be on board. I pulled my phone away from my ear when she squealed. "Oh my God, that's a brilliant idea!"

"I know." It took me the better part of a day and a half to come up with it. "So you'll help?"

"Of course I will. Just because my love life has gone down the tubes doesn't mean I want you to join me."

"I'm so sorry about Nell."

"Don't be. This has been an issue for as long as we'd been together. I can't be with someone who can't trust me." She cleared her throat. "Look, let's focus on you, Super Vixen."

"I should never have told you that."

"Shut up. I need to know all your weird, kinky shit. Now, tell me what you need me to do."

"Get a pen and an index card from the shelf under the printer."

"Yup."

"Okay, write *Day Twenty-one*. Today he's out of the office at one thirty—"

"I love that you know his schedule—"

"But he locks his office so you'll have to ask maintenance to open the door for you. Then just put it on his desk with the banana and leave the rest to me."

"Dare I ask what the banana is for?"

"It would scar you for life."

"Okay, not asking. You have to promise to tell me how this works out."

"In all the gory details."

"Go get him."

I still had a few calls to make, but now that I'd gotten things started, I had a good feeling that things were going to work out for the best. All I had to do was to seduce Eric and convince him that history didn't have to repeat itself. That we could have a relationship, maybe even a life together if things worked out. That he wasn't to blame for my mistakes.

That I didn't think what had happened was a mistake at all.

I was about to go in search of my red heels when my phone rang. It was probably a telemarketer, but I picked it up anyway.

"Is this Glenna O'Donald?"

"Yes."

"My name is Dave Matterson. I heard you might be looking for a new position."

I pulled the phone away from my head and stared at it for a moment. "How did you find that out? I haven't even finished compiling my résumé."

"We have a mutual friend. Eric Morris."

I found it suddenly very hard to stand. "Yes we do."

"I have an opening and I happened to be speaking to Eric about it. From what he's told me about you, I think you might be an ideal candidate for the role. Do you have a moment to talk?"

It shouldn't have surprised me that Eric had done something like this. He felt bad about what happened and would want to make reparations. That act, even though he tried to push me out of his life, made me love him all the more.

Now I just had to convince him that this—us—was worth fighting for.

25

I was buzzing with excitement. The red dress was slinky and soft and hugged my body in all the right places. Sure, it had been a bit of a splurge, but I was happy and deserved it.

Jasmine had been amazing in getting the card and the banana onto his desk while he was out of the office. She'd even stuck around pretending to be working until he came back from class. She'd texted me the entire sequence of events.

He's coming down the hall.

He's unlocking his door and going inside.

He's wearing that purple dress shirt that you like. No, the sleeves aren't rolled up.

Oh!

He's coming back into the hall. He's holding the card and looking around.

Shit, he's looking at me.

Sec.

That had been a painful five minutes of silence.

He came down and asked if I'd seen you. LOL he was carrying the banana.

This will rock! OMG you have to tell me how this turns out!
I had my fingers crossed that Jasmine's prediction would come true. If nothing else, I was going to give it my all. I wouldn't look back and wonder what might have been; I'd know one way or the other. No regrets.

Standing in the near empty banquet room in the top floor of the Reading Street Pub was intimidating. Yes, my card had the effect that I'd wanted—Eric called me. I didn't answer, which was part of the plan. Instead I texted Claude, who put part two of my plan into play.

That involved Eric coming to the pub to meet me.

He was five minutes late.

Claude had guaranteed me that there was no chance we'd be interrupted once the food had been served. He'd even volunteered to take care of the menu and the wine selection for me and promised to serve us himself.

"Eric has been miserable for too long now. If you're the woman who can make him happy again then I will help you no matter what."

The table was covered with a variety of appetizers, and a bottle of champagne was chilling off to the side. The lights were turned down and Claude had even created some mood lighting that gave the open space a sense of wonder and magic.

Now, if Eric would just show up, everything would be perfect.

Ten minutes past the time Eric was supposed to show, I started to wonder if he'd backed out. That my plan, as clever and sexy as I thought it was, wouldn't be enough to break past his fears. I couldn't sit, and standing wasn't something I could do when I wasn't a bundle of nerves, so I paced. The reclaimed wooden floor echoed as I strolled along, my heels clicking in an offbeat to the music being piped into the room.

The sun had set not long ago, the sky still held the remnants of the pinks and oranges, but I could see that they wouldn't last much longer. Soon it would be dark and the night would be in full swing.

"That's the most beautiful sight I've ever seen."

I turned at the sound of Eric's voice, to see him standing there wearing a suit and tie. "You came."

"I had to find out what this was for." He held up the banana. "I honestly forget what Day Twenty-one was."

All my tension bled away. I clasped my hands behind my back and came toward him.

"Wait. Stop." He held up his hand. "This will sound cheesy, but could you spin around? I want to see you dancing in the light, wearing that dress."

I grinned, giddy with excitement. Stretching my arms out to the side, I spun slowly at first, letting my momentum and the air catch my dress and flare it out like an opening flower. Then I kept going, simply enjoying the moment, the freedom. Great Glenna had always told me I needed to enjoy the time I had with the people I loved. If this wasn't something to love, then nothing was.

I nearly lost my balance, stumbling briefly before Eric caught me in his arms. Laughing, I leaned in and kissed his cheek. "Thanks."

"You're taller."

"I am."

"Another superpower you possess?"

"I'm in heels."

"I'm going to stick with superpower. You seem to have many of them." He tucked a lock of my hair behind my ear. "Like the ability to get me to come down here when I know it's probably a terrible idea."

The old me would have jumped in and told him that it wasn't a bad idea, that we could make anything work if we put our minds to it. The new me knew that wasn't exactly the case. He'd put the effort in with Grace and things hadn't gone the way he wanted. I had to show him that we could make this work.

Taking a step back I captured his hand. "How about we sit and have something to eat?"

"How could I say no?"

Like he had in the past, Eric pulled my chair out for me, bending to kiss my bare shoulder as he did. "I love this dress."

"Thank you. It was a gift to myself for getting a job interview."

He hesitated behind me before taking the seat to my left. "Oh?"

"Yes. It seems your friend Mr. Matterson heard about my sudden unemployment from a little bird and wanted to have a chat with me."

Eric lowered his chin to his chest, but it didn't hide his smile. "I don't want you to think that I didn't believe in you, that you couldn't get your own interviews. I've known Dave for a few years now. He's been trying to get me to leave academia and come to the private sector since I moved back to Toronto."

"Dave said as much to me when we talked. The more we chatted the more it became apparent that the job is something that I think I'll enjoy."

"Do you think you'll accept it?" There was an eagerness to him that lit up his face. It was cute. "You don't have to. Not on my account. I know you can find something else if you want it."

The funny thing was the position—dealing with market research and analyzing the impact of social media—was basically my dream job. "He said based on my skills that I'd pretty much be the team lead. He would want me to build the team, hire my own staff, and run the direction of the projects. The salary was more than generous."

Eric's entire body relaxed back against the chair. "Good. I'm really pleased for you."

"Well, he hasn't officially offered me the job yet, and I haven't officially accepted it, but yeah, I think things are going to work out."

Claude cleared his throat as he came into the room. Without saying anything, he popped the cork on the champagne bottle and filled our flutes. "Your meals will be along shortly."

Eric snorted and Claude flicked his ear on the way by. "I see the two of you are really mature."

"Believe me, it gets worse when there's wine involved." He held up his flute. "To new beginnings."

I took a sip of the champagne, enjoying the way the bubbles made my nose and throat tingle, before I reached beneath my napkin and removed the card I'd placed there earlier. I slid it across the table to him. It was upside down, so he had no way of knowing what was printed there. He'd have to flip it over.

He looked down at it, hesitating briefly before reaching to see. I placed my hand on his, stopping him. "Before you do that, I need to say something."

His gaze met mine, and all of the confidence that I'd come to associate with him, all of the brooding, all of the strength, was gone. All I saw was a man scared. Whether he was scared to hope, scared to try, or scared to have history repeat itself, I couldn't be sure.

My little speech suddenly felt as though it wouldn't be enough. That he wouldn't be able to accept what I needed him to so we could keep going. I curled my fingers around his hand and squeezed.

"I had a whole thing I was going to say. I was going to tease you, do a little sexy thing, and then when I had you where I wanted you I was going to tell you what my plan for the banana was. But I realized just now that despite how great the sex is between us, that's the easy part. The things that I think you struggle with is the everyday part. I know I do. I never felt good enough to reach out and take. I didn't do my PhD because I let Mickelson convince me that I wasn't ready. I didn't approach you before because I didn't think I was in your league. I never tried because I was scared. I don't want to be scared anymore."

Eric turned his hand around and laced our fingers. "You don't have to be."

"I know. And I'm not. I took a chance. The worst thing imaginable happened, I lost my job. That position was everything to me. But getting fired made me realize something: The world didn't end. I *am* stronger than that. I don't know if I'll take the position with Dave. Or if I take it, whether I'll keep it. I know I have options. What I don't want to do is find a replacement for you."

"Glenna—"

"Let me finish. Please."

He nodded.

"I talked to Grace." When he tried to pull away, I held him firm. "I know you'll probably be upset with me, but I needed to know. I needed to understand why you walked away from me. I thought everything had been going well and yes, losing my job sucked, but it wasn't the end of the world."

"It was to you. I ruined everything you'd worked for."

I leaned down and kissed the back of his hand. "No you didn't, and I think you know that. What happened to me isn't the same as what happened to Grace. But regardless, neither of those incidents were your fault."

"I was the one driving."

"And she said she was the one arguing. That the accident was more her fault for distracting you in the first place."

"No."

"Yes. She also told me that you wanted to take care of her afterward. Even though she'd broken up with you. I could tell when I spoke to her that she cared for you, but she knew the two of you wouldn't have worked. She wanted you to live your life and be happy."

"I know." He spoke softly. "Even when we were happy I knew in the back of my head things wouldn't last long-term. I wanted it to, hoped it would, but it didn't."

"I'm sorry."

"Don't be. It was the reason I left U of T and came to work at the college. I knew I had to move on, and to do that I needed to be away from her. Seeing her day after day was slowly eating me alive. Even if I didn't love her any longer, it was too painful to see her that way."

"If it's any consolation, she looked great. Happy."

"Good." He leaned back but didn't release my hand. "So am I going to be able to see what this is or not?"

"Yes, but I need to say one last thing before you do." Okay, this was it, the moment that I'd worked myself up to. The moment that would either make or break tonight. "I know we haven't been doing this whole thing for long, but I've been drawn to you for a while. Spending time with you, getting to know the man behind the professor mask you wore made me realize something."

"What?"

"That I have . . . feelings for you."

"What kind of feeling?" He lifted my hand to his lips and kissed the inside of my wrist. "Glenna? What feelings?"

My skin tingled from his heated breath. My breasts ached to be touched, to be kissed by him. He continued to kiss up my arm, moving closer until he was on his knees by my chair. "Glenna?"

I sucked in a breath as my wish came true and he ran his fingertips across my erect nipple. "I think . . ."

"Yes?" He slid his hand up along my thigh.

"I think . . ."

He cupped the back of my head and nuzzled the side of my neck. "Yes?"

"That I might love you."

He sucked in a small breath; the rush of air tickled my skin. "Really?"

"Yeah."

When he pulled back and I could look into his eyes, my heart danced at the sparkle I saw reflected back to me. "Thank you."

I didn't need to ask him how he felt about me. We hadn't ever been a proper couple. But I knew my own heart and I didn't regret my words. Great Glenna had encouraged me to take a chance on life and love, and that's what I'd done.

"You can turn the card over." I finished my champagne and poured some more.

Eric shook his head but complied. "Day One. Tell him how you feel."

"I thought it might be a good idea to start off on the right foot. Give ourselves a new beginning."

"And this?" He took the card Jasmine had written from his pocket and put it on the table with the banana.

"Well, there was no sense in wasting a perfectly good sex card. Besides, that's dessert."

"Claude better hurry up and get supper here soon. I'm not sure I can wait very long."

Despite our mutual impatience, we both managed to get through our meal. It turned out to be an extended form of foreplay. Claude would bring us a course, and the teasing would begin. I'd eat bits of bread using lots of teeth. Eric would pop an olive into his mouth, giving the end a tiny lick before devouring it. That had me squirming in my seat and wishing that I'd chosen to wear something other than the lace panties. I had no doubt that my pussy was damp enough to soak through the thin barrier.

"Is it time for dessert?" He picked up the banana. "Because I know I'm ready."

Yeah, I was more than happy to move my plan along to phase two. "I think that's an excellent idea."

"Shall I bring this?" He picked up the banana as he stood. "I'd hate to leave a key element for us to complete Day Twenty-one."

Rather than let him have all the fun, I took the banana and held on to it. "For safekeeping."

As we came down the stairs, Claude was waiting for us. "I hope everything was to your satisfaction."

"It was perfect." Even in my heels, I had to get up on my tiptoes to kiss Claude's cheek. "Thank you for everything."

"If it means this asshole finally comes to his senses, then I'm more than happy to help. Oh and Eric"—Claude punched his shoulder—"don't fuck up."

"I won't."

Eric led me to his car. "If it doesn't ruin your plans, I have a suggestion for where we continue the rest of our night."

"Where?"

He took a deep breath. "If you're up for it, I was thinking my place is closer than yours."

That was something I hadn't even hoped would happen. "Yes. Take me home."

"As you wish."

26

I don't know what I'd been expecting when Eric invited me to his place. A big condo? A monster mansion that a billionaire would live in? He was a professor. And while I'm sure he wasn't poor, he certainly wasn't swimming in cash either.

The brick town house was cute. There was a large tree with thick foliage that hung above the walkway that led to a small covered porch. It was enough to diffuse the light from the streetlamp on the road, casting interesting patterns on us as we walked by.

"Watch your step." He lifted me up over a raised stone. "I've been meaning to get that fixed."

"A real hazard." I didn't really mind being pressed against his side.

"The top step is a bit wonky as well." He actually sounded embarrassed.

"You're an evil villain. Shouldn't your lair have traps meant to slow down unsuspecting superheroes?"

He gave my side a gentle squeeze before unlocking the door. "I hope you're not allergic to cats."

"You have a cat?" Damn, how did I not know that?

"I don't, but my neighbor does. She'll sometimes crawl across the porch roof and pick at my window until I let her in. Crazy thing."

"You rescue cats from roofs. Careful, or you're going to ruin your evil reputation."

The front door was barely closed when Eric spun me around and pressed me against it. My hands flew to his chest and my lips barely parted before he devoured me with a kiss. I grasped at his body, wanting to pull him in as hard as I could. If there'd been a way that I could have dissolved against him I would have done it.

His mouth was greedy; his tongue plunged deep into my mouth. My skin felt electrified, tingling with the brush of his hands across the silk of my dress. When he cupped my breasts, a jolt of arousal shot straight to my cunt, making me moan and writhe against him. This wasn't going to be enough, not tonight. Yet, it would be easy to simply let him carry me to his bed and make love to me. I wanted that, God I really did. But tonight was about something more. Showing him that we could have this, have fun and our lives wouldn't fall apart.

It took effort, but I pulled back from him. "We need to stop or else you won't get your dessert."

He groaned and dropped his forehead to mine. "I don't care about food right now."

"I think you'll like this. It's on the cards, after all."

"Day Twenty-one."

I grinned. "Day Twenty-one."

"I'm stopping under protest." He stepped back and it was clear to see his erection tenting his dress pants.

"Noted. I promise you'll enjoy this."

I took his hand and started to lead him into the house, when I realized I had no idea where I was going. "Kitchen?"

"Wasn't expecting that. Straight down the hall and on the left."

It was with a sense of relief that I quickly laid eyes on his microwave. "Wait here, please."

I should have practiced my technique for what I was about to do. The bit of reading I'd done gave some guidance, but I didn't want to go too deeply down that particular rabbit hole on the Internet. Scary, scary things online. I peeled away one section of the banana from the bottom, leaving the stem whole. Then I carefully pulled the banana out and set it on the counter. Ten super-long seconds in the microwave was all it took for my prop to be ready.

When I turned back around to see Eric, he was wearing the most adorably horrified and confused expression. *Bless.* "Are you freaking out?"

He swallowed but didn't look away from the peel. "A bit."

I took a bite of the banana and collected the peel from the microwave. "Bedroom. And naked." I spoke between bites. This banana was actually a tasty one.

Eric shook his head but led the way up a narrow staircase to his bedroom. His room wasn't huge, but somehow he'd made room for a big bed and two bookcases. Old, dark wood trimmed the place and offset the light blue walls. It was charming and very masculine. "Brown and blue."

"Just like I said." He took off his tie. "I have a request. If that's allowed."

"Maybe." I licked up the remaining side of the banana before popping it into my mouth.

Eric licked his lips. "Can you keep the red heels on? They're sexy."

"A foot fetish, Professor Cyborg?" I winked at him. "I think I can accommodate you."

He started to unbutton his shirt, slowing down when he realized I was paying particular attention. "Didn't one of those cards say something about a striptease?"

"I think so."

"Why don't we tease each other?" His smirk matched my own. "Or don't you think you can resist my charms, Super Vixen."

God, I loved this man.

"Better hurry. You don't want your treat to get cold." I slipped one strap of my dress down so it hung around my biceps. Then I waited for him to remove his shirt before doing the same on the other side.

"Glenna—"

"Pants too, Professor."

I waited until he pushed them down, leaving him only in his briefs and socks before I undid the side zipper of my dress and let it slip to the floor with a near silent *whoosh*. I'd chosen to wear red lace panties and bra to match the red of my dress. Another little splurge for this evening. Eric growled softly, confirmation enough that I'd made the right choice.

"On the bed." I held the peel between my forefinger and thumb. "It's getting cold."

I'd never seen a grown man move that quickly before in my life. Before I crawled onto the bed, I paused long enough to pull his socks off, tossing them over my shoulder. He shook his head, smiling, but didn't argue.

"I have you in my grasp, Professor Cyborg. This is payback for the evil you'd inflicted upon me the other night."

"The vibrator?"

"No. For doubting that I cared for you. That I wouldn't fight for you." I bent down and licked a long trail up his thigh. "That I would turn tail and run at the first sign of trouble."

His face tightened, but the look in his eyes was pure lust. And maybe a bit of something else. I'd worry about that later.

I set the peel on the bed beside me and reached up to pull his briefs down. He helped just enough to make it easy for me, and then I forced him back to the bed with a single hand to his chest. "Don't move."

The peel had grown cooler than the blog I'd read suggested it should be. While it might not exactly feel like a pussy, I hoped it would be enough to give him a taste of something kinky and fun. Carefully, I slipped the peel around his straining cock and closed my hand around it. With his shaft cocooned in the peel, I began to slowly pump his cock with slow, smooth strokes.

"Jesus." He thumped his head against the mattress. "Glenna—"

I couldn't stop from giggling. *Thank you, whoever wrote these cards*. I wasn't exactly pushing him into the land of blissful craziness, so I bent my head and began to lick his balls and the insides of his thighs as I continued to stroke. I picked up the speed and cooed as his body began to shudder and twitch beneath me.

"Too fast." He reached for me, his fingers gripping my arm. "I don't want to come."

"Oh no. We can't have that. Your torture will last far longer than a few minutes."

I tossed the peel aside and repositioned myself so I could have better reach of his cock. Ignoring him as best I could, I licked a long swipe up his shaft. "Oh, it tastes like banana."

"I wonder why."

I sucked the head of his cock into my mouth, teasing the head with my tongue. It was the oddest flavor—banana and arousal, chased by a bitter aftertaste—but I quickly grew addicted to it. I put every ounce of want into my blow job. I didn't mind giving them in the past, but with Eric I wanted to take it from a *thing* to an art form.

The more I sucked and licked, the louder his moans grew. His fingers were buried deep in my hair, pulling and directing me.

His nails grazed my scalp as he cupped the back of my head. "Glenna . . ."

The popping noise I made when I pulled off him was obscene. "Yes?"

"My turn to be evil."

One moment I was draped over him, and the next I was flat on my back, my head partially off the side. I laughed when he rubbed his face between my breasts, mouthing at the sensitive skin.

"Curse you, Cyborg." I hooked my legs around his torso.

"You'll never escape me, Vixen." He kissed across the tops of my breasts. "Never." He nipped at my nipple through the lace. "Ever."

With a skill that I shouldn't have forgotten he had, my bra was swiftly removed and tossed beside the banana peel. Once he pulled my panties down, he lifted each of my legs and draped them over his shoulders. "I've wanted to do this again since our first time together."

There wasn't anything tentative about his mouth on my pussy. He sucked my clit into his mouth and teased it with his tongue. Without warning, he added two fingers and began to pump me hard and fast. I was wet and horny, too wound up from the evening's teasing. Eric pushed and coaxed with his mouth and hands until my orgasm blasted through me. I grabbed at his head, keeping him in place until the waves of pleasure finally subsided. Only then did I let him pull back, stroking his face when he smiled up at me.

"Evil man." I sighed.

"I'm not through with you yet."

It was an absolute treat watching him walk naked across the room and out into the hall. There's nothing better than seeing the body of a fit man in motion. He was back after a moment of rummaging around, condoms and lube in hand. "I wasn't expecting this tonight. I'll have to move these back into the bedroom."

Now, for the final part in my plan to seduce the hell out of him. "I hope you have extra lube there." I carefully got onto my hands and knees and shook my ass at him. "I believe you had a longing to engage in Day Twenty-four?"

He was on his knees behind me in a flash. But rather than jump to the whole *let's have butt sex* part, he kissed my ass cheek before biting it. "You will kill me."

"You'll love it."

Pulling at my cheeks, he kneaded the flesh. "Have you done this before?"

"Once. It was . . . interesting. You?"

"No. It's been a fantasy. Grace wasn't interested. Neither were my other lovers."

Okay, I shouldn't have been as pleased as I was about being the one to do this for him, but I totally was. "I'm happy to help, Professor."

"I'm going to take some time and play. Loosen your muscles. I've read that if I don't do that it can hurt you."

His hands shook as he squirted lube across my asshole. The one time I'd done this, I'd been a ball of nerves. My boyfriend had pretty much browbeaten me into trying it and, unlike Eric, he hadn't taken the time to get me in the right state of being. I was already relaxed from my orgasm, so his index finger slipped easily into me.

As it had that previous time, it felt weird. But Eric took his time, pumping in and out. After a minute, he added a second finger and started the process over again. What I wasn't expecting was for him to reach between my legs with his other hand and begin to play with my pussy. The mutual stimulation of both my front and back had me bucking against him in a matter of moments.

"You're tight and wet." He kissed my ass again. "I'm going to add a third finger."

With the additional digit in place, he began to flex and fan his fingers. The faint twinge of pain melted away and it took no time for him to move in and out of me easily.

"Put the condom on and fuck me." Sweat had broken out across my body. My muscles shook and I knew given enough simulation I would probably come again. If we didn't move things along quickly, that would happen without him even being inside me.

Eric withdrew his fingers and I turned my head so I could catch sight of him putting the condom on. He then placed one hand on my lower back as he guided his cock to my ass. I relaxed against the intrusion, adjusting as he moved into me with small, shallow thrusts. It was surprising how quickly he filled me and how little discomfort I felt.

Clearly my ex was an idiot.

He gave me a few steady thrusts before he did something unexpected. He picked up the banana peel and tore it open. Then he leaned forward and pressed the slick inner pulp to my clit. "Payback is a bitch."

"Fuck."

It was the strangest, yet most arousing thing I'd ever experienced in my life. I didn't know what to do, where to focus my attention. The fullness of my ass sent shivers through me, filling me in a way I'd never experienced before. The moist slide of the peel felt like water, satin; something alien and I loved it. Eric's thrusts faltered as he tried to fuck me and rub me off. It wasn't fair to either of us for him to do all the work.

I reached between my legs and took the peel from him. "Just fuck me."

The trade allowed me to grind my cunt against my hand, increasing the pressure tenfold. Eric in turn grabbed my hips, the change in position making his movements more fluid. Our moans mingled as we chased our mutual releases. His body shook and his fingers flexed repeatedly on my hips.

With my shoes still on, I had to be careful about moving too much and scraping the sides of his legs. I widened the space between my knees, which gave me more room to manipulate the peel against my clit and allowed me to push my ass higher into the air.

"Shit." Eric slammed into me as he roared out. My muscles clenched around his cock as it milked every bit of come from him.

It became hard to breathe, everything was too much. I was desperate to come again, but I couldn't manage it. Eric fell against my back, his cock still buried deep in me. I continued to frantically work the peel, but wasn't getting any closer to orgasm.

Eric reached around me and batted my hand aside. Without the peel, he slid his fingers between my labia to tease my clit. "So wet. Hard."

He set a pace far slower than I had. Pressing against the top of my clit, he worked small circles over the sensitive nub as he leaned in and sucked on my ear. "You're so beautiful. Full of fire. I've wanted this from the moment I shook your hand last year. Wanted to strip you bare and make love to you."

I closed my eyes and tipped my head back against him.

"I'd listen for your laugh. I'd sneak glances at your ass. I wanted you and your small-sized package of goodness to climb me like a tree and kiss me."

Hearing him vocalize one of my fantasies was the nudge I needed. My head fell forward and my back arched against him as I came. Eric kept rubbing, kissing, teasing my body as pleasure tore through me, melting me from the inside out until I couldn't hold myself up any longer.

"Stop. Please."

His hand fell away and he finally slipped his softening cock from my ass. I wanted to drop to the mattress, curl into a little ball and go to sleep. When Eric took first one, then the other shoe, I managed to hold still long enough for him to finish.

"I'll get us something to clean up with."

Before he went, I flung the banana peel at him. "Here."

There was a soft splat and I looked in time to see it stick to his chest for a moment before it fell into his hand. My giggles exploded from me and I couldn't stop, not even when he got back from the bathroom with a warm cloth.

"Roll over and let me clean you up." He shook his head as I squirmed beneath him. "You're crazy."

"Too late to get rid of me now, Professor. You're stuck."

"I don't mind." He scooped me into his arms, holding me close while he pulled the blankets back.

I hadn't suspected that Eric was a cuddler, but he set me down beneath the sheets before wiggling in beside me. "I hope you didn't have any plans for the night. Because I'm not letting you go."

"Nope." I turned in his arms and pressed my face to his chest. The soft hairs tickled my nose. "I do love you. I know this is probably crazy because we haven't been doing this long. When my Great Glenna died, she left me a letter. She told me that I needed to find the right man and once I did that I needed to hold on to him."

He stroked my hair and wrapped the strands around his fingers. "I think I would have liked her."

"I know she would have liked you. She was a cougar even in her nineties."

We were quiet for a long time after that. I might have drifted close to sleep because I didn't quite hear him when he spoke next. "Hmm?"

He kissed my forehead. "I said, I think I might love you, too."

I pulled back, needing to see his eyes so that I'd know for certain I'd heard him right. "You do?"

"Yeah." He cupped my cheek. "I thought after all that happened with Grace that I wouldn't be able to find what I'd had with her again. That it was a one-shot deal and I'd blown it. And in a way what we share isn't what I had with her. It's so much more."

I pushed him down and kissed him. "Oh good, because I'm not letting you go anywhere. Just so you know where you stand."

"That's fine by me. You're willing to put up with me. Apparently, I can be self-absorbed when I'm working. And an idiot when Claude and I get together."

"Are you kidding? I'm unorganized when I first wake up. I've been told that I snore and talk in my sleep. I laugh at dumb stuff and can be argumentative." I groaned when I realized I'd better come clean about all my quirks. "And I have a confession to make."

He cocked an eyebrow. "Oh?"

"I have this old corkboard that I use sometimes. I kind of took a bunch of index cards and put everything I knew about you on there when I was trying to figure out . . . well, things."

"Like Pinterest?"

"Except with fewer motivational sayings and nudes." When he started laughing, I knew that everything between us would be fine. It was then that I heard a loud howl at the window. Eric groaned and immediately got out of bed. "Was that the cat?"

"I have to let her in or else she won't stop." A fat orange and white tabby jumped into the room the moment he pulled the screen open. "Glenna, meet Fluffy. Fluffy, Glenna."

"Fluffy?"

"The couple next door claim that was her name when they rescued her. Who am I to argue?"

Fluffy jumped onto the bed and curled up by my feet. I was either accepted with little concern, or my presence was deemed unimportant. "Well hello, Fluffy."

"I can kick her out if you want."

"Hell no. I've always wanted a cat. Or a dog."

Eric smiled and gave the cat a quick scratch behind the ears before coming back to bed. "I think you and I are going to have a lot of fun."

I snuggled in beside him. "Me too."

Epilogue

There was a wonderful breeze blowing as we walked through the park. The temperature had risen back up to summer levels, resulting in a large number of families taking advantage of being outside. It was awesome to be amongst them, holding Eric's hand as we went.

We'd been officially dating now for a whole week. We'd spent almost every night together, mostly at his place, getting to know each other beyond sex. He'd even shown me the director's cut with the original ending of *Little Shop of Horrors*. I had to admit that a rampaging Audrey II and her horde was probably the funniest thing I'd ever watched.

Today we were on a mission. Well, *I* was on a mission. I'd dragged Eric along because now that he was officially mine I was taking every opportunity I could to simply be with him. And that meant him coming with me while I looked for a good place to leave some sex cards.

"I can't put them here. There are way too many kids."

"I told you we should have taken them to campus. No risk of the wrong people finding them there."

"My luck, Nell would be the one to find them and I'd end up getting sued."

Jasmine was thrilled about my relationship status change. She'd decided to move on herself and had signed up for an on-line dating service. I loved her to death and I wanted her to be happy. I hoped she found the right woman sooner rather than later.

There was a crowd of college-aged people running around a far part of the park. I tugged Eric along and we headed in that direction. "What do you think they're doing?"

"Looks like Ultimate Frisbee."

"That's perfect."

There was a bench close to where the group was playing. I'd never seen Ultimate Frisbee before and it wasn't the easygoing pitch and catch that I used to play as a kid. No, this was a strange mix of Frisbee, football, and—ouch, that dive—I don't know what else. We sat down and watched the teams play. It didn't appear to be a game, more of a practice. There weren't a lot of spectators, but the ones milling around all appeared to be older.

We stayed for a solid ten minutes before I reached into my purse and pulled out the bag with the index cards. I'd taken the time to clip them together so they wouldn't go all over the place and get lost. I'd also written a note that I'd attached as well. Given the possible history of where they'd come from, it only seemed right. I read the note one final time, just to make sure everything was as it should be.

To Whomever Finds This Package.
Hello! I hope you're the right person for this.
You'll need an open mind and an open heart. What
you have discovered is something that has helped
more than one person. It's opened minds, hearts,
and healed the past. Sounds big, doesn't it.

Ready?

They're sex cards!

Thirty days and nights of wonderful sex.

I know, you're probably thinking some sicko left these behind wanting to get off on knowing you'd find them. I want to tell you that it's not like that. These cards were written with love. They were originally for someone who'd lost their partner, written to help her find her way forward. When I found them, they helped me realize that the best things in life are the ones you go after.

They might help you discover something else. Something that had been missing from your life.

If this isn't your thing, no worries. Leave them somewhere for another person to find.

If you want to use them, then go for it!

Have fun!

I hope the magic that seems to be attached to them finds its way into your life. If it does, then keep the magic going. Keep the love and laughter going.

And don't forget to get laid. ☺

Be well and happy.

I placed the bag on the bench beside me. Eric gave my hand a little squeeze. "Are you sure about this?"

"I am. It's weird but I think now that they're out there, the good that has come of them will keep going."

He gave me the side-eye. "You know how that sounds, right?"

"Shut up." But I grinned at him. "Worst case they get picked up by one of the students over there and make the rounds at a dorm. At least I've done my part."

"Fair enough." He lifted my hand to his mouth and placed a kiss to the inside of my wrist. "Are you ready to go?"

I gave the cards one final look before I got to my feet. "I want ice cream."

"Of course, my little vixen."

"That's Super Vixen to you."

My heart lightened and my soul sang as we left the cards behind. Things would be very good from now on.

The wind had died down as the Frisbee game continued. The heat, unseasonably warm for this time of year, made it uncomfortable to stand for long. There was an empty bench, invitingly empty, waiting for someone to take advantage and rest.

Also waiting, the contents of a bag, sitting in a small neat pile. It stayed there for a while, over an hour, before someone finally noticed. A shadow descended across the bag. A hand reached out and picked up the bag.

A laugh as a woman read the note.

She hesitated for a moment before casting a longing glance at one of the players on the field. She smiled and slipped the cards into her pocket.

Acknowledgments

It's that time when I get to hold my hat in my hand and thank all of the people who helped make this book possible. Always, I have to start by thanking my crew: Kristina, Paula, Kimber, and Amy. I love you ladies! Huge thanks to Del, who is always there to answer my crazy IM pings and take on my "sanity" reads. I'll forever be thankful for your suggestion on this book, even if it meant "changing all the things."

My amazing agent, Courtney Miller-Callihan, is awesome. Not only does she get me, but she gets my writing. Thank you for somehow always knowing what I mean and finding the best homes for my work.

A super big thank-you to my editor, Esi Sogah. Both *30 Days* and *30 Nights* meant so much to me, and I'm so proud that they became what they are with your help.

And finally, I can never thank my husband and daughters enough. You're my inspiration to keep writing, even when I don't think I can. I love you.

Don't miss the book where it all started

30 DAYS

Available now from
Kensington Trade Paperbacks.
Keep reading for a sneak peek!

1

So, the thing about me being a widow at the ripe old age of thirty-five was that no one knew what to say or how to act around me. My couple friends still invited me over to their parties, barbecues and the like, but the conversations always drifted into the land of awkward. *Oh you look great. I haven't seen you since Rob . . . since the funeral. Did you do something to your hair?*

The few single friends I had tried to pull me into their world. I didn't quite fit with them though. While they were clubbing or barhopping trying to find the perfect guy, every time I met someone my brain automatically compared him to Rob. I wasn't *still* looking for that special someone—I'd found and lost him.

Being a widow is not quite the same as being divorced. I'd been quite happy being married, having regular, boring sex with my amazing husband, followed by eating cold pizza in bed while we watched the hockey game. It was what I'd always wanted. *He* was who I'd always wanted.

288 / *Christine d'Abo*

Seriously, fuck cancer.

As a result, I found myself on my own more and more. It wasn't a bad thing, really. I'd been with Rob since I was nineteen and we'd been friends long before we'd officially started dating. We'd grown up together, had the same interests, same fears. Hell, we used to speak in nothing but punch lines, only to dissolve into giggles together when no one else in the room knew what the hell we were talking about. Not having him by my side had forced me to slowly become a singular entity instead of a plural.

Being on my own was . . . strange. Rob had been gone nearly two years and I still found myself turning to say something to him at the weirdest times. Though over the past month that started happening less frequently. I couldn't tell you exactly how I felt about that. Guilty? Oh my God yes. But I knew it meant I'd finally started to move on. I hadn't told anyone about my mental shift. Instead, I found myself going to this quiet place in my head, speaking less, observing more. It was different. I guess I'd become different more out of necessity than any real desire to change.

We'd known his time was coming to an end and took the last month of his life to simply enjoy each other. It was on one of our various trips to the beach that he handed me The Envelope.

"What's this?" My fingers were damp from the ocean spray and sticky from the ice cream I'd just finished. "If this is some death letter thing, I can't read it."

He grinned at that. "Naw, it's not sappy or anything. But yes, it's for after I'm gone."

"Rob—"

"Lyssa, listen to me. I promise you it's not what you think." He huffed, puffing out his shallow cheeks. "How many guys have you slept with?" The breeze moved his shirt and the sun made his brown eyes sparkle. If he had any hair left it would have blown from his forehead. My heart ached to run my hands through his hair once more. "And if you say more than one I'll promise not to be pissed."

"Don't be an ass. You know you're the only man I've ever been with." We'd talked a lot about that after we'd gotten married. Rob had a small measure of guilt that I hadn't had a chance to sow my oats. Somehow he thought because of my limited dating experience I would get bored or grow to resent him.

The idiot.

"That's my point." He took my hand and pressed the envelope into my palm once more. "Don't open this until you're ready. Hell, you might not want to open it at all. Just . . ." He gave my hand a squeeze, but for the first time in a long while, he couldn't meet my gaze. "I know you said you didn't think you'd want to be with anyone else."

"I don't." The thought made me ill.

"Baby, you shouldn't be alone. You have too much light and love inside you. The thought of you being on your own, of not having anyone to share in the joy you have to give? No. I know you. There will come a time when you'll realize that you're ready to move on—"

"I won't."

"—and I know you'll feel guilty about that. You'll ignore the feelings for as long as you can, thinking that you don't need anyone. Then something will happen. You'll see someone and in that beautiful brain of yours you'll be all *nice ass, dude* and that will be it. You'll cry about it but you'll realize you're ready."

"Please. I wouldn't cry." Because it wouldn't happen. Ever. "Not over a nice ass."

He chuckled, finally looking me in the eye. "You'll cry. But then you'll remember this conversation and know that I was right. So I'm going to say *I told you so* now. Then I want you to take this envelope and open it."

"Rob—"

"It's about sex."

I stood there with my mouth open. "What?"

"Just some ideas I had for you about sex when I'm gone. Getting back on the horse. Riding the cowboy. That sort of thing."

I wasn't ready to think about him being gone, let alone wanting to have sex with someone else. "I don't want to talk about this anymore. Seriously, shut up or I'm going to punch you."

"Okay."

He didn't let me forget about the envelope. He tried to get me to talk about it, but I would always cut him off. When I shoved it into a pile of papers in the closet, it found its way back onto my dresser. That box in the basement of papers that was older than me? Materialized on top of my desk. The recycling bin? Back onto the counter. I could have continued to play that game, but then Rob took another turn for the worse and all thoughts of envelopes and what they contained were the last things on my mind.

The cancer won.

And I was suddenly alone.

It really wasn't as bad as I'd first assumed it would be. I thought a lot about Rob, and missed him terribly for the better part of the first year. I functioned, worked, went out, but that was more of an automated response than actual living. There'd been more tears than I ever thought possible. My chest ached and my stomach churned. When I didn't feel ill, my mind wandered. I couldn't pretend to have any focus. My friends and the people at work never called me on my distraction.

Then I started to emerge from under the darkness and began

to live once more. I still missed Rob, thought about him daily, but the tightness in my chest eased. That's when the guilt kicked in. At least he'd already told me it would.

I stopped going out to our friends' homes for a while. They'd begun to get used to me as a singular—Alyssa—and not a plural—Rob and Alyssa. With their ease came my anger that they were all still couples. Their lives hadn't been shattered and swept away without their permission. They'd smile, laugh, and all the while I wanted to scream at them.

So I stayed away.

It helped. I was able to catch my breath, cry, hit things, and slowly my brain adjusted. I could be allowed into public once more, no longer a danger to happy couples.

One thing that helped was changing up my routine. I'd re-arranged all the furniture in our condo, painted the walls, even put up some new pictures. Rob would have hated them. I wasn't a fan myself, but it served its purpose. I started going to a new coffee shop half a block farther away from our building. I saw new people as I went, had to train a new barista named Len, smiled at a street performer who always played the same three songs on his guitar. It was good.

By the time the beginning of June rolled around, the tension had bled from my shoulders. It had taken me nearly two years, but I knew I was going to be okay.

That was when it happened.

A new guy moved into the complex.

Our building was a renovated school, each unit composed of three converted classrooms. Rob loved that we had a working water fountain just outside our front door. For fun, we'd mentally labeled the condos by classes. We were English because of the sheer number of books we had. Mr. and Mrs. Le Page were French, the Chin family were Home Ec, and on and on. The new guy had moved into Tourism, the condo owned by some company that let their out-of-town employees stay there for extended periods of time. It was just down the hall on the side opposite our place.

No, *my* place.

And he had a nice ass.

I knew this because my first sight of him was him bent over, pushing a large box through his front door. His jeans were stretched tight as his long legs worked against their load. I don't know how long I stood there, but it was enough that I hadn't unlocked my front door and he must have felt my gaze on him. He looked over his shoulder and smiled.

My body shivered. Even with the distance between us, I felt the intensity of his gaze.

Then I heard Rob's chuckle in my brain, that little one he'd give me when he knew he'd won an argument. I had to get in before I looked even more the idiot. I waved to the guy and immediately fumbled with my key. I knew he was watching me, which made the entire process of opening the door a monumental task. *Click, whoosh, bang* and I was safely inside. I pressed my forehead to the door and contemplated the probability of dying from embarrassment. Given my current state, upward of forty percent chance of death.

The bastard *did* have a nice ass.

It was in that moment that I remembered my conversation with Rob at the beach and his envelope. I was guilty, but that guilt wasn't nearly as strong as it had once been. With my hand pressed against the wood, I pushed away and slowly made my way to the bedroom. The envelope had taken up residence in my underwear drawer—I knew Rob would approve—deep beneath my panties and socks. I hadn't thought about it for quite some time, but rather than feel sad about the prospect of opening it, I had a strange tingle of anticipation.

I held it in my hands as I sat on the edge of the bed. The stains from my ice cream–coated fingers were still on the envelope. Chocolate with fudge. I ran my thumb across them.

Nothing else adorned the front of the envelope, no indication of what may be inside. I huffed, then licked my lips before I finally slipped my finger beneath the edge and tore the paper open.

Hidden inside was a single piece of paper wrapped around a bundle of index cards. I ignored the cards for the time being and spread open the paper. I took a moment before I could read the note. This was something new from Rob and my heart broke a little bit more. Those invisible fingers squeezed at my chest.

> *Alyssa.*
>
> *I love you. I know you love me. I'm glad you're ready to move on and start having some fun once again. I also know you well enough to realize you'll only go so far before you stop. Don't do that. And for God's sake, don't get into a serious relationship right away either. I always thought you hadn't taken enough time to figure out who you were as a person before we hooked up. We jumped into being a couple and lucky for us we worked and it was awesome.*
>
> *You always said you never regretted being with me so young, but you also didn't date anyone else. You didn't sleep with anyone else. I took that experience from you and I always hated that you didn't get to explore. I wanted to give you my permission to go out there and experiment. Have fun. Fool around and don't feel the least bit guilty about it.*
>
> *I thought I might also offer you some suggestions on how to get started.*
>
> *Humor me, okay.*
>
> *I've had a lot of time on my hands recently.*

*When you weren't here, I started this little project.
I call it Alyssa's 30 Days of Sex. Please don't have
sex thirty days in a row because I'll be jealous. Not
really. If you can do that go for it. Seriously though,
jealous.*

*Anyway, even if you don't use any of these
cards, I had a lot of fun imagining you enacting
them. You'll read them and think OMG boy
dreams! That's cool. They are. Change them up if
you want.*

*Even when you weren't with me, you made me
happy. I'm going to stop now before I get sappy. Go
get laid and enjoy the kinky sex.*

Love you, baby.

Rob.

I laughed. It was such a Rob thing to have done. I had no
difficulty picturing him coming up with ideas for his cards
while going through his chemo. Come to think of it, that ex-
plained most of the Internet pop-ups I'd been forced to clean
off his laptop after he passed.

Sex cards. He wrote me freaking sex cards. I fell in love with
him all over again. My best friend and lover was giving me advice
on how to hook up with other people from beyond the grave. The
idea was a mix of weird and sweet, the perfect descriptor for him.

My fingers shook as I flipped through the cards. Tears filled
my eyes, but I couldn't stop myself from giggling. If he were
still here, I would have punched him on the arm for confusing
the hell out of me. I kept laughing as I flipped through the stack.
He didn't actually expect me to do some of these? Threesome.
Public sex. Get tied up. Have sex with a vibrator in my ass.

Actually, that one sounded interesting.

Eventually I went back to the first card and looked at it

closely. On the top of each one he'd printed *30 Days of Sex*, and directly below it, the day it represented. This one had *Day One* written across the top and only one word written in his messy scrawl in the middle of the card. While it appeared to be the simplest to complete, I had a few doubts about starting on this insane game.

Masturbate.